SINISTER
SCENES

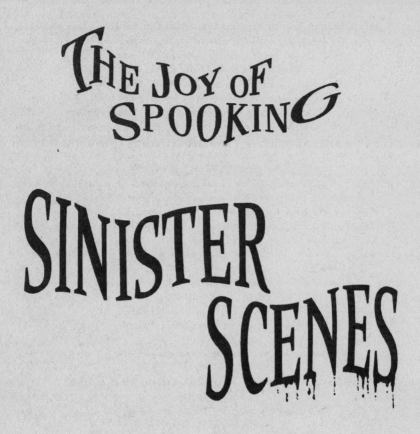

THE JOY OF SPOOKING

SINISTER SCENES

P. J. BRACEGIRDLE

Margaret K. McElderry Books
New York London Toronto Sydney New Delhi

MARGARET K. McELDERRY BOOKS

An imprint of Simon & Schuster Children's Publishing Division

1230 Avenue of the Americas, New York, New York 10020

This book is a work of fiction. Any references to historical events, real people, or real locales are used fictitiously. Other names, characters, places, and incidents are products of the author's imagination, and any resemblance to actual events or locales or persons, living or dead, is entirely coincidental.

Copyright © 2011 by P. J. Bracegirdle

All rights reserved, including the right of reproduction in whole or in part in any form.

MARGARET K. McELDERRY BOOKS is a trademark of Simon & Schuster, Inc.

For information about special discounts for bulk purchases, please contact Simon & Schuster Special Sales at 1-866-506-1949 or business@simonandschuster.com.

The Simon & Schuster Speakers Bureau can bring authors to your live event. For more information or to book an event, contact the Simon & Schuster Speakers Bureau at 1-866-248-3049 or visit our website at www.simonspeakers.com.

Also available in a Margaret K. McElderry Books hardcover edition

Book design by Debra Sfetsios-Conover

The text for this book is set in Adobe Caslon.

Manufactured in the United States of America

0712 ARC

First Margaret K. McElderry Books paperback edition August 2012

2 4 6 8 10 9 7 5 3 1

The Library of Congress has cataloged the hardcover edition as follows:

Bracegirdle, P. J.

Sinister scenes / P. J. Bracegirdle.—1st ed.

p. cm.—(The joy of Spooking ; bk. 3)

Summary: When the star of a horror movie filming in the town of Spooking disappears, twelve-year-old Joy Wells steps into the role—and into real-life horror when her costar gives a terrifying and unscripted performance.

ISBN 978-1-4169-3420-2 (hardcover)

[1. Motion pictures—Production and direction—Fiction. 2. Horror films—Fiction. 3. Missing persons—Fiction. 4. Spirit possession—Fiction. 5. Blessing and cursing—Fiction. 6. Horror stories. 7. Supernatural—Fiction.] I. Title.

PZ7.B6987Sin 2011

[Fic]—dc22

2010045267

ISBN 978-1-4169-3421-9 (pbk)

ISBN 978-1-4424-2643-6 (eBook)

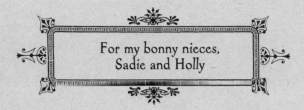

For my bonny nieces,
Sadie and Holly

A fog poured inside the cemetery gates, rushing in like a ghostly tide. Over mounds and gullies the white vapor rolled, swallowing up markers and swirling around monuments, all the while pursuing a girl with straight blond hair. Striding unknowingly ahead, she held her hand up to her ear, black raincoat swishing as she tromped over the untold number of souls buried beneath her.

Stopping suddenly, she broke the deathly silence.

"I already told you where I am, Marty!" she yelled. From within her curtain of unnatural-looking hair, a hidden phone appeared—an expensive model, tucked into a pink leather sleeve. Holding out the device, she began yelling directly at it. "Thanks to you, I'm in some disgusting graveyard in the middle of nowhere, that's where!"

The girl put the phone to her ear again as a voice could be heard pleading with her. Listening, she nodded impatiently for a while before suddenly shaking her head furiously.

"I know it's in my contract!" she shouted. "But that's your job, isn't it—to get me out of things? Otherwise, why even bother having an agent?"

The tiny voice began speaking again, this time with a

noticeably stern tone. As the girl listened, the fog began circling her ankles, then swirling up around her legs like a supernatural flood.

"Marty, I don't care!" she finally interrupted. "Right now I should be at home, getting ready for the Teens Say Awards tomorrow night! But no. Instead I'm on the other side of the country, taking promo pictures for a movie that doesn't even start shooting for another month!"

A crow landed atop a nearby monument, a tall granite obelisk covered in luminous green moss, as the voice on the phone continued speaking. With beady eyes the bird watched the girl as she began shaking with rage.

"No. You listen to me, Marty. I've had enough of this treatment! I'm the one working here, making all the money! But do you care? Do my parents care? No. Instead everyone is bossing me around, telling me what to do all the time!

"Well, I'm sick of it. Do you hear me? I'm sick of it! And this time, I swear, I'm really running away. And then we'll see how you all get along without me!"

Before the tiny voice could say another word, the girl stabbed the phone with her finger and cut off any reply. She then looked up at the perched crow.

"What do you think?" she asked the unblinking creature. "Do you think they'll learn their lesson?"

The cemetery rang with a woeful caw.

"Well, that's just your opinion, birdbrain."

There was a black blur as the crow took flight. The girl glanced back at the dead screen on her phone. Maybe it was a bad move. Her phone connected her to everything: her friends; her parents; her publicist; her stupid boyfriend, Jacob; and her even stupider agent, who did at least sometimes call with good news. But she had to make a point, she decided. Let them all sweat it for a bit. Maybe then they would start appreciating her more, instead of taking constant advantage.

The girl dropped the phone into the black depths of her large purse. Flinging the heavy bag over her shoulder, she began looking around for the photographer. Was he mad at her? Probably. But who cared.

He was nowhere in sight, nor were his assistants or the makeup artist. And where was her bodyguard? Just because he had the flu didn't mean he could spend the whole day sitting in the limousine.

By now the fog had reached up to her waist. "Did somebody forget to switch off the smoke machine?" she shouted into the gloom. "Hello?"

There was no reply.

Looking around, the girl spotted a stone angel holding a sword. It wasn't the slightest bit familiar to her, she decided, so she headed off in the other direction, careful not to stumble over any hidden headstones.

Before long she came across a large stone vault with its heavy iron door hanging open. There was some sort of light inside. Was this the next location they were supposed to shoot in? How gross!

Whatever, she told herself. The sooner they got it done, the sooner she could get back to the airport. With a loud theatrical sigh she disappeared through the narrow opening, her purse barely able to follow.

"Hey there, puppy dog! What are you doing in here? Are you going to be in the photo with me? *Come* here. *Come* here, boy. . . ."

There was a terrible clang as the iron door swung shut behind her.

CHAPTER 1

It was always the same dream, night after night.

She was a pilot—the aviatrix—slim in an olive green flight suit, looking beautiful despite her leather flight cap and goggles. Climbing up the ladder alongside a silver propeller plane, she paused to wave to the crowd gathered nearby beneath a string of colorful fluttering flags. With a cheeky wink she then hopped into the cramped cockpit and took her place at the controls.

To cries of delight the aviatrix then opened up the throttle. Casting an eye toward the red and white wind sock, she noted it was blowing a stiff northeasterly. She then released the brakes.

Twin propellers roaring, the gleaming airplane began pulling away. Above the noise came more hearty huzzahs. But before long the cheers turned to gasps as she hurtled down the runway. "Pull up!" someone shouted. "Pull up!"

But the aviatrix just frowned. Squinting at the instruments through her grimy goggles, she saw something she didn't like, a gauge against which she repeatedly tapped a fingertip. Nevertheless she roared onward. Glancing up, she finally pulled back hard on the yoke and, with only a foot of runway remaining, left the ground. Wings shuddering, the airplane began climbing, higher and higher until it appeared to onlookers like a silver dagger slicing through the sky.

From her position at the controls, the aviatrix looked out at the world. Far below, the carpet of swaying palm trees became shadowy reef and then an endless expanse of glittering turquoise. High above, the yellow sun burned brightly in a cloudless sky.

She smiled, blissfully alone in this singular universe. Alone she would remain until, many hours later, a sandy landing strip appeared out of the twinkling infinity.

Except it never did.

The dazzling blue turned to darkest night as Joy Wells yelped in fright. Arms out, she sat up in bed, still braced for impact with the great blue sea that had an instant ago been rushing up to meet her.

It had all seemed so real.

Joy could still remember every detail. From helplessly watching the fuel gauge dip until the needle shuddered below empty, to hearing the engines sputter and die. With nothing more to be done, she had then closed her eyes, tracking the plane's descent by the sickening sensation in her stomach.

The shattering impact had awoken her.

Fortunately, it was only a dream, Joy assured herself. It was late at night and she was in her bedroom, she confirmed by the soft glow coming from Fizz's aquarium heater. From down the hall she could hear her father's snoring, and the familiar scratching of a branch against the shingles of her home at Number 9 Ravenwood Avenue.

After flipping over her drenched pillow, Joy lay back down. As her heart slowed its thumping, she stared up into the black nothingness until she finally fell back into a fitful sleep.

The next morning Joy arrived at the breakfast table looking shadowy-eyed and exhausted.

"What's wrong, dear?" her mother asked upon witnessing the haunted look she had given her piece of toast. "My, oh my. You look absolutely awful today."

If the repulsed expressions on their faces were anything to go by, Joy's brother, Byron, and her father both appeared to agree.

Joy flopped forward over the table, her long blond hair trailing in the butter dish. She grumpily relayed how she'd been suffering from the same recurring dream for the past few weeks, a terrible one that felt curiously real, as if she had been somehow witnessing events that had actually transpired.

"Ah," Mrs. Wells replied once her daughter had finished. "They're called night terrors. I used to get them too when I was about twelve," she confessed. "They're basically nightmares but a lot more vivid and much, much harder to wake up from."

"Can you die from them?" Byron inquired, his mouth ringed in raspberry jam.

"From what?" his mother asked.

"From a night terror."

"No, Byron," Mrs. Wells assured her son.

"Are you sure?" the boy asked. "Because Gustave says you

can actually die if you dream you're falling but don't wake up before you hit the ground."

Horrified, Joy turned to her mother, awaiting a confirmation or denial of Byron's friend's claim. Because when it came to medical facts, Mrs. Wells was considered the authority in the family. Although not a physician, she did have a PhD in philosophy, which meant she was still allowed to call herself a doctor. Which, she boasted, meant she could get dinner reservations just as easily as any practitioner of actual medicine.

"That is complete nonsense," Mrs. Wells informed her children. "A dream is nothing more than the processing of memories and subconscious information," she recalled vaguely from an article she'd once read. "It's absolutely impossible to get physically hurt from things that just exist in your imagination."

"Yeah, but what if the shock of going splat gives you a heart attack or something?" Byron persisted. "That *could* happen, couldn't it?"

"Well, I guess so," Mrs. Wells admitted. "But I'm sure it's really, really unlikely. Especially when it comes to healthy young people like you and your sister."

"Phew," Byron said, exhaling. "Because sometimes I like to dream I'm flying, and I go pretty high . . ."

Joy shook her head wearily. Having slammed into the sea at least a dozen times now, she probably had nothing to worry about. "Anyway, I never used to get bad dreams," she continued. "So why now?"

Actually, the statement wasn't strictly accurate. Having

spent many nights reading horror stories by flashlight, Joy was pretty accustomed to nightmares. Usually they featured terrifying creatures bristling with claws and fangs, or mind-bending supernatural occurrences that defied both sense and reason. However, these were the kinds of dreams she enjoyed most. They were like cool little movies where she got to be the star.

"Night terrors can start at any age, dear," Mrs. Wells explained. "They're usually caused by exhaustion and anxiety. To be honest, since you're so sensitive, I'm surprised you didn't start getting them earlier."

"Sensitive?" Joy shrieked. "Me?"

"It's not an insult, dear. It's just a statement of fact. Wouldn't you agree, Edward?"

"Your mother's right, pumpkin. You are very sensitive," Mr. Wells mumbled from behind his newspaper. "Is there any more coffee, Helen?"

"That was the last cup."

"Oh shucks. Really?"

"You guys are out of your minds," Joy protested. "I am *not* sensitive! Actually, I'm the total opposite of sensitive!"

"You're completely insensitive?" her mother offered with a wry smile. "Well, true enough. Sometimes you can be like that, too."

Joy stomped a foot, rattling the breakfast dishes on the table. Why did everyone always feel so free to comment on what sort of person they'd decided she was? And of all things to accuse her of—being sensitive? How ridiculous! If anything, being forced to go to school down in Darlington had given her a pretty thick skin, she had always reckoned.

But why bother arguing? So long as her parents didn't start dragging her down for more therapy sessions at Darlington General, they could pretty much say whatever they wanted.

"Well, I'm sorry you feel that way," Joy said, regaining her composure. "I just don't agree."

"And I'm sorry if you took my observation as a criticism," Mrs. Wells insisted. "Really, these discussions are only meant to illuminate, my dear, to help you develop and refine your own personal philosophy. I think you might be wise to take a note from the great thinker Michel de Montaigne: 'Of all our infirmities, the most savage is to despise our being.'"

Joy bristled. Out of all the dusty catchphrases Mrs. Wells had seen fit to shake out over the years, few got under her daughter's skin quite like those of this particular dead French dude. Each one seemed to come out of the blue like a little nuclear missile that, despite her best defenses, Joy could never knock out of the sky. Even the man's very likenesses were annoying. She had discovered this while looking him up on the Internet, his portraits all capturing the same sad face perched atop a white ruff as if on a serving plate.

Maybe it was time for Joy to change up her tactics a little bit.

"'My life has been full of terrible misfortunes,'" Joy quoted, using her best impersonation of a cockatoo. "'Most of which never happened.'"

"Another great thought from Monsieur de Montaigne!"

Mrs. Wells squealed with delight. "And perfectly recalled. As I keep saying, your mind is a steel trap, my dear. Please do yourself the favor of putting it to good use."

"Uh-huh," Joy replied, unsure whether or not to be pleased with the results of her experiment.

"Anyway, perhaps I'm being hard on you, sweetheart," Mrs. Wells admitted. "For once you do have a pretty good reason to feel a bit anxious."

Joy's eyes snapped open wide. Why the sudden turn-around? "What do you mean?" she demanded.

"Well, you are about to graduate, darling. That has to be fairly upsetting."

"Upsetting?" Joy laughed, whacking a spoon off the table and snorting on top of it. "I'm graduating from Winsome Elementary, a dump I can't wait to get out of."

Mrs. Wells rolled her eyes. "Yes, yes. Everyone knows how much you hate your school. But look at it this way: At least at Winsome you already know your enemy. In junior high who knows what will happen?"

"What do you mean?" Joy demanded to know. "What could happen?"

"Oh, probably nothing," Mrs. Wells answered. "In fact, I'm sure everything will be fine. That said, what if you end up feeling just as unpopular and persecuted as you did at elementary school? Or what if it's even worse—"

"Hey, wait a minute," Joy interrupted. "I thought you told me that junior high is when all the teasing stops, when everybody starts getting really serious!"

"Did I really say that?" Mrs. Wells put a hand over her

mouth to cover a laugh. "I'm sorry. Maybe that was just wishful thinking. Anyway, all I am saying is that it is enough to give anyone in their right mind nightmares."

That was just great, Joy thought, glaring at her mother. It was bad enough that she was having night terrors, but did such dread have to come out in the full light of day? Were there any hereditary family illnesses her mother thought she should know about while she was at it?

Now Joy was scared. What if whatever new world lay ahead of her turned out to be even worse than the current one? She had been so excited about finally leaving Winsome Elementary that she had never really considered what possible horrors could follow.

"Speaking of nightmares, Edward," Mrs. Wells said, turning her attention to her husband. "Are you going to mow the lawn today?"

"The lawn?" cried Mr. Wells. "What on earth for?"

"I thought we decided last night that we would have Byron's birthday party in the backyard this year."

Eagerly anticipating his ninth birthday, Byron somehow managed to smile around the third piece of toast stuck in his mouth. There was just something about the number nine that was so much less lame than the number eight. At least in his opinion.

"Well, sure, but that's not for another two weeks," Mr. Wells replied. "What's the big rush?"

"Have you looked at the state of the lawn lately?" Mrs. Wells demanded. "A herd of buffalo could be living in there and we would be none the wiser. In fact, I don't think it's been mowed once since last summer, if I recall correctly."

"That's because we had a really rainy fall," Mr. Wells explained, folding his newspaper irritably. "You can't mow wet grass. It just clumps together and clogs up the blade."

"Well, whatever. I just wouldn't leave it to the last minute, Edward. You know it's always much more work than you expect. Better to get it under control now and then do a quick pass before the party."

Mr. Wells took a swig from his mug and once again discovered it empty. Grumbling, he then turned to his son. "I think good old Byron here is getting more than old enough to add mowing the lawn to his growing list of skills," Mr. Wells said, ruffling the boy's dark mop of hair. "Hey, would you like to start earning yourself a bit of pocket money, Son?"

"Not really," Byron answered honestly.

"Honestly, Edward, are you even being serious?" cried Mrs. Wells. "There is no way a seventy-pound child can push a thirty-pound mower through four-foot-high grass."

Tuning out her family, Joy looked down at her breakfast. She was feeling a bit hungry now and took a bite of cold toast. As she chewed, her thoughts returned to her night terrors. Even if her fears about graduating were the cause, it still didn't explain the dream itself, she decided. What could plummeting into the sea possibly have to do with heading off to junior high?

On this matter Joy decided not to further consult her mother, who had fortunately given over her full attention to the upcoming gardening duties of Mr. Wells. Having already heard enough about how alternately sensitive and insensitive she was, Joy didn't need to listen to a bunch of lame metaphors involving fears of crashing and burning, and how you had to sink or swim in life.

Anyway, Joy felt pretty certain that she had already worked out the most important part of her dream: the identity of the person in whose body she kept finding herself trapped. Her name was Ms. Melody Huxley. And for the past two weeks, Joy had been reliving the last moments of her life.

Joy had first learned about Melody, who was one of her greatest idols, while rummaging through the forgotten old trunks in the cellar. Joy had been instantly fascinated by the woman who, like her, had once occupied 9 Ravenwood Avenue. With her knees going numb on the cold cellar floor, Joy had spent hours piecing together what she could of the woman's extraordinary life. Rifling through old possessions and examining faded photographs, she had marveled at the contradictory images of the beautiful socialite and blood-thirsty game hunter, traveling the globe wherever wildlife and wet bars coexisted.

But that was before Joy had finally learned the full extent of the woman's amazing life.

For it had turned out that the former resident of Number 9 was in fact a famous female aviator. And what was even more startling, just like Joy's other idol—legendary horror writer Ethan Alvin Peugeot—the pioneering airwoman had also infamously vanished without a trace.

The revelation had come curiously enough via a special bulletin from the E. A. Peugeot Society. A huge fan ever since having been bequeathed a first-edition compendium of his work, Joy had been a proud member of the literary fellowship for the past year, during which an unshakable belief had taken hold of her. Finding uncanny similarities between the setting of Peugeot's stories and Spooking itself, Joy had become convinced that he had once lived in her hometown.

But as the notorious recluse's whereabouts were uncertain even in his own day, no one appeared to know much about him. He would appear unexpectedly at his publisher's office before disappearing again. And when he eventually failed to resurface, an entire century would pass without the mystery ever being solved.

So it happened that Joy had decided to take the case for Spooking directly to the Society itself. By documenting the considerable evidence, she would prove once and for all that the town was once home to the great author. But despite her best efforts, Joy had been unable to deliver her arguments before a stunning revelation from the Society brought everything into question.

According to the special bulletin, the startling discovery had been made in Steadford Mines, a popular tourist town a few hundred miles away. Plucked from the basement of an old lakeside cottage, a bundle of correspondence and an unpublished manuscript had been discovered bearing the distinctive handwriting of the author.

The correspondence itself, the bulletin had explained, consisted exclusively of love letters penned to someone known as "My Sweet Semiquaver." Joy had been delighted to learn that the previously unknown manuscript was entitled "The Crimson Pool."

But even more astoundingly, further investigation had revealed that the cottage was once the summer residence of another celebrity—the world-famous female aviator Ms. Melody Huxley.

The shock had been so great, Joy had immediately passed out. Upon regaining her senses, Joy had believed the connection to be too much of a coincidence. How could the former resident of 9 Ravenwood Avenue have come into possession of the private writings of Ethan Alvin Peugeot? Joy had promptly ransacked her house looking for any clues, but had found nothing.

Unfortunately, there were few leads to follow. Ms. Huxley's own disappearance proved equally baffling. She was presumed lost at sea when her propeller plane failed to arrive at a small island in the middle of the Pacific. With no wreckage recovered, some sort of tragic error of navigation or mechanical malfunction was presumed by her many mourners and admirers.

But as often happens in such cases, some people began offering more outlandish explanations. A few even began suggesting that Ms. Huxley had in fact survived by crash-landing on a remote island. Some claimed she had lived out the rest of her days in complete solitude, while others said she had been adopted by a tribe of natives who'd revered her as a goddess.

The latter theory was later supported by the discovery of a small camp on a remote island, with a nearby altar of worship fashioned from the remnants of an aircraft of the same era. But arguments had quickly raged over whether or not Ms. Huxley's airplane had possessed sufficient range to reach the site.

Still others maintained that she had secretly been a foreign spy and had slipped away on an enemy submarine to escape justice. Some even argued that a series of lights spotted in the sky by rescue teams suggested that the airwoman might have been abducted by aliens.

After reading all the evidence, Joy had not initially been able to decide which theory she believed. Each had its merits—especially the one about the UFOs, in whose existence she most definitely believed.

However, that was before her night terrors had started. Now she felt in her heart that Ms. Huxley had simply run out of fuel and slammed into the ocean.

Still, it was a horrible notion. Somehow the idea of her idol living out her life as a tribal queen, in secret exile somewhere, or even hurtling through the vastness of space alongside a bunch of almond-eyed abductors seemed much more comforting to Joy than the thought of her lifeless body slipping silently into the briny depths of the sea.

Equally upsetting, it also meant that Melody's secrets had sunk to the bottom of the ocean with her, the most important of which was her connection to Ethan Alvin Peugeot—a man last seen alive when she had been but a mere girl of seven. It was a mystery that weighed not only on Joy's mind, but on those of everyone at the E. A. Peugeot Society.

However, just because Peugeot had stopped appearing in public didn't mean that he had stopped existing. Joy speculated that he could have easily lived out the rest of his days in secret on her very doorstep and at some point met Melody here.

Unfortunately, no one was interested in this possibility, nor in any other of Joy's many theories. Not her parents, nor her teachers—nor even her usually loyal brother, Byron, it seemed lately. But what did it matter? It was the truth, Joy knew, and all she had to do was prove it.

Unfortunately, no one seemed the slightest bit interested in her latest belief that Melody Huxley had once lived at Number 9. Even Joy's own parents were unable to properly assess clear photographic evidence, having been already driven to the edge of sanity by her Peugeot obsession.

"I'll agree, the woman does look a bit like her," her father had conceded, scarcely able to contain a yawn. "But from my work on old deeds with Pennington, Plover & Freep, I can tell you that Huxleys once positively abounded in this area. Now, if this person really was *the* Melody Huxley like you think, why are there no pictures of her at the controls of an airplane?"

To that question Joy had no good answer. But now tormented by night terrors over the mystery, she felt more determined than ever to find out.

But first she had to go to school, she knew, looking up at the clock. Which unfortunately was yet another realm of nightmare—Winsome Elementary.

Groaning, she got up from the table and shuffled off to brush her teeth.

CHAPTER 2

Hunched like a buzzard, the clerk perched on a stool behind the shop counter. He yawned—an overlong gaping-mouthed demonstration—before violently ruffling his own black hair in an effort to revive himself. But it was no use. Propping his pallid face on his hands, he closed his eyes. As he breathed slowly, a calm expression began washing over his sharp features, until his tortured face transformed into what looked like a waxen death mask.

Just at the moment the clerk began snoring, a wild high-pitched squealing rang out. Leaping up in a panic, he threw out his arms in self-defense. Eyes wide, he searched frantically for whatever was making the terrifying sound.

The source was a figure holding a guitar up to the twin speakers of a massive amplifier.

"WHAT DO YOU THINK YOU'RE DOING?" the clerk shouted, somehow cutting through the earsplitting noise.

A red-haired teenager turned around, causing the screeching to immediately cease. The young man then shrugged. "I was just wondering if this amp does feedback."

Even at this point in his short retail career, the clerk was accustomed to indulging moronic questions, and perhaps in another mood he might have explained the theory behind what he knew was properly known as the Larsen effect. However, having been startled from a brief but dead sleep, the man's thread of patience snapped instantly. "It's a sound loop, you idiot. You can do it with any input and output!"

Towering full height over the counter, the clerk's slender frame was nevertheless menacing. Thrown into shadow, the teenager shuddered by the amplifier. "Sorry," he all but blubbered. "I didn't know."

"Well, you do now! So knock it off or I'm banning you from the store!"

"I said I was sorry," the young man replied sullenly. Nevertheless, he respected the demand, dutifully flicking the amp's standby switch before carefully removing the patch cord and returning the guitar to the wall where he'd found it. Trembling, the red-haired boy then began leafing through a book entitled *101 Head-Melting Riffs! A Hands-on Tutorial.*

Glaring, the clerk sat down again. It must be four o'clock, he guessed—the hour when the high school students started drifting in. The darn kids never bought anything, but instead tried out every guitar in the store while waiting for turns on the infernal dance machines at the arcade opposite. The clerk assumed that teenage girls must prefer good dancers to good musicians these days.

How depressing, he thought. But that was the way of things now.

Still, there was one upside, the clerk thought as a few more kids entered. The appearance of the spotty-faced slouches marked the final hour of his shift. Which meant that within the hour he would escape the cramped confines of Electric Eddie's House of Shred in its far-flung corner of the Darlington Mega Mall.

He returned his head to the comfortable cradle of his upturned palms. The clerk sighed, however, to see a grown-up customer entering the store. Sitting at attention, he then watched the man navigate the guitars hanging like stalactites from the ceiling. The man sported a business suit, the clerk noticed. Hmm, perhaps he might end the day with a decent sale after all, he mused. Which would shut up the store's manager, Collin, at least.

But suddenly the man's cherubic face came into view. The clerk gasped and then ducked to the side, desperately trying to conceal himself.

The effort proved useless.

"Phipps?" the customer called out in an uncertain voice. "Is that you?"

Emerging from behind a display case of harmonicas, Octavio Phipps tried to adopt a dignified posture. But he failed, hunching over instead like a black question mark.

"Hello, Mayor MacBrayne," he said, cringing as his ex-boss stared at his name tag in disbelief.

It had been three months since Phipps had been fired from the mayor's administration, during which time his anger and resentment had not diminished in the slightest. How could he have deserved such treatment, especially after everything he had done for the city? Using the limited power and influence of his modest post, Phipps had been nonetheless shaping a bright future for Darlington—from a position of complete shadow! All this he had done, not only at great risk to both his liberty and safety, but while simultaneously covering up the mayor's incompetence. And to what credit or recompense?

None.

Nevertheless the effort had felt worth it to Phipps. For he'd had a greater purpose—to completely undermine Spooking, to redevelop and remodel it until its very likeness was wiped utterly from the earth.

But then had come the disaster at the town's old asylum.

Phipps's original plan had been ingenious enough—to evict the asylum's operators and remodel the property into a combination health spa and plastic surgery clinic. It was his firm belief, and he had convinced the mayor, that such an exclusive facility would transform Spooking, leading to all sorts of interest and opportunities in the otherwise scabrous old town.

It was with this plan in mind that Phipps had connived to admit his old bandmate Felix as a patient to the mysterious asylum. By spying on the asylum's activities, the mayor's assistant had been certain he could manufacture a case for closing down the operation.

But when the hospital administrator, Dr. Warshaw, and his staff had turned out to be themselves criminally insane, Phipps had received a desperate call from his inside man, Felix. Despite rushing to his aid, he had been too late and found himself taken prisoner. Only moments away from being surgically turned into a brainless robot like his poor friend, he had narrowly managed to escape—just before some inexplicable force destroyed the property.

Even months later Phipps could not explain what he had seen that night as he'd fled across the grounds. He'd witnessed great flaming missiles arcing across the sky and exploding against the brick building. In a matter of minutes the projectiles had leveled the structure and set fire to the property.

And so it happened that the once glittering investment opportunity—and a venture eagerly anticipated by a close personal friend of the mayor's—had been reduced to a worthless ruin, the bulk of which had been swallowed up by the earth itself.

Touring the aftermath, Phipps had found himself at a rare loss to explain what exactly had happened.

So Mayor MacBrayne had promptly fired him.

After a month of sitting around in his underwear, Phipps had finally been forced to look for another job. However, with his reputation apparently preceding him, he'd discovered that he could secure no interviews, at least not for any positions at his previous level of endeavor.

Despairing, Phipps had begun hoping that his curse would finally take him, and like his father he would simply vanish without a trace. Like all males in his family, he had been thus afflicted since birth, for some crime of an ancestor's. Soon it would take him, and he would be gone from the earth forever. But his body cruelly remained in the material world. Starving, he had soon become desperate.

Phipps had finally accepted a retail job selling musical instruments. Having helped out for years at his father's store, it seemed a fairly logical option and somewhat less odious than being reduced to flipping burgers or folding sweaters. Besides, he was an accomplished musician whose extensive training and expertise would surely make the work mere child's play. But most importantly, who from his past life would he ever run into, working at a place like Electric Eddie's?

"So how are you, buddy?" the mayor asked in a tone that made Phipps feel like he was being visited in a home after suffering massive brain damage.

"I'm fine, sir, thank you."

"I'm glad to hear it," the mayor said. "Er, so you work here?"

Phipps looked down at his oversize T-shirt emblazoned with the store's logo—the silhouette of a shaggy-haired dude wailing on a guitar—and then looked back up at the mayor. "Yes, sir."

"Wow. I mean, I remember you saying your family had a music store up in Spooking once upon a time, so I guess it makes sense."

"My father was a luthier," Phipps replied haughtily. "He made fine handcrafted stringed instruments. These items are slapped together in the hundreds of thousands by mindless drones who work for ten cents an hour."

"Really?" said the mayor, looking around the store in admiration. "How amazing. They all look pretty sharp."

"Is there something I can help you with, Mayor?" asked

Phipps. "I never knew you were an axe man."

"No, no." The mayor laughed, looking at the guitars like they were indeed fierce weapons he might injure himself on. "I'm just birthday shopping for my nephew. To be honest I don't know why I'm bothering. The spoiled kid's already got two of everything. His mother—my sister-in-law—is a real piece of work, lemme tell you. But my wife says guitar is his latest thing."

"Ah. Well, then, can I help you pick something out?"

"Yeah, sure." The mayor's stubby fingers picked at a price tag dangling from a candy-apple red instrument. Letting it go with a snap, he made a face. "You got anything for under fifty bucks?"

"I'm sure we can find you something," replied Phipps, gesturing to the glass counter between them.

The mayor approached, staring dumbly for a moment at the variety of accessories. Watching him, Phipps was about to make a suggestion when the man suddenly thumped his palm against the counter.

"So, I'm going to come out and say it," said the mayor. "I made a mistake, firing you like that. And I want to make it up to you."

Phipps didn't answer, but instead squatted down and began rifling around the accessories. He could feel his face going red. What was the mayor's game now?

The truth was that for the first time in his life, Phipps was finally accepting his lot. Approaching his fate, he found himself almost reveling in each fresh humiliation that life threw at him. It was kind of funny after all, he now saw, in a darkly humorous way. So funny that lately he even woke himself up at nights, cackling madly over it.

"Why? Isn't my replacement working out?"

The mayor frowned. "Well, I wouldn't say that exactly. Miss Sparks is a very good assistant—very conscientious, organized, reliable..."

"Miss Sparks?"

"Yeah, I know, I know. I hired a woman," the mayor said, shaking his head. "I don't know what I was thinking either. Well, that's not totally true. I was arguing with the missus at the time and thought a lady assistant might shake her tree a bit. Or at the very least get her off my back about the golfing for a couple of months. But anyway, it didn't work out that way."

"No?" replied Phipps, putting a box on the counter.

"In fact, it blew up in my face!" said the mayor, scowling. "The two of them are practically best friends now! My wife calls the office all the time, and Miss Sparks puts her straight through every time. I can't get a moment's peace these days!"

"Ah," said Phipps, remembering the various excuses he used to offer the mayor's wife when the man didn't want to be found. *He's currently chairing a budget meeting. He's currently in session, tabling a motion. He's currently ensconced in arbitration.* It was no small skill to make the mayor's activities sound so boring that there was no chance he would be quizzed on them later.

"But that's not the worst of it. Her priorities are completely out of whack," the mayor groaned. "She has me going everywhere these days—to press conferences, to council sessions, to budget meetings. . . . A mayor's job isn't in the details; it's in the overview. You knew that, Phipps!"

Nodding in time to the man's complaints, Phipps felt an evil spark of joy. Perhaps this was the best revenge he could have hoped for; that his termination had led to the mayor actually doing some work for a change. The corners of his mouth turned up at the thought.

"You knew what I was best at," said the mayor, not noticing. "Meet and greets. Cocktail parties. Getting people interested in spending their money around Darlington. That's the sort of thing I should be doing, right?"

Unable to come up with a polite response, Phipps just shrugged.

"Anyway, the thing is that I can't get rid of her. She's the daughter of my best buddy at the club," the mayor whined. "But if I could, I would, Phipps, my boy. And hire you back in a second."

Phipps glanced at the heavy wood-encased metronome to the immediate right of his hand, considering whether or not to bounce it off the top of the curly head now inclined toward him. But it somehow didn't seem worth his job. "I appreciate the sentiment, Mayor," he said.

"Thanks."

"Now, your nephew. Do you know whether he plays electric or acoustic guitar?"

"Electric, I'm guessing, because it's really loud, according to his fat-faced mother," said the mayor. "So, what do you think? Do you have anything in stock that makes it even more painful?"

Phipps raised a thoughtful eyebrow and pointed to the box on the counter. "Mayor, let me introduce you to your new best friend, the Fuzzinator 5000," he said.

"Is it loud? Is it ugly?"

"Oh yes."

"Done deal," said the mayor, pulling out his credit card. "Listen, Phipps . . ." The mayor paused, his wide forehead crinkling under his curls. "Are you sure you're happy here?"

"Quite," his ex-assistant lied.

"All right, then," replied the mayor. "But look, if there's anything I can ever do for you, let me know, okay?"

After completing his purchase, the mayor then departed. At the exit he paused and fixed a look on his old employee. A look of pity.

Phipps grimaced.

Still, at least Phipps had finally sold something today, which would hopefully make Collin less grumpy. Unlike the mayor, his new boss was an unflagging taskmaster, Phipps had discovered, who was never satisfied with any amount of effort. Besides delighting in reminding Phipps that if he had time to lean, he had time to clean, Collin took great joy in pointing out that his three-month probation was far, far from over.

With this thought in mind, Phipps fetched some spray and began removing the mayor's greasy fingerprints from the counter, until the surface was shiny enough that he could see himself reflected back in it.

He stared at the shadowy eyes set in his narrow face. What was he doing? he asked himself. He had once been on track to be someone—a musician, an artist. And in doing so he had been certain he would eventually leave some enduring legacy to the world, no matter how small.

But instead here he was, wearing a name tag in the middle of a mall.

"Hey, Octavio!" barked a voice. "What's the deal-i-o?"

Phipps looked up and saw the portly figure of Collin, who now stood before him eating a limp-looking burrito wrapped in wax paper. In the crook of his arm was a drink the size of a paint can.

"Pardon me?"

"You're on cloud nine, and there are customers in the store."

Phipps glanced over his shoulder at a group of teenagers gathering around the red-haired boy, who was now back playing an appalling hammer-on at high volume. "Customers?" Phipps repeated. "You call those kids customers?"

"Are you kidding me? Those little brats are loaded. Now, go over and see if you can't sell them something before they head off and blow it all at the arcade."

"Yes, sir—"

Phipps stopped, staring at the man cramming a burrito into his face. Addressing his superior as "sir" was a habit dating back to his days at City Hall. The mayor's appearance had obviously triggered the reflex.

"I mean, yes, *Collin*," he seethed, circling the counter.

CHAPTER 3

With the end of the school year in sight, most of Winsome Elementary had degenerated into a state of lawlessness. Resembling prisoners in the middle of a violent overthrow, pupils poured into the halls after each bell, raging and screaming, ignoring the frazzled shouts of their teachers as they pushed and shoved a route to freedom.

In Joy's class, on the other hand, the atmosphere had become unusually subdued. Perhaps it was because the windows were now open, Joy hypothesized, drawing everyone's attention to whatever fluffy cloud or singing bird happened by. Or more likely it was because they were graduating and everyone was now simply running down the clock, careful not to make any mistake that could end up in a repetition of the year.

Regardless of the cause, whatever flickering flame of interest had sustained the class from September onward had now completely fizzled out. Even the most compulsive brats and bullies couldn't find the strength to inflict misery on others, Joy had noticed. And since she was their usual target, this meant uncommon bliss. For once she could rest her eyes without the fear of a wet missile hitting her painfully off the temple.

Further adding to Joy's delight, the year had finally put a puncture in their teacher Miss Keener's overinflated pep. Slumped over a desk covered in cruise ship brochures, Miss Keener would stare into space for long spells until some fearful pupil finally made a noise to startle her.

Then again, the poor woman had been pining ever since the departure of her teacher's assistant, Murray. Leaving behind a bouquet of yellow carnations, the tattooed giant had completed his requirements and departed, never to be seen in the halls again.

Gone along with him were Miss Keener's cheerful *Good mornings*, her daily dietary lectures, and the cringe-worthy pageantry of her magic top hat, where she'd once insisted on fishing for students' names. Instead she had become like a robot, Joy observed, constantly switching off to save what little charge remained in her battery.

The hot sun blazing through the open window like an alien stun weapon only added to the general torpor in the room that day. Yawning widely, Miss Keener suddenly rose to her feet.

"I have to go . . . ," she began, struggling to form the words against her uncooperative jaw, "to the office."

Then, instead of issuing her usual instructions about students remaining in their seats and the penalties accruable, the teacher left the class, staggering slightly.

The lack of such an explicit warning would have normally caused the class to erupt into chaos. However, this time hardly anyone even registered her departure. It was Tyler, Joy's most hated tormentor, who finally roused himself enough to notice their lack of supervision.

"Yo, Seth!" he shouted over to a friend, whom Miss Keener had purposely relocated across the room earlier in the year. "Did you hear the news?"

Doubting that any of Tyler's cronies were ever much up on current events, Joy wasn't surprised when Seth said no. Still, she decided to monitor the exchange in case it was a signal to start some sort of barrage on her. Fortunately, this time it wasn't.

"They're gonna make a movie here!"

"A movie? Where?"

"Where?" he imitated unflatteringly. "Where do you think? In town, dumb-face."

The rest of the classroom became immediately interested. "A real movie? For real?"

"No, for fake," sneered Tyler. "Yes, for real," he declared, inflating with enough pride to make Joy wonder if he thought he was getting a producing credit.

"I heard it too," said Melissa.

"It's true," Nathan confirmed. As everyone knew, Nathan's father worked as a security guard at the local newspaper, making him the most credible source available for confirming any fact.

"Cool! What's the movie about?"

"I heard it's about vampires."

"I heard it's about zombies."

"Actually, I heard it's got both," Tyler informed them.

Hearing this, Joy could not help but say something. "Vampires *and* zombies?" she cried out. "In the same movie?"

"Yeah. Doesn't it sound awesome?"

"Actually, it sounds moronic," Joy declared. But it figured. Vampires and zombies were the two monsters even Joy couldn't stand lately, mostly because every girl at Winsome had somehow come under the impression that they made good boyfriends. Pale and pensive with six-packs, they craved not blood and brains apparently, but chocolate and kisses. Joy was outraged. What was happening to the world? Even Cassandra, the classroom's girliest girl, had abandoned her beloved ponies in favor of the latest big-screen hunk, some walking cadaver named Curtis.

Hearing Joy's outburst, Tyler's lips peeled back in disdain. "Why? What's wrong with it, freak-show?"

Joy refused to be intimidated on matters of obvious logic, especially when they pertained to horror entertainment. "How can you put vampires and zombies in the same movie? They are from two totally different kinds of stories."

"It's easy," scoffed Tyler. "Just make a war between the two."

"A war?" Joy felt her voice fall just short of a full-on shriek. "Come on. Zombies can't fight wars. They can hardly use a door handle or take an escalator."

"So? There's always a lot of them."

"Oh, please. Even one self-respecting vampire is going to kick an entire army of zombies' butts."

Joy was happy to hear the rest of the class begin murmuring in agreement for once. However, Tyler would never lose an argument that gracefully, she knew from experience.

"Well, you would know, Spooky," sneered Tyler. "Since your mom's a vampire and your dad's a zombie."

Joy felt her face burn as the class broke out laughing at her. It was exactly these sort of moments that she was so hoping would be over in junior high.

Still, she couldn't help but picture her mother baring her fangs while Joy's shadowy-eyed father shuffled after her, moaning.

It did fit, she had to admit.

The snickering quickly died down, however, as the discussion returned to the movie. "Hey, do you know if anybody cool is in it?" someone asked Nathan.

"My dad said Penny Farthing is supposed to be in it," he answered.

There was a squeak of delight from a few girls. "I love her!" said Cassandra. "Even though she did blow off the Teens Say Awards last month, which was lame. She won for best kiss and didn't even bother recording an acceptance speech!"

"She's actually a bit of a jerk," her friend Missy reported.

"My dad said some big rock star is in it too, but I never heard of him," Nathan added. "My mother was pretty excited, though."

"Who is it?"

"It was a dumb made-up-sounding name. Teddy something."

"Teddy *Danger*?" someone asked.

"Yeah, Teddy Danger, that's it."

Joy's head turned with a snap. The name struck her as very familiar, but she couldn't remember why.

"Ugh, my parents like that guy. He's old!"

"Man, I was hoping it would be someone cooler than that."

"Who's Teddy Danger?"

"He's a singer," Tyler replied. "A punk rocker."

"Yuck," said Cassandra. "Punk rockers spit at their audiences."

"And have dumb hair!" Tyler added. "And like slam dancing!" The boy began a demonstration, careening across the room and smashing into desks.

The door opened. Miss Keener entered, holding a steaming Styrofoam cup in her hand. "All right, children, simmer down," she said, without noticing that several desks were no longer even pointing forward. "Tyler, I thought I told you to stay in your seat," she then protested.

"You never actually said so, Miss Keener," the boy informed her gleefully.

But instead of arguing the point further, the teacher just sighed and collapsed into her chair.

So they were making a movie, thought Joy. In Darlington? What sort of movie could anyone possibly want to make here—in what had to be the most boring location on the planet? But with special effects being so good these days, maybe it didn't really matter. Maybe they could paint the whole place blue and digitally fill in a more interesting city later.

Byron seemed suitably impressed to hear the news about

the movie as they waited in line for the bus home.

"You think everything is dumb," her brother pointed out. "It sounds cool to me."

"Yeah, and I seem to remember you thinking that moronic Kiddy Kingdom was cool," Joy reminded him. "Even after those kids almost beat you to death with foam-covered sticks."

The memory of little Lucy Primrose's birthday party at the medieval-themed function room still haunted Joy. It was just such a typical Darlington experience—loud, lame, and phony in the extreme.

It was also there that she had first come face-to-face with Morris Mealey, she remembered as she spotted the odd little boy leaving the school. As usual he wore a bow tie and had his hair neatly plastered into a side part. Joy wondered if he still hated her for wrecking the city's plans for building a water park over Spooking Bog. Probably. After all, it was Morris himself who had come up with the idea as part of a school contest.

Apparently he did still harbor some resentment, Joy quickly learned. Catching sight of her, the boy pinched his face in complete disgust and made a rude hand gesture.

Byron meanwhile was offended by his sister's slight regarding his fighting abilities. "Hey, I was outnumbered," he explained of his inability to bludgeon his way into the play castle. "Besides, you should thank me for taking you to Kiddy Kingdom, since that's where you got to meet your boyfriend, Louden."

At the mention of Lucy Primrose's big brother, Joy's face

turned instantly red. "Louden is not my boyfriend," she said furiously under her breath.

"Well, that's what everybody thinks anyway."

Fortunately, Joy knew instantly that there was no way her brother was privy to what anybody thought outside of his own grade. However, such misinformation was still worrying, no matter where it was coming from.

Just then the Spooking bus arrived, spewing out even more black smoke than usual. A second after the children got on, it drove off at high speed.

"Anyway, if the rumor is true, Mom will be excited," Byron added as they roared toward Spooking Hill.

"What?" Joy cried. "Don't tell Mom anything about it!"

"Why not? She's a big Teddy Danger fan."

It took a moment before Joy realized that Byron was talking about the movie. "Wait a second. Who is he again?"

"Don't you remember? When Mom smashed into that guy's car?"

A chill went through Joy. "You mean Mr. Phipps?"

"Yeah. She got all excited because he looked like the singer Teddy Danger."

Of course! He was that old punk rocker, the one with the spiked hair like a hedgehog! Joy had looked him up on the Internet afterward, confirming that he did indeed share a resemblance with her mortal enemy, Mr. Phipps.

Joy squirmed to remember the incident with her mother and the man who hated Spooking so much he couldn't even say its name without sending spit flying. Flirting outrageously after the accident, Mrs. Wells had cast some sort of spell over him, it had appeared. Mr. Phipps had then inexplicably let her off without having to pay for what looked like a lot of damage.

"It's just a little dent," he had insisted while beaming at Joy's mother. "Don't worry. It's easy enough to fix."

The dent in Joy's already fragile psyche, however, could never be repaired. It was one thing to see her mother flashing teeth and flapping her eyelashes at a man who wasn't Joy's father. But it was quite another to see her making doe eyes at the most villainous individual Joy had ever had the displeasure to meet.

Because even though Mr. Phipps had helped her escape almost certain death at the asylum, Joy couldn't help but remain hostile toward him. After all, the black-suited mayor's assistant wanted to destroy Spooking. That much he had made very clear. And his creepy insistence that he was somehow her friend, somehow trying to protect her from the future, had only made her stomach lurch more.

It was an assertion that Mr. Phipps had made twice now. Once after Halloween, when Joy had had the misfortune to run into him the day he'd moved back to Spooking and his childhood home above the music store. And a second time, in the gloomy old schoolhouse where Joy had learned that her mysterious friend Poppy was in fact not of this world.

On that occasion he'd also predicted that he was about to be fired from his job at City Hall, which had come true. A few days later Joy had spotted him from the bus while heading to school. He'd looked haggard as he'd sat out on his front balcony above the old music shop. For weeks he had appeared there each morning in the same threadbare bathrobe, motionless no matter the weather, staring blankly out at the cemetery opposite.

But no longer.

The bus reached the summit of Spooking Hill. As they roared past the cemetery, Joy looked out the window and once again saw no sign of life at the old music store. Just as it had been earlier that morning, the balcony was empty, and the evil black car was missing from the driveway.

Could the mayor have given him his old job back? The possibility filled Joy with renewed dread. If so, it meant that Spooking was no longer safe, and that something terrible was coming, she was certain.

Pulling into the outside lane, the bus overtook a limousine. "Hey, look!" said Byron as they whizzed by. "Do you think someone famous is inside?"

"This is Spooking, Byron," said Joy. "What on earth would anybody famous ever be doing up here?"

"Hey, wait a second," said Byron. "I thought you said that guy E. A. Peugeot lived here."

"Yeah. So?"

"Well, isn't he famous?"

"That's different," Joy sighed. "He's dead."

CHAPTER 4

As the school bus sped off into the distance, the white stretch limousine signaled to turn left onto Weredale Avenue. With the ungainliness of an ocean liner, the overlong vehicle made the maneuver and headed up the oak-lined street.

With shadowy abandoned-looking residences reflected in its tinted windows, the limo drove to the very end, where it tentatively climbed the steep drive of a large old house. Drawing up by a double garage, the car then stopped.

A moment later the driver got out. Putting on his hat, he walked to the rear of the car, where he then opened the back door and stood aside.

A man in a leather jacket climbed out, his hair having the appearance of a sterling silver sea urchin.

"I still can't believe they picked me up in a white limo!" Teddy Danger complained again as a tiny pink-haired woman emerged behind him. Glaring back at the gleaming vehicle, Teddy kicked the gravel with a heavy boot laced up to his kneecap. "I look like a schoolkid going to his graduation dance!"

"It's just a car, Teddy," the little woman said.

"Oh yeah? Well, what if someone saw me at the airport? Or even worse, took a picture?"

"I'm sure no one could have seen you getting picked up on the tarmac," the woman assured him, struggling with several pieces of luggage.

Her name was Molly Sinclair. She had been Teddy's assistant for two years now—two long years without a vacation worth even speaking about.

"They better not have. Celebrities don't ride in white limos, you know. They ride in black ones. It's common knowledge to anyone in the entertainment business!"

"I will call the company and make sure there's a black one put aside for you tomorrow," Molly assured him.

"Because there's no way I'm setting foot inside that monstrosity again. I'm serious."

"I said I would call and tell them!" she insisted.

The driver dumped the remaining suitcases onto the pavement. Then, without a word, he got back into his monstrosity and drove off, leaving the pair standing alone on the drive.

"You're going to have to get those," Teddy said, gesturing to the bags. "My back is killing me. Which reminds me, I'll need a massage therapist as soon as possible." Teddy turned and looked up at the house. "Really? This is the place the studio rented for me?" he demanded, his spiked hair adding to his look of shock.

"What's wrong with it?" Molly asked.

"What's wrong with it?" Teddy shot a glare at his assistant. "Molly, use your eyes. It looks like the haunted house ride in an amusement park! Did they know it's for me, music legend Teddy Danger, and not some stupid actor?"

"Of course they know it's for you," Molly insisted. "It just wasn't easy finding somewhere with ten bedrooms like you asked for—"

"Eight bedrooms," her boss immediately corrected. "I asked for eight bedrooms."

"We only need two, Teddy!"

"Hey, we're here for two months, and I have friends who are coming to visit. Where are they supposed to sleep? In bunk beds?"

Molly sighed. She'd really hoped that this time she might get a break from Teddy's friends, a bunch of brain-damaged brats who couldn't even make themselves toast without setting something on fire.

"Well, I'm afraid this is the best property they could find anywhere near the set," she declared. "So you and your buddies will just have to make do with it. Anyway, I'm a bit surprised you're complaining. I thought you of all people would appreciate its Gothic vibe."

Teddy looked up at the looming mansion. "Gothic, huh?" he replied, taking in the menacing exterior. He then turned, looking down the block at the other houses. He had to agree that the property was in better condition than its immediate neighbors at least, each of which looked on the verge of total collapse.

"All right, then, I'll make do. To be honest, compared to the squat I used to live in, this place is practically a palace," Teddy added, striding up the flagstone path toward the front door. "Did I tell you how we once had to electrify the fire escape just to stop skinheads from attacking us?"

Molly rolled her eyes. Teddy loved to talk about the old days and how edgy his life was back when he was *still paying his dues*, as he put it. He sometimes even liked to show her the thin white slash on his side that he said he'd gotten from a knife fight, a mark that looked suspiciously like her own appendix operation scar, she'd noted.

Quickly gathering up all the bags, she followed after him.

Teddy looked disapprovingly down the long sloping front yard, which despite its recent clipping still appeared choked with weeds and clover. Back at his own home he would never have stood for such a thing, having once fired a gardener for potting a plant in the wrong variety of soil.

It was then that he caught sight of something standing in the center of the lawn. A thickset dog, staring back at him while in the process of showering the grass in urine.

He stopped. "Hey, you. Shoo!" he shouted at the broadheaded animal that resembled the attack dogs that currently roamed Teddy's property at home. Finishing his business, the dog curled his lips back, showcasing the unbelievable number of teeth crammed into his maw. Teddy, scared, hurried on. Glancing back, he was relieved to see the dog hopping off with surprising speed despite a missing front leg.

"Did you see that freaky thing?" he called back to Molly. "I've thought of a good name for it: Tripod! What do you think?"

"Leave the dog alone, Teddy."

The ancient wooden porch creaked as they mounted the

stairs. Teddy tried the heavy oak front door and found it locked.

"Keys?" he demanded.

"Under the mat," Molly panted, still laden with suitcases.

"Ah." Teddy bent over to recover an old-fashioned skeleton key. He fumbled around for a moment and then managed to unlock the door. It swung inward on its own power with an ominous creak, revealing a pitch-black interior.

"Ladies first," Teddy said.

Pushing past him, Molly strode into the dark entranceway. It was a wide oval foyer, she saw as her eyes adjusted to the gloom. After dumping the cases on the large rug at its center, she found a light switch. High above, an enormous chandelier lit up the area.

Teddy finally entered the property, leaving the front door open.

"I guess it seems swanky enough," he declared, casting his eyes over the collection of antique oil paintings adorning the paneled walls. "Whoa, check her out!" he exclaimed.

Molly craned up at the large portrait in a gilded frame, hung high above the hearth. It was of a striking dark-haired woman, gazing into a crystal ball and seeing something apparently delightfully uncertain. "She looks like some kind of fortune-teller," she said.

"Yeah, the hot kind," Teddy clarified. "You know, I haven't had a tarot card reading in a while, actually. See if you can arrange one for me." He sighed at the brooding image, then turned to the onyx-colored staircase with a carved wood balustrade that swept up to the second floor.

"I guess I'll go up and check out the master bedroom."

Teddy headed up to the second floor as Molly flopped down, exhausted, on one of the suitcases. This could be a long couple of months, she thought, listening to his big boots clomping around upstairs. And why did they have to come so early when filming didn't even start for another two weeks?

Probably so Teddy could get a few acting lessons, she reminded herself.

But at least it was a pretty big house. Unlike at the endless hotels Molly was used to staying in while Teddy was on tour, hopefully here she could at least find a room that did not connect directly to her employer's. Smiling at the prospect, she closed her eyes for a moment.

Just then she heard something. It was a moan, she was certain, issuing from deep within the house. Sounding like a fetid rush of air from a great slumbering monster's throat, it raced through unseen rooms and halls in seeming pursuit of her.

Molly jumped in fright as the front door suddenly slammed shut.

"Hey, come check it out!" shouted Teddy from the landing, holding a bottle of something in his hand. "I've got a wicked four-poster bed like a king or a lord or something!"

"I will be right up, Teddy."

"And the studio left out a bottle of nice champagne," he added, peeling off the foil. "Oh, and I've picked you out a room. It's right across the hall from me so you don't have to go far in case I need something."

Molly's head dropped toward the floor as she pinched her eyes shut.

There was a sudden pop, immediately followed by the sound of breaking glass as the champagne cork hit the chandelier.

"Whoopsies," said Teddy.

CHAPTER 5

"**B**ut of course you're going," Mrs. Wells informed her daughter that Saturday before lunch. "It's the graduation dance. You have to go."

Joy had suspected this might be her mother's attitude. And despite her best effort to conceal the upcoming event, she had apparently not sufficiently crumpled up the reminder notice when she had thrown it away. She should have known better. Despite being a tenured philosophy professor, her mother had the eyes of a police detective, especially when it came to emptying trash cans.

"What do you mean I have to go?" Joy demanded. "Why?"

"Because if you don't, you'll regret it for the rest of your life," Mrs. Wells warned gravely.

Joy looked at her mother, wearing a pensive expression. Since Joy was already hoping for an unnaturally long life, she had to weigh the possibility seriously, she decided. So she began picturing herself as a housebound old woman, bitterly wishing she had shaken her booty in a hot gymnasium with people she considered mostly bullies and bozos.

It just didn't seem likely.

In fact, she couldn't picture herself having to shoulder

any sort of regret past the weekend, much less to her death-bed. Because let's face it: This wasn't a med school or a space academy she was graduating from. This was Winsome Elementary, the bane of her last seven years of existence. And she already had her own private celebrations planned, which involved skipping and shrieking with glee.

"I think I'll pass, thanks," said Joy.

"It's not up for discussion. As parents we have to make decisions about your well-being, and this kind of milestone is too important to miss out on. If it's your clothes you're worried about, don't worry, dear. We'll head down to the mall this afternoon and pick you out a nice new dress."

"A new dress?" cried Joy. "Are you even listening to me? I don't want to go!"

Mrs. Wells looked at her daughter with a pained look. "Joy, you may not realize it, but you are a very pretty girl. And I'm certain that if you have a more open attitude, a few boys will even ask you to dance. And then you won't feel so self-conscious about being there, hanging around the punch bowl."

Joy snorted. "You just don't get it!" she raged.

At the same time, the question of whether or not Louden Primrose was going sprung to mind. And instantly Joy felt mortified.

Louden was the only boy at school whom Joy had been even vaguely friendly with this final year of elementary school. He had even volunteered to come up to her house in Spooking to work on a project together, something no one she knew from Darlington had ever done before.

The visit itself had proved to be somewhat of a nightmare, Joy felt. Showing him around her dilapidated house, she had experienced a newfound self-consciousness. Joy had silently cringed as the boy's eyes had seemed to alight on just about every inch of chipped paint and each hole in the walls, and as his toes caught on every piece of torn carpet and warped floorboard.

But most embarrassing had been her parents. Wringing their hands nervously, they'd grilled Louden on every detail of his family's life before fussing around him like he was a foreign prince uncertain of local customs.

The only relief had come when they had finally gotten down to do their schoolwork up in the library, one of the few relatively presentable rooms in the house. But then her mother had popped in, bringing them each a glass of water. Reaching for one, Joy had been horrified to see that the water in each glass was brown, with flotillas of rust flakes patrolling their surfaces.

She had gasped as Louden had slurped it back without a word.

Later, when Louden's parents had come to pick him up, Joy had smiled back falsely as he had insisted how great it had been, seeing where she lived, and then had further suggested she might come hang out at his place sometime. Joy had politely accepted the offer, all the while knowing there was no way she was ever taking him up on it. She had already seen the Primrose home on Sunnyview Street, which she and Byron had visited last Halloween. Inside and out it couldn't have been more unlike Number 9 Ravenwood

Avenue. And there was no way she was going back there now. Ever.

So it had happened that Joy had begun creatively rebuffing each and every one of Louden's efforts to make conversation at school. Fearing he might reiterate the invitation, she would jerk her face away the moment the boy's glance turned toward her. And at lunch and recess she spent an inordinate amount of time loitering in the girls' washroom.

But now, with the graduation dance looming, Joy found herself wondering if Louden had a date. He probably did, she guessed, since he wasn't shy and made the other girls at school giggle a lot. Not that it mattered, since she didn't care anyway.

Ignoring Joy's protests, Mrs. Wells kept insisting that Joy would be much more excited about going once she'd gotten a look at herself in proper evening wear. "You know, I think something in a deep blue or indigo would go really well against your blond hair, don't you think? And if you promise to be careful, I can lend you one of your grandmother's antique necklaces. . . ."

Joy grunted in surrender. Having never met her grandmother, Joy had always cherished the feeling of connection she got by trying on her jewelry. And though her mother and grandmother had endured a pretty stormy relationship from all reports, it was clear to Joy that Mrs. Wells missed her own mother dearly. So the last thing Joy wanted was to appear ungrateful for the offer.

In the end, she decided that trying on a few dresses that day was probably much easier than arguing about it for the rest of the month. Joy would make up her mind about the dance closer to the night. She could always fake being sick once again by mixing her mother's alabaster face powder with a glob of petroleum jelly, and giving herself the sweaty blanched pallor of someone about to drop dead.

That afternoon Joy clung on for her life as the family station wagon skidded around the vast parking lot of the Darlington Mega Mall. Her foot hard on the gas, Mrs. Wells whipped along the rows of cars, looking for a parking spot with the same determination with which a shark might hunt a seal pup.

"There we go!" Mrs. Wells finally exclaimed. "I told you we'd find something closer."

Having to exhale first, Joy barely squeezed out through the narrow opening left by her mother's abominable parking job. They then walked the short distance to an entrance.

"This is so fun, isn't it? Having a mother-daughter shopping day? Maybe you can help me pick out some flats for the summer while we're here."

"Okay," Joy replied with fake enthusiasm. It was proving to be hard work, hiding her foul mood and overall sense of indignation. Maybe it was the offer of letting her wear one of her grandmother's necklaces, but something made Joy unusually careful of her mother's feelings.

Nevertheless, to Joy, Saturdays were precious. They were one of the two days a week that she got to spend completely away from Darlington. The idea of squandering a Saturday on a trip to the mall was just too much to bear. The mall was basically the center of the universe down there, a distillation of everything Joy hated about the city. Were it not for the movie theater, Joy figured she could happily live out her entire life without setting foot inside the place again.

But she did like Sergeant Popper's Popping Corn Emporium, she admitted to herself as its mouthwatering aroma wafted through the automatic doors.

Having never parked near this entrance before, neither Joy nor Mrs. Wells were familiar with this part of the mall, which was dimly lit and somewhat deserted. It was only the smell of popcorn that identified their rough whereabouts. Joy peered into Trick Shotz, a large shadowy hall where men were busy playing pool. Turning, she then looked into the shop opposite. There she was shocked to glimpse a familiar face.

Joy recognized him instantly. It was Mr. Phipps.

Swallowed up in a gigantic black T-shirt, the mayor's former assistant looked rail thin, she noticed. He was pacing impatiently behind a customer trying out a V-shaped guitar. His once carefully assembled hair was now an unkempt bush.

Looking out, his eyes met Joy's.

Startled, she waved. Why did she just do that? This was the self-proclaimed scourge of Spooking, the man hell-bent on remaking the town into a mini version of Darlington.

Still, he didn't look much like a scourge now. And wasn't he also the man who had saved her from the masked giant's clutches in the asylum? Who had then distracted the mad doctor and crazed nurse so she could escape?

It was almost certain that she owed him not just a wave, but her very life.

In the second before Joy and her mother continued on, Joy saw the man halfheartedly raise a hand in reply. And in his tortured face she saw a person burning with humiliation, wishing he were anywhere else.

It was the same look that she saw often in the mirror of the girls' washroom at Winsome.

"Who were you waving at, Joy?" her mother asked.

"No one," she said. "I mean, just someone I know," she answered.

Joy felt her heart stop as her mother skidded to a halt. "Do you want to stop and say hi? We're in no big rush, you know."

"No!" Joy cried. The last thing she wanted was to have to speak to the guy, never mind having to watch her mother purring in his presence again. "Please. Let's go," she begged, yanking her mother's wrist.

But then a queer little smile crossed the face of Mrs. Wells. "Was it a boy? Was it Louden? He was cute. Hey, maybe he'll ask you to the dance!"

"Omigod, no! Can we just go? You're embarrassing me."

"All right, Joy. Sheesh."

Joy continued dragging her mother into the depths of the busy mall, leaving Electric Eddie's far behind. Joining the bustling crowd, they worked their way to the escalators and climbed up and up until they reached It's a Girl Thing, a clothing retailer catering to young ladies.

And though Joy had never been so relieved for an opportunity to change a subject, she soon found herself running out of things to say about a series of flouncy-looking dresses.

"I don't know," said Joy over the blasting music, making a face at the emerald green number her mother was currently holding up. "They all look too poofy to me."

"They're just dresses, dear."

"Maybe they're just dresses to Miss Universe. To me they're too poofy."

"Well, I don't know what universe you are living in, but in this one, girls like dressing up for dances like this. Why don't you just try one on? How about the one you didn't completely hate, the one with the empire waist and velvet top?"

Joy sighed and took the discarded dress back off the rack. Indigo blue, it was the plainest of the dresses with just a thin detail of beading, which was why Joy had not rejected it completely out of hand. Looking again, she realized it was not completely unlike a dress she remembered Melody Huxley once wearing in one of her faded old photos. She'd been at a glitzy casino, grimacing horribly at either her particular hand of cards or the smoke curling up from the giant cigar dangling from her lips, but otherwise looking fairly spectacular.

Joy, however, soon found out she looked far less like a glamorous gambler and more like a sour-faced kid wearing a dark blue sack. Stepping out from the changing room, she reluctantly gave a twirl at her mother's instruction.

"Well, I think you look lovely. Let's get it."

Sighing, Joy glanced at a nearby mirror. Maybe she was wrong. Maybe she did look a little like Ms. Huxley, without the cigar, of course. Joy then noticed a couple of girls from her class in the store. It was Cassandra and Missy, browsing a display of bangles nearby. Before Joy could slip out of sight, they both turned and saw her standing there in the blue dress.

Eyes wide with surprise, the girls turned to each other and began whispering.

Joy retreated back into the changing room. That was it, she decided. There was no way she was going to the stupid dance at all, much less in this dress. But there was no use in discussing it right then with her mother. So, back in her regular clothes, Joy left the dressing room, handing over the roughly folded dress.

"I'm going to wait outside," Joy told Mrs. Wells.

"Is something wrong?" her mother asked, immediately noticing her red face.

"I'm just hot."

"Okay, dear. It looks like there's a bit of a line to pay, so don't wander too far."

Joy agreed and then began heading out of the store, hoping to avoid running into her two classmates again. Glancing to the side, she saw they had moved on from the bangles and were now examining colorful scarves with skull prints on them. *Wait a second*, she thought. Skulls? First vampires and zombies, and now skulls? Whatever happened to puppies and ponies?

Horrified, Joy hurried out. The thumping dance music left behind, she let the soothing sounds of soft rock wash over her as she leaned over the railing and looked out at the central hub of the Mega Mall. From the top gallery she peered into packed stores lining every level, hawking what seemed like every good and service imaginable.

She stared up at the giant skylight high above, and followed the path of its golden light as it bathed the food court below. Staring down at the seething mass of diners, she laughed to herself, thinking how much like ants they looked, crowded over a fallen crumb.

Joy felt suddenly dizzy and took a step back. A hand fell onto her shoulder.

"Phew, that didn't take too long," said Mrs. Wells. "Well, dear, you are all set for the dance now. I just realized it's your brother's birthday coming up. Do you mind helping me pick him out a present before we go looking at shoes?"

"Okay, Mom."

"Any ideas where to start?" Mrs. Wells asked her daughter.

They looked at each other before their eyes sought out the same massive storefront far below: Electronica Veronica.

Without any further discussion they made their way to the escalators.

CHAPTER 6

Having spent the last six days in a row working at Electric Eddie's, Phipps drove home, barely able to keep the car on the road. He was exhausted, and his feet were throbbing. But worst of all, no matter how hard he tried, he just could not get "Smoke on the Water" out of his head.

It was an occupational hazard, Collin had informed him.

Phipps wasn't even supposed to work Saturdays. Sleeping in that morning, he had been awoken by his manager, who had called to inform him that the usual guy had called in sick.

"So?" Phipps had replied, grinding a fist into his sleepy eye. "What does that have to do with me?"

Apparently, he had then learned, it was part of his probation to prove not only that was he reliable, but that he was good in a pinch.

Hearing the tires spinning on the gravel shoulder, Phipps's eyes snapped open. He was falling asleep at the wheel, which was a very bad thing while ascending the crooked road up to Spooking. With a quick jerk he narrowly averted a death plunge down a steep rock incline and then continued up to the summit. Within a minute he had passed the cemetery and pulled into the drive of his home.

The faded sign for Luthier Lorenzo screeched in the breeze as he got out of the car. Phipps glared at the front of his father's old music shop. What would have happened if he had listened to his father and gone into the family business? Hardly anyone played the lute anymore, or the harp, or the mandolin—three of his father's flagship instruments. He would have been long ago wiped out by the likes of Electric Eddie's.

And if his father had still been alive, he would have blamed his son, no doubt. He'd never been able to do anything right in his eyes, ever since he'd become a man.

"Why do you want to go and study music?" he'd demanded of his son. "You can already read music and play it beautifully."

"I don't want to just read music, Father. I want to write it."

"Why? All the best music has already been written. By geniuses. Do you think you're a genius, Son?" he'd asked mockingly. "That you're Mozart with a Mohawk? Or a blue-haired Beethoven?"

"Maybe not," the young punk Octavio had sneered back at him. "But at least I'm not a pompous old shopkeeper!"

Such were the pair's daily exchanges before Phipps had finally gone away to the city, to music school, breaking his mother's heart and further hardening his father's. He had never seen either of them again.

Until now, that is, as their hovering ghosts lurked forever in the corner of his eye. He had to sell this place, he thought. But he was no closer to putting the ugly two-story building back on the market. And no closer to moving into even the cheapest studio Darlington had to offer. Not on his current wages.

Putting his key in the door, Phipps stopped, hearing the unusual sound of heavy vehicles approaching. He turned, seeing a convoy of gleaming white trucks lumbering toward him. As they rumbled past the old shop, he managed to make out words on several of them:

STAR TRAILERS.

The convoy continued on without slowing, heading into town.

What was all that about? he wondered. Phipps had lived in a big city for many years after leaving Spooking, so the sight seemed somehow familiar to him. Then he remembered seeing the very same type of vehicles parked around the old squat down at the waterfront, blocking off streets for days at a time as they set up blazing lights and other equipment.

It was a film crew, he was certain, rolling into Spooking. But for what purpose?

Phipps went inside. Flicking the light switch by the front door, he discovered that the power was out. Swearing, he slammed the door. It had been very windy that morning, he remembered, which kept blowing the power line to the building loose. The electric company had just been up and had told him it was fixed.

However, this was Spooking, where no one bothered to do a good job of anything. He would have to call them again. Previously he would have shouted down the phone, reminding them whom he worked for, making threats until a repairman was dispatched. But no longer. *Do you know who I am?* he imagined himself now demanding. *I'm the guy who changed your son's guitar strings!*

He decided to eat before calling. Going into the lightless kitchen, he fumbled around the cabinets until he found something edible, and then fished around in the drawers until he had finally retrieved a can opener, a spoon, a book of matches, and a candle.

Sitting down on the couch, he lit the candle. Softening the end with the flame, he then stuck it straight to the coffee table on one of the few bare spaces remaining. He then opened the can, revealing what looked like some sort of stew.

It was his first candlelight meal in years, he realized.

Phipps took a bite and chewed. Making a face, he then checked the label again to make sure he hadn't accidentally bought dog food. No, it was supposedly fit for human consumption, he saw.

The dirty spoon clattered onto the coffee table.

Phipps turned on his phone to call the electric company. He was amazed his phone still had a charge, but then again he hardly used it anymore. To his further surprise there was even a message for him.

It was from Miss Sparks, the mayor's new assistant.

"Hello, Mr. Phipps," she said after introducing herself. "Sorry to disturb you on the weekend, but I'm wondering if you can give me a call."

What could she possibly want from him? he wondered.

Perhaps she had lost the key to the mayor's private washroom, or needed to know what color of tie made the mayor look least like a crook. Feeling angry, he decided to ignore the call. Instead he dialed up the electric company and listened to a recorded voice informing him that office hours were now over.

Upon hanging up, he discovered that he could no longer resist calling Miss Sparks back.

"Thank you so much for getting back to me so promptly," she said, answering on the first ring. "You know, I've heard so many great things about you."

Phipps grunted, wondering what possible sort of positive impression his replacement could have of him. After all, he had been fired. And surely his name had come up among the other gossipy workers down at City Hall, who had almost to a man and woman universally despised him and had surely gleefully celebrated his undoing.

But the truth was that Phipps hadn't taken the job to make a bunch of friends with whom he could talk about television around the watercooler. He had been there to build a city, a towering modern testament to urbanity. He had been there to scour the area of such worn-down blights as the neighborhood whose postal code he currently shared.

"What can I do for you, Miss Sparks?" he asked, putting his feet up among the stained newspapers and wrappers on the coffee table.

"I'm calling on behalf of the mayor, of course," she said. "He said he ran into you the other day down at the mall."

"Oh?" Phipps could feel his hackles going up. Did the

mayor mention where he had run into him, working as a lowly clerk in a grimy music store? And was that a smirk he detected, her voice ever so slightly pinched by it?

"The mayor told me you are a talented musician. And that you used to have a band years ago?" she asked.

"Uh-huh," Phipps replied, amazed that the mayor recollected even that much about him.

"What were you called?"

"The Black Tongs." He sighed, glancing at his awaiting supper, which despite its acrid smell was now making his mouth water.

"Really?" she said with unexpected enthusiasm. "You were in the Black Tongs."

"Yes. Why?"

"I knew I'd heard your name before," Miss Sparks said cheerfully. "I actually saw your band way back a couple of times. You guys were great!"

"Really?" replied Phipps. He then listened as Miss Sparks recounted the days when she too had been a young punk rocker, her hair bleached, wearing plaid skirts and combat boots and sticking safety pins through her nose.

Brightening, Phipps then found himself laughing along with her at how such a total conservative type as the mayor had now twice hired ex-punk-rockers as his assistant.

"Oh, didn't you know he had his own band?" Phipps even quipped. "MacBrayne Damaged. They were pretty hard-core, actually—"

Miss Sparks laughed so hard she had a coughing fit. "It was such a shame you guys never put out a record," she lamented once she had regained her composure. "I was looking forward to buying it."

"Yes, well. Unfortunately, we broke up just as we were about to."

"Really? That stinks. Oh yeah. Didn't somebody in your band go off with someone famous?"

The Tongs' old front man felt his mood suddenly sour, remembering how his best friend and songwriting partner had indeed left him in the lurch and gone off to join another band. But as if that hadn't been bad enough, the band he'd joined had been . . .

"My bass player, Felix," said Phipps. "He ended up playing with Teddy Danger," he told her.

But his rage quickly subsided. With a pang of guilt Phipps remembered how he had involved Felix in the whole business at the asylum a few months ago, where his friend had ultimately perished under a pile of bricks.

It was all his fault Felix was dead, he knew. Just like it was his fault that Vince, his old guitar player, had met his grisly end in the bog not long before.

If they had all just stuck with the plan and made their record, none of it would have happened, he was certain.

"Anyway, I guess that's enough reminiscing," said Miss Sparks after the long pause, her voice turning businesslike once again. "I'm calling because the mayor would like to offer you a position."

Phipps yanked his feet off the table and sat up. "A position?" he said with disbelief. "Back at City Hall?"

"Not a permanent one," she added hastily. "It's only a

contract, I'm afraid. But perhaps the mayor can find you something in the administration once the contract expires. I know elections are coming up, for example, so there might be something in the campaign office."

"Certainly, certainly." Phipps didn't care. He would do anything to get out of Electric Eddie's, to get out of his prison down in that stinking loop of the mall's intestines. But this was better than just anything. It was a chance to get back into city affairs, where he could begin amassing power and wielding influence again. But that assumed the mayor wasn't offering him a position washing cars in the motor pool. "So what's the contract?" he asked nervously.

"Well, I can only imagine you heard the big news that they are making a movie in town."

"Uh, no," said Phipps, who had been avoiding reading the newspaper since his termination. But instead of just canceling his subscription, he had each morning dutifully taken his copy inside, where it had then been thrown onto an ever-diminishing number of surfaces.

"It's a big-budget horror movie called *Blackthorne Inn*. They're shooting it up in Spooking."

The trucks that had driven by! He had been right—it was a film crew. "A horror movie, you say?" Somehow the title was familiar to him.

"That's what I'm told. Anyway, the mayor tells me that you know the neighborhood well. You grew up there, I hear?"

"I did," Phipps answered, squirming to admit his darkest shame to a complete stranger. He looked around at the squalid living room and cleared his throat. "Actually, I'm living up here again for the moment, renovating and selling my parents' property. It's just a temporary arrangement, however."

"Well, here's the situation," Miss Sparks continued. "We're looking for someone to act as a special liaison officer representing Darlington city, someone who can help the movie people and assist the location manager with any problems. This is a big production, as I'm sure you can imagine, and will bring a lot of money into the city. And who knows? If the studio has a good experience shooting here, one can only imagine what future benefits it might bring."

"One can only imagine," Phipps agreed. But the truth was he was already five steps ahead, imagining benefits he was certain none of the dull functionaries in the MacBrayne administration had the slightest foresight to envision. If they played their cards right, Darlington could become a moviemaking destination, he thought. By its very distinction of being completely unremarkable, it could stand in for any location, really.

And then there was Spooking. Unlike Darlington it was an extremely unique place. With its creepy cemetery and scary-looking houses, it was just begging to be in the movies. Surely it had no equal in the entire country. There could be good money to be made just renting out the whole town to film production crews. Unable to contain his excitement, he stood up and began pacing around the room.

But wasn't there an even greater secret about Spooking to be revealed? The town had a great and mysterious history after all, thanks to his own famous ancestor. Revealing the truth could generate huge interest in the terrible town on the hideous hill.

Phipps walked to the front window and looked out at the cemetery, its stones turning purple in the evening light. Yes, by proving this, he could truly make a mint. He could even sell the shop for a small fortune, he was certain, seeing that it occupied the very ground where the literary man's cottage had once stood.

But no. This was a fact that he could not endure coming to light, he decided almost as soon as he'd thought of it. He could not bear to witness it, to see some pathetic hack whose actions had forever cursed future descendants suddenly celebrated on his very doorstep.

Besides, what would Phipps ever need a fortune for, cursed as he was, thanks to that same man.

Even just thinking about vanishing these days, Phipps could almost feel it happening to him. The phone suddenly felt like a brick in his hand as he felt himself coming undone, his very particles straining against whatever influence kept them together in the form of a person.

Was this it? he wondered. The moment he would turn to vapor like his father? And if so, what then? Would he ever find his way out of the apartment above the old shop and float up into the atmosphere, his bodily elements condensing on flecks of dust until he became a tiny part of some enormous cloud, and then became droplets of rain, and then a puddle in the mud before being borne away to rivers and lakes and oceans?

"Mr. Phipps?" Miss Sparks called down the phone. "Are you still there?"

"Yes, yes, I'm here," Phipps answered, his tired body coming instantly back to him. "Of course I'm interested in the position. You know, I have always had a lot of ideas for Spooking, but this is by far the most intriguing project I have ever had the opportunity to work on."

"Well, why don't you swing by the mayor's office Monday and we can discuss things further. Would you like me to send a car for you?"

"No, no," replied Phipps. He looked down at the black monster in the driveway, its chrome grill grinning back at him. "I will take my own car."

"I look forward to meeting you."

Phipps hung up. *Finally*, he thought. *The pendulum is swinging in my favor again.* Standing in the window, he stood gazing out at the cemetery, watching the stones go dark before his eyes.

A flashlight came on outside the gates, Phipps noticed, held out by a small-statured man. Training the beam at the ground, the man walked in a slow circle before finally squatting down. He then began running his fingers along the dirt, examining something of apparent interest. A minute later he abruptly stood up. Brushing his hand off on his trousers, the man then strode with purpose into the lifeless grounds.

Phipps watched suspiciously until the light finally vanished among the gravestones.

CHAPTER 7

That evening at home Joy sat at the kitchen table thumbing through the spring-summer catalogue her mother had brought home from It's a Girl Thing.

"Just have a look at what they have," her mother had begged her. "It would be so nice to get you out of those morbid old clothes you wear and into something a bit more cheery."

While Joy was quick to point out that Ms. Melody Huxley's wardrobe comprised classic garments that never went out of style, she did have to admit that her tweed outfit was becoming rather stuffy and uncomfortable with the approach of summer. The weather had never seemed to bother Ms. Huxley, on the other hand. In fact, according to her pictures, the intrepid traveler had worn the exact same ensemble whether on a camel in the middle of the desert or standing over a dead polar bear in the Arctic.

According to Joy's parents, people were just made of harder stuff back then.

But even if Joy was feeling open to getting some new clothes, this whole "cheery" thing was an entirely different matter. And it wasn't just her own fashion sense. Had her mother been in some sort of walking coma when they'd been out shopping? Other than the hideous evening dresses they had so painfully lingered over, Joy had seen absolutely nothing cheery in stock.

And it wasn't just her imagination, she now confirmed. Leafing through the pages, Joy once again marveled at the macabre themes permeating young fashion. Even with her own considerable interest in death, danger, and destruction, Joy found the idea of swathing herself in skulls and snake prints completely ridiculous.

That said, she did spot a button-down with the toxic waste symbol motif that was kind of cool.

Bored, Joy turned her attention to her parents, who were busy trying to come up with something for dinner. Both tired and cranky, they were locked in a familiar struggle, a spectacle that Joy for some reason morbidly enjoyed. As always with such passive-aggressive death matches, Joy put her imaginary money on her mother, who could bring her husband to a fury of frustration with the seemingly most innocent of actions.

This time it was by removing a large jar from the fridge and placing it on the counter.

"So that's your suggestion?" demanded Mr. Wells. "That we have dill pickles for dinner?"

"I don't know, dear. I thought we could have them on the side. At least I'm trying to come up with something. Do you have a better idea?"

"I guess I will have to make my famous spaghetti, then," Mr. Wells said in a defeated voice. "You can always chop up a pickle and put it on top, if you like."

"Oh, now, that does sound good," said Mrs. Wells.

Watching the two of them, Joy remembered Tyler's insult, calling her parents a vampire and a zombie. Mrs. Wells stood back, wearing all black and greedily sipping from a long-stemmed glass what could have easily passed for blood. Mr. Wells, meanwhile, sporting a ratty old cardigan with holes in the elbows and a pair of frayed chinos, looked positively gray as he began rifling through the fridge.

Joy shivered in horror as an awful moan emerged from the vegetable crisper.

"We are out of mushrooms," Mr. Wells reported in utter despair. "And onions."

"I never keep onions in the fridge, dear. There are plenty of them with the potatoes in the pantry."

"It doesn't matter. We are still out of mushrooms. And I simply can't make my famous sauce without mushrooms!"

"Well, then, why not make one a bit more obscure for a change?" Seeing her husband's glare, she sighed. "All right, no spaghetti, then." She pulled out a recipe book and began flipping halfheartedly through it. "Here, this looks good. Potato frittatas. Do we have any eggs?"

From behind the fridge door came another moan.

"Oh, enough already," said Joy irritably. Even she was starting to get hungry now, and at the current rate it would be breakfast before the contest had a winner. "I'm going down to the freezer to get a frozen pizza. Is that okay with everybody?"

"I guess we could do that," said Mr. Wells, shutting the fridge door.

"If that's what you kids want," agreed Mrs. Wells, who closed the recipe book with a thump and slid it onto a shelf.

"Well, I think I speak for Byron when I say we were both hoping to eat tonight."

Pleased to have resolved a conflict for once, Joy went out to the hall. There, a locked door led down to the cellar. It seemed strange, she thought, the habit of always keeping the door bolted. After all, there was no other way in. So why had someone ever bothered putting a bolt on in the first place?

Unlocking the door, a number of terrifying possibilities came to Joy's mind. Could there be some sort of hidden passageway down there, perhaps snaking its way to Spooking Cemetery to emerge from an airless tomb?

Joy had read about such tunnels in *The Compleat and Collected Works of E. A. Peugeot.* According to one particular story, "Denizens of the Underworld," there was an entire city buried deep beneath the town, inhabited by a race of shadowy troglodytes whose lightless world rendered them unable to reproduce. Unlike the gibberings, Peugeot's carnivorous sewer dwellers, these gray humanoids were peaceful enough, snatching children from the surface not to eat them but simply to supplement their ever-dwindling population.

On the other hand, maybe the cellar door was kept locked because of the large drain set in the floor. That made the most sense. Having already braved the sewers searching for Fizz, Joy knew firsthand how vast the system was, and how it led to all sorts of otherwise inaccessible locations across town. Which meant anything could find its way into their house, really.

Then again, the drain wasn't that big. But what if some kind of serpent or perhaps swarms of man-eating rats got in? Maybe the bolt was a good idea.

Joy snapped on the ancient light switch. Far below came the pop of yet another exploding lightbulb. *That's just perfect,* she thought, peering down the darkened stairwell. Now there was only one bulb left.

She began descending the wooden stairs, which had worn into shovel blades over a century of use. Their slippery sheen made Joy immediately regret not putting on shoes, as did her arrival upon the stone floor of the cellar. Landing on what felt like an ice rink, she became painfully aware of a hole in one of her socks.

Luckily the one light remaining dangled directly above the freezer. A coffin-size monstrosity, its terrible rattle could be heard from all the way up in Joy's bedroom. Proceeding on her tiptoes, she crossed to the ancient appliance and with a grunt opened the lid.

Inside, a thick layer of frost made its contents indistinguishable. Looking at the frozen plain, Joy thought again of the picture of Ms. Huxley standing over the poor dead bear. It was a bit of a shame that her idol was such a remorseless animal killer, but at least dogs and horses remained in her good books.

At the thought, Joy glanced toward the far end of the cellar, where boxes and trunks sat stacked upon shelves. These were the forgotten possessions of the home's previous owners, among which she had spent countless hours cheerfully rifling. Reclaimed by the gloom, they now emanated an unsettling menace.

There was something in there she needed to get, Joy remembered.

Hands aching, Joy dug down through plastic wrapped leftovers. Finally exhuming a three-cheese deep-pan deluxe, she slammed the lid shut and turned back toward the trunks.

Stepping carefully, Joy cast an inky black shadow ahead of her. Before long she felt swallowed up by the cold and blackness as if slipping under the surface of a muddy lake at midnight. The frozen pizza tucked under one arm, she put a hand out in front of her and felt her way toward the trunks. Holding her breath, she inched forward, her very heartbeats slowing to a stop as an eerie hush fell over the cellar.

Then there came a sickening crunch underfoot.

Joy screamed.

Back in the safety of her bedroom, Joy could not stop herself from shivering. No matter how hard she tried, she couldn't shake the cold fear she felt, replaying her horror in the cellar over and over again.

It had happened as she'd been trying to find the collection of trunks, blindly groping in front of her as she inched forward in the dark. But she never reached them.

Normally Joy wasn't particularly afraid of the dark. In fact, she had squeezed into enough crypts and down enough holes to last most people's lifetimes. But this time she'd become overwhelmed with a terrifying sensation, as if she'd been slipping down the gullet of a great and terrible worm-beast that had parked itself against the foundation of her house.

Terrified, she'd considered turning back. That was when a large beetle had scurried underfoot. The beetle had exploded instantly under her weight, and the resulting mess of pulpy insect guts and shell had gotten her right through the hole in her sock. She'd then fled, screaming.

A hulking dark figure had caught her at the top of the stairs.

"Hey, where's the pizza?" her father had demanded.

Joy had held out her empty hands uncertainly, recalling how she'd dropped the box in fright. But there was no way she was going back down to feel around for it on a floor full of scuttling creatures.

"There were none left," she'd lied.

Mr. Wells had uttered another groan as he'd staggered off back toward the kitchen.

So Joy had no idea what dinner would be or when it would be ready, not that she much cared. She had lost her appetite, somehow still detecting the sour tang of the flattened beetle even with a fresh change of socks.

And unfortunately, for the first time in her life, fear had caused her to fail in her mission.

For a while Joy had kept the diary of Ms. Melody Huxley upstairs, buried among the various newspaper clippings, half-finished projects, and other curios piled on her desk. Its secrets, however, were held by a thick leather strap attached to a tiny but sturdy brass lock. Joy had never found the key among the woman's effects.

And though it probably would have been easy enough to slice through the enclosing strap with a heavy pair of utility scissors, there was something about Ms. Huxley's adventurous spirit that had prevented Joy from doing so. Was it not a form of desecration to simply strong-arm her way into its deceased owner's presumably most personal thoughts?

No, Joy could only feel good about reading such private contents by accessing them by means of special finesse.

And so, with the help of a bent bobby pin, Joy had been teaching herself lock picking. After all, it was a skill that Peugeot's recurrent hero, Dr. Ingram, had so often found of use, gaining access to all manner of forbidden places.

But despite several hours of fiddling, she had made no headway. Looking up tips on the Internet had taught her that there were many more types of locks than she ever cared to learn about. Then, in a moment of weakness, she'd found herself with the scissors in hand, her knuckles white as she'd pressed the blades against the resisting strap.

Feeling mad at herself, she had thrown the scissors onto her bed in disgust.

So it had happened that in order to avoid future temptation, Joy had returned the leather-bound journal back to the trunk where she'd found it. But now with the mystery of Melody Huxley's life so linked with her own, it was imperative that she retrieve it.

Yet why did the cellar suddenly hold so much terror for her? A place where she had once sat happily for hours, rummaging through mold-covered boxes? Surely it wasn't just the blown lights that were freaking her out.

It was then that Joy realized that beyond her boundless inquisitiveness, her insatiable curiosity, there were some secrets that still filled her with dread. What would the diary finally reveal? What if she didn't like the answers?

CHAPTER 8

The front lawn of the old Shew Inn buzzed with black-clad crew members busily setting up lights and dolly tracks and running heavy cables through the tall grass. High atop a crane a technician adjusted the camera angle as a man in a baseball cap examined the shot through a monitor below.

"Would you just look at this frame?" exclaimed Director Templeton Cray, perching his sunglasses on the brim of his cap. Dressed in blue jeans and cowboy boots, he was lean and athletic-looking despite the tinges of gray in his wild hair. "It looks just as described in the book. What an amazing coincidence!"

A couple of colleagues joined him at the monitor and began nodding in wonder and agreement.

"I don't want to jinx things, but I'm telling you, I feel like this is going to be the best book-to-movie adaptation in the history of cinema!" the director proclaimed.

Standing back at a safe distance from the hubbub, a black-haired man in a dark suit looked on. Hands clasped behind his back, he wore the thin smile of someone very pleased with himself.

"Thanks again for showing us this place," the director called over to him. "It's perfect. We couldn't have asked for better!"

Mr. Octavio Phipps waved a hand modestly. "Not another word about it," he insisted. "On behalf of the city of Darlington, I am just glad to be at your service."

And it couldn't have been more true, Phipps thought, especially after having swung by the Mega Mall earlier that day. He had been working as special municipal consultant for a week before being forced to make a morning detour to return "company property" to Electric Eddie's.

"What? You thought you could just keep your uniform?" Collin had demanded incredulously over the phone. "No freebies!" he'd spat down the line. "It's standard operating procedure for quitters here at Eddie's!"

The trip, however, had not been completely without pleasure. Looking immaculate in his freshly pressed suit, Phipps had quite enjoyed throwing his balled-up T-shirt straight into Collin's face.

"Oh, and I nearly forgot," he had then sneered, slamming down the name tag with such force that he'd almost broken the glass counter. "This should come in very handy should you ever hire another Octavio."

Smearing the countertop in greasy fingerprints, Phipps had turned on his heels to leave.

"Don't think you can come back and expect an employee discount!" the furious manager had croaked after him.

Chuckling to himself, Phipps had then driven straight to the set, where the first day of principal photography was getting under way. There he would continue to make himself available to the production to advise on locations and regulatory matters.

But despite his gladness, any humility was merely for show. In truth the director should be kissing up to him, Phipps thought smugly. Because without his insider knowledge, no movie scout could have ever found this unbelievable location.

In fact, very few people knew about the curious property these days. Dating back almost two hundred years, the inn was supposedly an exact replica of a hostelry located high in the Bavarian Alps. However, it had been hidden from view for the better part of a century behind towering hedges, and had been ringed on all sides by thorny briar. Phipps himself had only happened upon it by sheer accident as a boy.

It had happened one day while ten-year-old Octavio Phipps had been playing in the cemetery. At that time he'd preferred the quiet company of the dead to the living bullies that stalked Spooking Park. But as the sun had begun waning, Octavio had become suddenly gripped with an unstoppable craving for licorice strings.

His pockets chiming with change earned at the music store, he had set off toward Mortimer's Old-Style Sweet Shop, which back then had still operated at the center of town. Seeking a safer route that avoided passing in front of the park, Octavio had squeezed through a fence near the paupers' burial ground. There he had emerged in the shadow of the strangest-looking house he'd ever seen.

Cut to shreds by the briar, the boy had stood dabbing

his cuts as he'd gawped up at the unexpected discovery. Ridiculously ornate, the enormous structure had looked like something fashioned out of gingerbread rather than lumber and shingles, and then decorated with candy and piped white icing. Nevertheless there had been something about the look that had resonated with evil. In fact, it had been exactly the kind of place where a witch would live, lying in wait for stray youngsters she could boil.

Spooking had long been plagued by witches, or so the elder Mr. Phipps had once warned his son. Remembering how his own grandfather had run afoul of one, the terrified boy had crept forward. Thankfully, the gingerbread house had appeared to be unoccupied. And so, after fighting his way through yet more thorny briar, young Octavio had simply continued on his quest for sugary treats.

With the exception of one other occasion, Phipps had never revisited the property. And he had forgotten altogether about the place he now knew as the Shew Inn until recently, when he had come across the name while leafing through old real estate records.

Even with chain saws it had taken the movie crew several hours just to reveal the drive leading up to the property. But as Phipps had assured them, the effort had proved worth it.

The years of neglect had taken their toll on the building, however. Despite its whimsical architecture, the inn now positively throbbed with an unsettling malevolence, and creaked evilly in the lightest of breezes. Standing at odd and ominous angles, the premises were clearly not safe to enter.

But that didn't matter, the director had explained. They

were only interested in shooting the curious exterior. The interior scenes in the movie would be shot at various locations around Spooking, and then edited together to make it look like it was all one house.

Ah, show business, Phipps had delighted quietly. Nothing more than a string of lies crafted into something everyone would believe. He had been stupid not to make it his career.

Soon everything was ready, and the crew was ready to roll. It was just an establishing shot of the inn, Phipps understood from listening in, with no actual actors appearing in the scene. Mr. Cray sat down in a folding chair and drank water as the assistant director took over. "Quiet on set!" the man shouted. "Picture up! Camera rolling! And, action . . ."

The sun was getting hot. Feeling thirsty, Phipps looked around, trying to find out where everyone was getting the ice-cold bottles of water they were guzzling. Having no luck, he wandered back toward his car, where he had left a half-drunk iced coffee he'd splurged on as he'd left the Mega Mall. It was probably warm now, he guessed, but who cared. It was still coffee, wasn't it?

Standing by the open car door, Phipps read the coffee label again. Specifically the beverage was billed as an iced mocha-caramel Frappuccino, he confirmed before taking a swig. Grimacing, he spat out a mouthful of what tasted like boiling river mud.

"No good?" a gruff voice asked him.

Phipps turned, startled. Behind him stood a short older man wearing a blue blazer and a lime green golf shirt. The man's graying hair was carefully greased back into a 1950s rock-and-roll pompadour, and he wore rolled-up blue jeans and sneakers. Despite his small stature, he appeared none-theless imposing, like a grizzled old bulldog.

"The drink," he said, folding his arms. "Not to your liking?"

It was only then that Phipps recognized him. He was the guy Phipps had seen wandering around the cemetery with a flashlight.

"It's gone warm," Phipps answered. "I shouldn't have left it in the car."

"Hmm. Bad idea," the man told him. "At least on a scorcher like today."

Phipps smiled politely at the incredibly dull observation, hoping their conversation was at an end. But instead of moving on, the man just stood there with his arms folded, eyeballing him. In turn Phipps stared back with equal inten-sity, waiting for the man to state his purpose. But he did not do so.

"Can I help you with anything?" Phipps finally felt obliged to inquire.

But the man just shook his head. "I don't touch them myself," he said, apparently ignoring the question.

"I beg your pardon?"

"Those fancy coffee drinks. I make sure to avoid them."

"Really," Phipps replied, bored beyond belief. "And why is that?"

"For one, they cost an arm and a leg. But worse, they're full of chemicals. Look at them. I can see the list from here, right there on the side."

Sighing impatiently, Phipps held the bottle up to his face. The drink did indeed contain a terrifying number of undecipherable ingredients, among which "sodium hexa-metaphosphate" was far from the hardest to pronounce. Just by reading the exhaustive list of unidentifiable additives, Phipps felt his tongue begin to swell and itch.

"That's why I lug this baby around," the man said.

Phipps looked up to see the man open his jacket to reveal a plaid thermos, below which the handle of what was plainly a gun became visible.

"Hot drinks, cold ones—it's my choice. Either way, one is always ready to go. Heck, I'll even stick some sort of hearty soup in there iffin I feel like it."

"Excuse me," Phipps interrupted irritably, nevertheless feeling nervous now that he knew the man was armed. "But what exactly is your business here?"

"My business?" the man repeated. "Well, that depends who is doing the asking."

"My name is Octavio Phipps, and I'm the special munici-pal consultant from Darlington."

"Sounds fancy. What does it mean?"

"It means I'm assisting the production with local matters. This is a closed set, as I understand it, and all authorized visitors are supposed to check in and be registered." In truth Phipps had no idea what the policy concerning visitors was, but it sounded believable coming out of his mouth.

"I don't have anything to do with the movie," the man admitted. "Well, not directly anyway. I'm a detective, you see," he explained.

Phipps took the creased and coffee-stained card from the man, managing to read:

Mr. Leon Loveday, Esq.
Private Detective and Personal Security Expert

Phipps immediately wrinkled his mouth at the pompous-sounding title. "Do you mind my asking what you are detecting, then?"

"Hmm. That depends. Who did you say you are again?"

"Mr. Phipps. The special municipal consultant from Darlington."

"Oh, that's right. Well, in your case I'm detecting a whole heckuva lot of hoo-haw." Mr. Loveday laughed. "But what I'm supposed to be investigating is the whereabouts of a missing person last seen in this area."

Missing person.

With the terrifying words still ringing in his ears, Phipps struggled to keep his composure. Was it Vince or Felix that the man was looking for?

It hardly mattered. For either disappearance he could be held equally responsible. After all it was Phipps who had hired his old colleagues, involving them in his underhanded schemes to destroy Spooking, and ultimately delivering them up to mortal injury.

But who could have hired a private investigator to find one of them?

Taking a breath, Phipps tried to calm himself. There was no need to panic. He had concealed everything to do with their visits, he was quite certain, and had carefully disposed of what few personal effects they had left behind. He had even manically wiped down his entire car and home for stray fingerprints one night after watching a crime drama on TV.

And yet still it would be impossible to hide. These days there were cameras everywhere, he realized in shopping malls and in parking lots, on highways and at stoplights. If the slightest suspicion ever fell on him, it would be easy enough to locate some sort of grainy footage that showed Phipps driving each of his two unfortunate associates around town.

And then he would have a lot of questions to answer.

But no, it didn't have to go that way. *Stay cool*, he told himself. How would a completely innocent person respond?

"A missing person, here?" Phipps said carefully, his face creased with concern. "That's terrible! Is there anything I can do to help?"

But at his words the detective's eyes snapped open for some reason. Loveday peered at the tall man for a moment, an eyebrow raised suspiciously. Phipps swallowed hard as Loveday then went to fish something out of his inside pocket. Phipps felt his stomach clench as he once again glimpsed the gun.

"Look familiar to you?"

Phipps glanced down. It was a scrap of magazine, he saw with surprise, torn from the pages of *Celebrity Informer*.

"It rings a bell," he declared.

"Oh, really?" the detective said hopefully.

"'Lose Forty Pounds in Forty Days'?" Phipps read out

loud. "'While Eating Whatever You Want'? Of course. But while I've seen this advertisement before, I do not buy its outrageous claims for an instant."

"Huh? Wait, no," the detective replied, quickly flipping the sheet over.

On the other side was a glossy picture of a well-known young starlet, wearing skinny jeans and teetering on high heels as she exited an airport. With one eye closed and her mouth hanging open, she had not been captured in a particularly flattering moment.

"Have you ever seen her anywhere?" Mr. Loveday demanded.

"I must confess that I have," Phipps confirmed, shrugging. "But I'm not sure where. To be honest her films don't really appeal to me. What's her name again?"

"Her name is Penny Farthing," growled the little detective. "And I don't mean have you see her in movies. I mean right here, somewhere around this puny town of yours."

"Are you asking if I have ever seen a B-list celebrity running around Spooking? Most certainly not." Phipps laughed, feeling increasingly relieved. "But perhaps that will change," he added. Looking back toward the set, he saw the camera sweep down from up high again in what would surely be a pretty dramatic shot. He realized he still had no idea who was starring in this ridiculous-sounding movie, but hopefully it would be someone really big. Someone whose star power could help bring all sorts of attention to Spooking.

"So you're sure you've never seen her?" the detective demanded again. "Maybe talking to somebody, or wandering around the place? Maybe without makeup, or wearing a wig . . ."

"I am quite sure I have never set eyes on Miss Farthing," Phipps insisted haughtily, "unless you count her appearance in similarly trashy periodicals I sometimes glance at whilst checking out of the grocery store."

The bulldog frowned but nevertheless did not seem convinced. "Well, if you do see her, or if you remember anything, I'd appreciate it if you'd gimme a call at the number on my card." After flashing the revolver one last time, Mr. Loveday buttoned up his jacket. He then turned and sauntered back down the drive.

Phipps watched the man's retreating back with unease. Though he had not the slightest clue what was up with this Penny Farthing character, the idea of a private investigator wandering around town made him feel very uneasy. He thought back to the cemetery, where he had already seen the man poking around.

Wait a minute, Phipps thought with a gasp. The crypt where he had hidden Vince's leather jacket along with Felix's duffel bag of belongings! What if Loveday found it?

There was no need to worry, he assured himself. There were easily twenty other crypts scattered around in the cemetery, each of them shut so solidly that a person would need a crowbar to open them.

At that moment Mr. Loveday stopped and turned around.

"Excuse me, Mr. Phipps," he called back. "You wouldn't happen to know where I could find a hardware store around here?"

The question filled Phipps's veins with ice. "I'm afraid there are no such stores in Spooking," he told the man truthfully.

"All right, then, what about down the hill in Darlington?"

"I suppose so. But I really couldn't tell you where."

Mr. Loveday shook his head. "Wow. Some kind of consultant you turned out to be. I guess I'll just have to find it myself."

"I'm sure you'll have no problem," Phipps replied, his voice beginning to waver.

"I'm sure I won't," Mr. Loveday agreed. "I'm a detective, as I mentioned. And my business is finding things."

CHAPTER 9

ad Byron been hoping his own birthday party would match the pomp and pageantry he'd experienced down at Kiddy Kingdom when he had attended Lucy Primrose's own celebrations, he would have been sorely disappointed. But fortunately, he'd already made known a preference for something a bit more low-key, which was in truth a bit more realistic.

Held in the backyard, the party had a modest number of guests, including Byron's best friend, Gustave, and a few other kids.

"Where's Poppy?" Byron asked, looking around the small group eating chips and cheese puffs at the picnic table.

Joy swallowed hard. Unlike her brother, she had not seen Byron's watery-eyed little admirer ever since their harrowing adventure in the asylum a few months before.

"She isn't coming," she finally explained.

That much was certain, at least if Mr. Phipps was to be believed. And for once Joy had taken him at his word. After all, Peugeot himself had frequently written of such beings—mysterious ethereal forces that were no more than psychic echoes from other eras.

For Poppy was only an apparition, having haunted the neighborhood for more than a century. So Mr. Phipps had relayed after discovering Joy inside the old schoolhouse where the little phantom made her home. But upon learning Poppy's otherworldly secret, her spirit would forever cease to appear to a person, the man had then further explained.

Hearing this, Joy had been dismayed. So she had hidden the truth about Poppy from her brother, hoping that the ghost-child might still appear to him—at least whenever Joy herself wasn't around. Because rather than as a mere translucent smudge glanced in the corner of one's eye, Poppy manifested herself in full high-definition color and, what's more, could carry on a pretty decent conversation. Which made Poppy a perfectly viable playmate, something hard to come by in Spooking these days.

And Joy's plan had worked perfectly. Until now. Byron and Poppy still enjoyed long afternoons together at the park, and it appeared that Byron was developing a reciprocal crush on Poppy. It was a development Joy was certain would end in heartbreak.

"Did you invite her?" Byron asked.

"I did, but she said her family was going away on vacation," Joy said by way of explanation. "She sends her best wishes, though."

"When did you ask her?"

"A couple of weeks ago," Joy replied.

"That doesn't make sense," Byron immediately objected. "I saw her on the merry-go-round just last weekend."

"Did I say 'weeks'?" Joy laughed awkwardly. "I meant days. They left on Thursday, I think."

It was useless, Joy knew. Sooner or later the little playground spirit was going to make her look like a liar—or worse, like an evil sister interfering with her brother's love life. How she wished she could still speak to Poppy, even for just a few minutes so they could get their stories straight. Or better yet, get her to leave Byron alone completely.

It would be sad, but sometimes love was like that.

Luckily for Joy, the revolting sight of Gustave with a pair of cheese puffs shoved up his nose distracted her brother enough that she had no further explaining to do. She turned, instead admiring the unusually tidy backyard, which had just been mowed for the first time that year.

Having left the job to the last minute, her father had struggled mightily to accomplish the task earlier that day. Barely able to push the groaning mower through the tall sopping wet grass, he had managed to run over two extension cords and mangle three of Byron's lost knight figures. Too exhausted to rake, Mr. Wells had left the damp cuttings exactly where they had dropped. Joy thought they looked like big green loaves of bread.

Also left to the last minute was starting the barbecue, Joy saw, which was causing an argument.

"It's called timing, Helen," Mr. Wells protested. "If we light it too early, the coals are cold by the time things are ready to go."

"Yes, dear, but now we've got to wait an hour until they

are hot enough. Which means the children's parents will probably be here before you get cooking."

"It won't be an hour, I promise you."

"Shouldn't the coals be stacked up in more of a pyramid shape?" Mrs. Wells asked. "That's what the picture shows on the bag. And I really think you should use more fire-starting fluid. Otherwise we are going to be here until midnight."

"Helen, do you mind? I do know what I'm doing." Mr. Wells pulled the trigger on the butane barbecue starter, but no flame came out. "Now what's wrong with this thing? It's not even clicking!"

"The safety switch is on," Mrs. Wells informed him.

With a grunt Mr. Wells finally ignited the coals.

Knowing that the hot dogs and hamburgers were not soon forthcoming, Joy headed over to the picnic table to get a snack before the swarming little buzzards devoured everything. Seeing Gustave's orange-ringed nostrils, she stopped herself from eating a cheese puff but instead helped herself to a handful of chips and a plastic glass of cream soda.

Looking around the table, Joy felt an unexpected pang of jealousy. At least Byron had a few people his own age at his party. On Joy's last birthday her only guest had been Madame Portia—the owner and operator of the Happy Fates Retirement Estates—who had accompanied them to an Italian restaurant in Darlington. There the highlight had been a group of tone-deaf waiters gathering around to sing "Happy Birthday":

Buon Compleanno a te,
Buon Compleanno a te,
Buon Compleanno Joy
Buon Compleanno a te!

Joy had been mortified. Adding to her embarrassment, Madame Portia had then made some sort of insulting comment about their singing in Italian, leading to a full-on shouting match. After then waiting a fruitless hour for dessert forks, the group had been forced to collect their cake and leave.

Grabbing a few more chips, Joy now left the picnic table, her ears buzzing from the high-pitched voices shouting over one another. Oh yes, this was going to be yet another long and painful party.

Nevertheless, Joy soon found herself wishing that Byron had invited Lucy Primrose. For one, the prim little princess was a pretty good alternative to Poppy, possessing admittedly quite lovely strawberry blond hair, not to mention a material existence that science could easily prove. But equally fortuitous, Joy could have suggested that Louden come along with her. She kicked herself for not having thought of it earlier.

Then again, Joy wondered whether Louden would have appreciated the invitation. He was an unusually polite individual, Joy had observed, and as such a bit hard to read. In comparison most kids at Winsome wore their feelings not just on their sleeves, but taped to their foreheads as well. But not Louden. So despite his claims of enjoying his visit to Spooking, she really had no idea what he thought. For all she knew he had gone back to school and snickered to everyone about her cruddy house and overgrown backyard.

Wasn't it nice here now, though, with the lawn all mowed? Joy wished she could have let Louden know that it was safe to return. Then Mr. Wells put a match to the barbecue, which with a *poof* ignited into a fireball.

And Joy realized that it probably wasn't all that safe.

Mrs. Wells decided that perhaps it would be best to open the presents early, just in case they were chased inside by bats later. Somewhere nearby there was a huge nest of them, the Wells family knew from terrible experience, and as soon as the sun dipped behind the trees they came rushing out by the hundreds, squeaking and careening across the backyard. Even Joy, who'd read that they would never accidentally fly directly into a person, found her hardened nerves stretched taut by the stream of flying rodents swooping past her face.

Byron tore his way unceremoniously through several gifts before coming to the big present Joy and her mother had picked out at the Mega Mall. Feeling the telltale shape of the blister pack through the wrapping paper, his eyes lit up.

"I think I know what it is!" he shouted, delighted.

Seeing his excited face, Joy felt rather proud of herself. She was often too caught up in her own thoughts to listen to what Byron had to say, but somehow one sentence had stood out above his incessant blabbering:

"I think I want a walkie-talkie for my birthday."

Such were the words that had drawn Joy to the display in

Electronica Veronica. The walkie-talkies were sold in pairs, Joy and her mother had subsequently learned, and even the most modest set had a range of more than twenty miles. They were certainly reasonably priced enough, Mrs. Wells had remarked after Joy had positively guaranteed they were exactly what Byron wanted.

"Yeah! Wicked cool!" her brother cried once the two bright yellow devices were finally freed by Mr. Wells from their prison of packaging. "Come on, Gustave. Let's try them out!"

The rest of the children chased after the two boys as they went barreling across the property.

"Well, that was a hit," Mr. Wells observed.

"I know!" Mrs. Wells replied. "I'll tell you, Edward. They were probably the cheapest thing in the entire store," she added quietly.

"I guess they are a bit pointless these days, with cell phones and everything."

"Walkie-talkies." The name sounded like the kind of thing a four-year-old would come up with, Joy thought. Still, as neither she nor her brother had a cell phone, she could see how they could prove useful in a variety of adventuring situations. And while she had no idea how big Spooking was, she was pretty sure it spanned a lot less than twenty miles.

"This is Gustave," said the white-haired boy, tearing back through the backyard with a walkie-talkie held to his bright orange lips. "Come in. Over."

"This is Byron," came the crackling reply. "Come in. Over."

"Roger. This is Gustave. Over."

"Roger that. Byron here. Over."

Of course, they were only as useful as whatever you had to say, Joy noted.

"See? The coals are coming along beautifully and it hasn't been going even ten minutes," said Mr. Wells, heading inside to finally make the burgers.

"I guess I'll throw together some kind of salad for the grown-ups," said Mrs. Wells, following.

With the backyard now deserted, Joy found herself completely bored. She examined the rusted swing set, wondering if it would hold her weight. It looked pretty doubtful.

"Some party this turned out to be," she said under her breath.

Spotting a cloud of mosquitoes drifting her way, Joy decided to get out of there. Slipping down the side of the house, she headed out front, to find the street completely empty, with no signs of life other than distant shrieks and the distorted chatter of the walkie-talkies. Perhaps a stroll around the block might eat up some time before dinner, she thought.

Joy headed off down Ravenwood Avenue. There her path crossed that of a man she had never seen before, who was wearing a jacket and a bright green golf shirt.

"Penny?" he said, approaching. "Is that you?"

"Pardon me?" Joy replied.

"Sorry. I thought you might be someone else," he said. "Actually, I don't mean to bother you, but I was wondering if you've seen this girl around anywhere." He showed Joy a picture ripped out of a magazine.

"Penny Farthing?" Joy exclaimed. "The teen actress?"

"She might be wearing a blond wig, which is why I stopped you. And most likely dark sunglasses the size of dessert plates."

Was the guy out of his mind? It seemed probable.

"I'm sorry, but I've never seen her around here," Joy insisted, continuing past him.

"Well, thank you for your time anyway, young lady," the man called after her before walking off in the opposite direction.

Feeling confused, Joy headed up the Boulevard, looping back toward the other end of her block. She didn't often see strangers walking the streets of Spooking, and it made her feel uneasy. Which was funny, because she could pass a hundred people she didn't know down in Darlington and never give it a second thought.

Rounding the corner, Joy could still smell the acrid stench of fire-starting fluid and see the black tower of smoke drifting up from their barbecue. As she began walking down the Boulevard, she was suddenly overtaken by a few white box trucks that she had also never seen around town. What was going on? On the side of one of the vehicles, Joy glimpsed an unfamiliar company name and the picture of a movie camera.

Hold on a second, she thought. The movie! Didn't someone in her class say Penny Farthing was going to be in it? If that was true, then that could mean only one thing.

They must be making the movie in Spooking!

Cheering out loud, Joy sprinted along the Boulevard and back down toward Ravenwood. This was the best news ever! Finally Spooking was going to be in the spotlight. There couldn't be a better time for her to prove that the town was noteworthy, the home of both a famous author and a famous aviator. Maybe they could even make a documentary about Spooking to use as a special feature on the DVD!

Joy's mind was buzzing with possibilities as she arrived breathlessly in the backyard. The rest of the partygoers had returned to the picnic table, where they were now desperately awaiting the burgers currently catching fire on the barbecue.

"Hey, guys. Guess what. They're making the movie right here in Spooking!" Joy shouted.

"What movie?" asked Mr. Wells, flipping a patty with a flourish. "Oh, bother!" he shouted as the burger then slipped between the thin bars of the grill and was lost, sending a column of flame into the air.

"The movie! Something about vampires and zombies. I don't know. All I know is a guy just asked me about Penny Farthing, and there are movie trucks driving all over the place! Spooking is going to be famous!" Joy declared.

"Well, that's very nice, dear," Mrs. Well said.

"Oh yeah, and Teddy Danger is in it," Joy suddenly remembered.

"Teddy Danger?" her mother repeated. "Where did you hear that?"

"The kids at school said so. It was in the newspaper."

"Did you hear that, Edward!" cried Mrs. Wells. "Teddy

Danger is coming to Spooking! Isn't that exciting?"

"It's absolutely thrilling," Mr. Wells agreed flatly before flipping another blackened patty. "Oh, cripes, not another one!"

"I wonder if we'll get a look at him!" Mrs. Wells continued. "Or if I can get him to autograph a few of my records!"

"Gather round, children. Get your burgers before they all burn to cinders," Mr. Wells called. Famished, the children cried out in delight before surrounding the cook.

Taking a paper plate, Joy stood at the back of them. Finally her life felt like it was changing for the better. Not only was she graduating from Winsome, but there were great things on the way for Spooking.

Her night terrors, she thought, surely were over now.

CHAPTER 10

The production had wrapped for the day, and the special municipal consultant had just been taking his leave when he saw her, a raven-haired beauty in a pinstriped pantsuit, talking to the director. His body tingling, he'd walked straight up and interrupted them.

"Audrey," Phipps breathed.

The woman turned, startled. "Octavio!" she cried with a smile.

Phipps seized her hand and wrapped it in a drenched palm. Her delicate tapered fingers were rigid with astonishment.

"How *are* you?" he gushed, cringing to hear himself sounding like one of the teenage girls who infested the Mega Mall. "I mean, it's been a long time," he added in a voice with a more masculine timbre.

"It's been much too long," Audrey said. "It's so great to get the chance to come home, even if it is just for work."

"Do you two know each other?" the director asked with surprise.

"Once upon a time," Phipps replied.

"We used to be tennis partners," Audrey explained. "Back when we were teenagers."

Phipps nodded, finding it hard to take his eyes off his old flame, now grown from the girl who had once broken his heart into a woman. Except for a few crinkly laughter lines around her eyes, the designer suit, and her tasteful makeup, she did not look even a day older to him. She was still just as breathtaking as the last time he'd seen her, glimpsed through the window of a fancy restaurant in the big city. But he'd become a grimy impoverished musician by then, and had slunk off into the night without her spotting him.

"Oh yes, of course," said the director. "I'd forgotten that you actually grew up in this town, Audrey."

"You forgot? Well, surely you remember that it was my suggestion to shoot the movie here, at least," she chided comically.

"I do, I do," the director insisted. "And I am so thankful. Without you we never would have known about this wonderfully eccentric old town that's really making our project look great."

"Well, it is on a map, believe it or not, but I'll take the credit all the same," she joked.

"But I've got to give equal props to your tennis partner here. Without Mr. Phipps we would never have known about this property, which we're actually going to use as the exterior of the evil inn. It's absolutely amazing, isn't it? What a special place."

"It most certainly is," agreed Audrey. "Especially since it's where I once tried to kiss Octavio. But unfortunately, he turned me down. . . ."

Phipps turned, the blood draining from his face. He had

no such memory. To his knowledge he had brought Audrey here only once during their whole friendship, to escape a rainsquall that had surprised them while they'd been strolling around the cemetery.

Thinking back, he could still remember how badly he'd cut himself, holding back the thorny briar with his bare hands to afford his love safe passage onto the property. After sprinting across the lawn, they'd sheltered under the building's enormous eaves, drenched and laughing, until the storm had passed.

But there had been no kiss that he could recall.

Then he began remembering the occasion in detail. Audrey, shivering, had cuddled up to him, putting her arms around his neck. But he had not reciprocated. Fearing his bleeding hands might ruin the moment, Phipps had kept his balled-up fists in his pockets, out of sight. He'd stood there, staring out into the rain, reeling at the feeling of her warm breath on his cheek, and at the softest brush of her lips.

But their touch had been an accident, young Octavio had quickly decided, brought on by Audrey's shivers. And so he'd just gone on standing there, like a statue, until she'd finally released him.

The rain had stopped soon after.

The director was still cackling at Audrey's admission when Phipps returned from this recollection. At the horrible realization of his own stupidity, his face felt hot.

"Well, I can see you two have a lot to catch up on, so I'll leave you alone," Mr. Cray was saying, raising an eyebrow. But first he turned to Audrey and lowered his voice. "Thanks again so much for coming out to handle this personally. We really have to get moving on finding their replacements—because this is the kind of crisis that could kill the whole production."

"I understand, Templeton. I will keep you in the loop," she replied.

"A good evening to you, Mr. Phipps," said the director. "I would suggest not letting her get away a second time," he added jovially before walking off.

Audrey turned to Phipps. "Why such a red face, Octavio? We were just kids."

"Is my face really red? Because I'm not embarrassed. It must be the sun," he explained. "I've been out in it all day."

Audrey smiled but didn't push the matter further. "Anyway, I'm surprised to see you here. I thought I'd heard you moved away years ago."

"I had to come back, unfortunately," Phipps said. "My parents passed away."

"I heard. I'm so sorry." The woman's eyes went instantly bright with tears. "They were always so nice to me. What a pair of sweethearts."

"Thank you. They were very fond of you, too."

It was an understatement. His parents had fawned ridiculously over Audrey whenever she dropped by, usually for a cool drink after a long summer tennis session. His mother would always set out trays of baked treats as his father lavished her with weird wooden crafts he'd made for her in his workshop: letter openers, doorstops, shoehorns. As Phipps cringed, Audrey would laugh between bites of brownie, promising to cherish whatever bizarre gift always.

Then, whenever she left, Phipps could hear his parents in the kitchen, making excited plans for their eventual wedding.

Nothing had disappointed his parents quite as much as his losing Audrey, he'd always known.

"Anyway, after I'd seen to their affairs, I ended up staying on and getting a job with the Darlington city council."

"And is that what you're doing now?" Audrey asked.

"Well, I'm on more of a consultant basis really, acting as go-between for the city and the movie production. But up until recently I was the assistant to the mayor himself," he boasted.

What a lame brag, he then realized. "Until recently"? Could he make it any more obvious that he'd been fired?

"Well, it sounds like you've really done well for yourself."

"I keep busy," he said, and shrugged. "But it's not exactly show business. Speaking of which, what do you do?"

"I'm a casting director," Audrey said. "I'm not usually on set, but there's a bit of an emergency they want me to handle."

"That's too bad."

"Well, it's actually nice to be on location for once, and to get a chance to visit home. Like I said, it was my tip that got them looking at Spooking. They were searching for a special location for the shoot, and I couldn't think of anywhere more perfect."

"For a horror movie?" Phipps laughed. "I bet you couldn't.

The town's even more terrifying than ever, to be honest."

Audrey laughed. "Oh, Octo, you don't know how much I've missed your sardonic sense of humor. I was hoping you might be here," she added. "I know it's weird, but I kind of knew I would see you. Whenever I think about Spooking, I think of you."

Phipps smiled awkwardly. As much as he thrilled to hear the confession that his long-lost love still occasionally thought of him, the idea that she associated him with a freakish backwater town made him feel sick to his stomach.

And just how exactly did Audrey see him now? As the same gawky boy who had once chased after her like a puppy? He looked across to the gingerbread house, and thought again about the supposed kiss under those eaves. No, it was just a story, he decided, something to tease him with.

Phipps felt the welling of a familiar anger. Audrey had no idea of all the places he'd been, of all the things he'd done since she'd last seen him. The woman had not the slightest conception of who he was anymore.

As dark thoughts began overwhelming Phipps, they were interrupted by a shout.

"Is that you, Octo?"

The voice was familiar—hatefully so.

"I don't believe it!" Teddy Danger roared, jogging up. "It's Octo Phipps!"

If Phipps had felt hot with embarrassment before, he now found himself going cold. "Teddy," he answered.

"Oh, so you remember me?" cackled the sweaty-faced man wearing a red tracksuit and white headband. "Heck,

I'm sure you do. I'm the guy you said what about? Would never make it in the music business?"

Phipps took a jovial punch to the shoulder that nevertheless sent him staggering backward.

"I really don't remember ever saying that," Phipps protested.

"Hey, I'm just teasing you," said Teddy. "But you did say it," he quickly insisted, waggling his finger. "We may be getting older, you and I, but my memory is still perfect."

"Well, that's good to hear," Phipps replied, sickening himself with the grin he now wore.

"Oh, and if it isn't the gorgeous Miss Audrey?" Teddy asked, turning away. "How delightful to see you again!" he declared in a British accent. "I was just jogging by and thought I'd check out the set. But I would have run double time if I'd known you were here."

Phipps swallowed hard to see red blotches instantly appear above Audrey's neckline, just as they once did whenever he used to embarrass her.

"Nice to see you again, Teddy," she said. "How are you settling in?"

"Not too badly. The accommodations are a bit ramshackle, but as my friend here will testify, I've lived in worse. Remember that squat we stayed in down by the docks, Octo?"

Phipps nodded. He did remember the Black Tongs' squat, of course—a derelict old factory building they had lived in rent-free for a couple of years, until it was almost knocked down while he and his bandmates were sleeping in it. However, he did not remember Teddy staying there, except for perhaps on a couple of occasions when it was too late and the buses were no longer running.

"Oh, it's just that your assistant mentioned there were a few things you were unhappy with," Audrey reported.

"Unhappy?" Teddy snorted. "With what?"

"She mentioned that you were upset that there wasn't a pool," the woman replied.

"Don't listen to Molly," scoffed Teddy. "No, if I wanted a swim, I'd have stayed at home with my own two-hundred-foot wave pool. I'm just happy to be here, working on such a fantastic project. Besides, when you're a runner like me," Teddy said, unzipping the front of his red tracksuit, "the whole world is your pool."

Phipps clenched his teeth. What did that even mean?

But despite himself he felt a growing sense of awe. Teddy was an actual celebrity after all, and the very fact that this huge star knew his name was a source of swelling pride. Because in the end, who was Phipps really? He was the man who had once been an idol—a god—in the eyes of the young fool who would later become the legendary Teddy Danger.

It was a good thing to remind himself.

The fact, however, had evidently been forgotten by Teddy himself. Finishing up his conversation, the aging rock star turned to regard Phipps. With his head held back, he began looking straight down his nose at him. His lips curled into the trademark sneer appearing in his every promo photo for the past twenty-odd years.

Audrey seemed not to notice. "Well, if there's anything

I can do to help make you more comfortable, please let me know," she said.

"Hmm," said Teddy. "Maybe a spot of dinner a bit later, love?" he asked, again employing a faux British accent. Phipps looked on in horror as the red blotches on Audrey's neck began looking like angry bee stings.

"Perhaps in a few days," she replied, beaming at the offer. "But I've got a bit of a busy schedule at the moment."

"Sure, sure," said Teddy. "Let me know. Oh, there's Templeton. I'm just going to have a word with him . . ." Without a further glance at Phipps, Teddy jogged off toward the director.

"Hey, so you know Teddy?" asked Audrey.

Phipps made a face as if chewing a rusted old battery. "Yeah," he admitted. "But not as Teddy Danger. I knew him before he was famous, back when he was plain old Ted Wannamaker."

In truth no one had ever called the future megastar Ted. No one except for Phipps himself, that is, who'd done it specifically to annoy him. While a figure of fun for the entire band, Teddy had particularly infuriated Phipps with his constant questions and proximity. He'd been like a black hole that sucked all of the cool out of the room.

But no matter what manner of abuse Phipps would heap on the pathetic creature, Teddy would always come slinking back.

"He was a bit of a pest, to be honest, and used to follow me around everywhere."

"Follow you around? Why?"

"I don't know. He was a fan of my band, I guess," Phipps said. "Which makes sense since later he pretty much ripped our whole sound off—"

"I never knew you had your own band, Octavio!" Audrey interrupted. "What were you called?"

"The Black Tongs." For once Phipps felt exactly like Ted Wannamaker, hanging around backstage, desperate to impress. He searched her face for a glimmer of recognition of the name, since she had lived in the very city where his posters had covered every pole and bit of hoarding in the metropolitan area. But there was nothing.

"Good for you," she said, smiling. "You were always a talented singer and musician, even as a teenager, I remember."

"Thank you." Phipps shuffled around, hoping to move on to another topic. Because there was no way anything he ever did was going to even begin matching up to the multiplatinum record sales of Teddy Danger.

But Audrey persisted in picking the painful scab. "Did you guys ever put out an album?"

"Well, we were actually in the middle of making one, but then I lost my bass player and we broke up," Phipps explained.

"Oh, what a shame."

"Yes, it was." Phipps decided not to elaborate further on the departure of his best friend and songwriting partner, Felix. The betrayal had been unbearable, and Phipps had not written another song since. Instead he'd disappeared, until finally drifting into cover bands, spending years playing at weddings, birthdays, and bar mitzvahs. Anything to keep away from Spooking.

"So anyway, what's the crisis you have to handle?" Phipps asked, changing the subject.

Audrey lowered her voice. "We're trying to keep it quiet, but it seems we've lost both of our young costars at the last minute. One of them came down with appendicitis, and the other one has gone completely missing."

"Missing?" Phipps repeated quietly.

"Yeah. Penny Farthing. She was last seen just across the street from your place, shooting promotional material in the cemetery. Apparently she pitched some sort of fit on the phone and told her agent she was running away."

Like everyone else in the country, Phipps had heard enough about the troubled young actress to last his lifetime. "Do you have any idea who you are going to replace them with?"

"Well, the studio didn't like any of the kids they auditioned back out on the coast, so they're expecting me to pull a couple of unknowns out of the air locally to replace them. I need a boy who looks around eight and a girl who passes for twelve." Audrey sighed. "It's not going to be easy, I'll tell you. At this rate I'm going to have to go around to a few schools at recess and stake out their playgrounds."

Phipps raised an eyebrow. "A boy of eight and a girl of twelve, you say?"

"Do you know anyone? I'm not just looking for cute kids. I need youngsters with a real flair for drama."

Phipps smiled at this.

"Oh, I think I have your actors," he said, drumming his fingers together. "In fact, I think I have the absolutely perfect pair for you."

CHAPTER 11

"How are you guys doing back there?" the taxi driver called over the blaring radio. "All buckled in?"

"No!" shouted Morris, still struggling to free his belt from the depths of the plastic-covered backseat. Adding to his discomfort, his allergies were on edge, and the pine tree air freshener dangling from the rearview mirror was making his eyes stream.

"But it's not even a real tree, dear," his mother insisted.

"It has some sort of essence in it, like one big concentrated tree," he insisted.

"Oh, Morris. Just relax, please," she said as the taxi pulled away.

"Mother, you still haven't told me what's going on," he complained, finally securing himself.

"Like I said, there's no need to worry. We're just going to an appointment," Mrs. Mealey answered, her lips still fixed in the same queer smile she'd worn for the past two days.

"Worried?" Morris repeated. "Why do you keep insisting I might be worried?"

Morris considered himself fairly used to being dragged around to appointments. Since he'd been forced to attend weekly sessions with a play therapist for the past year, he was used to interrupting his day to answer a bunch of personal and sometimes awkward questions. But this was a Tuesday, and his visits with the pretty and kindly Dr. Daisy were normally on Thursdays. So he was a bit worried, come to think of it.

Why shouldn't he be? He had never seen his mother this excited. She was wearing what looked like a brand-new dress and had even pinned her hair up into a bun.

"Did we win the lottery or something?" Morris demanded.

"No, Morris. Well, not exactly. Why so curious?"

"I just want to know where we are going, that's all."

"We're going to an office, I suppose. Suite 405. But I've never been there before, dear, so I don't really know anything more than you."

"But *why* are we going there?"

"Honestly, Morris." Mrs. Mealey laughed. "If questions were dollars, we wouldn't need the lottery. We'd already be living in a solid gold mansion by now."

The taxi let them off in front of what was indeed an office building, an ugly five-story structure perched atop a depressing-looking strip mall. On the way in, Morris scanned the tenant directory in the lobby.

SUITE 405: CEREBUS PRODUCTIONS, he read. The name meant absolutely nothing to him.

"Press the button, Mother," said Morris, catching up to her outside the elevator.

"Whoops! Sorry."

Above, the shaft rang out with alarming clunking sounds.

Finally the doors opened and they stepped into the coffin-like interior. Morris glanced nervously at his mother as they rode up to the fourth floor. Usually she was terrified of elevators and quietly prayed the entire ride. This time she was singing to herself.

The doors opened. Morris followed his mother, still humming the unrecognizable tune, as she wandered up and down the quiet halls. Eventually she located the nondescript office suite and ushered her son inside, where a stone-faced receptionist took Morris's name and asked them both to have a seat.

"What are you doing, Mother?" he demanded, yanking his head out of range of her fussing fingers.

"I'm trying to make your hair look more natural. You look a bit serious with that side part."

"So what? I am serious."

"I just don't want you to be typecast," she explained, reaching for him again.

"Leave me alone, please!" he snapped, swatting away her hand. "And what does that mean, 'typecast'?"

At that moment the office door opened. A pretty lady appeared, holding a sheet of paper. "Morris Mealey?" she read. Seeing the waiting room otherwise empty, she beckoned to the boy still busy plastering down his hair.

"Good luck, dear," Mrs. Mealey breathed into her son's ear before shoving him to his feet.

Whatever this was about, it was now clear to Morris that he was going it alone. Feeling nauseated, he approached the woman, who stood in the doorway wearing a stiff smile.

Was she a psychologist, Morris wondered, or some other kind of therapist?

From the look of her it seemed unlikely. Running his tongue across his twisted incisors, Morris had a sudden flash. She was an orthodontist, surely. Hadn't his mother been threatening him with braces for years now? But stepping into the cramped little office, Morris found the room devoid of any facilities beyond a desk and two chairs. Even the walls themselves were completely bare except for two grimy squares that showed where pictures had once hung.

The pretty lady had him take a seat in a conference chair.

"So, Morris Mealey," she declared cheerfully. "That's quite a name."

"It's Morris M. Mealey, actually," the boy corrected automatically.

"I see," the woman replied. "What does the M stand for?"

It was a question no one had ever bothered to ask before, Morris realized. "Mordecai," he shyly admitted.

The pretty lady made a face of approval. "I like the sound of it. Now, it says here that you are nine?" She looked up at Morris doubtfully. "Really?"

"I know I seem a bit older. But yes, I am nine."

"Actually, I thought you were more around eight, because of your size. But never mind. Being a bit small for your age can be a good thing."

"A good thing?" Morris scoffed. Of all the things he considered to be exceptionally fortunate about himself, being small was not one of them. "How?"

"It's always good to be able to play a bit younger, but be

a bit more mature. It means you can take direction better, which is always appreciated."

"Ah," said Morris, feeling impatient. What was this person going on about? Even with his politeness to elders being a well-honed reflex, he felt a growing disrespect that began to strain his face. When was she going to get to the point? What did she want from him?

"Okay. I want you to try saying this," the pretty lady said, flipping open a bound sheaf of paper. Her finger traced down lines of circled dialogue. "'Agnes, you gotta listen to me!'" she bellowed so loudly that Morris flinched in his seat. "'I think Daddy is turning into some kind of monster!'"

Heart thumping, Morris stared back as the pretty lady handed over the stack of paper. He looked down and saw it was a story of some sort, with dialogue spoken by someone named Alfred.

"What do you want me to do?" he asked.

"Just try reading it at whatever pace feels comfortable," she said in a normal voice. "But make it sound dramatic. You know, like you are starting to get a bit upset," she added. "'Agnes, you gotta listen to me!'" she repeated. "'I think Daddy is turning into some kind of monster!'"

Mrs. Mealey sat in the waiting room, chewing her nails. She had heard what sounded like the woman shouting a few times, and then Morris responding at the same volume. After a few minutes the door finally opened. Looking pale and confused, her son wandered out.

"Thank you both for coming in," the pretty lady called

over to Morris's mother. "We'll be in touch."

It was only in the elevator that Mrs. Mealey finally spoke. "So," she began breezily, "how did your audition go?"

Morris turned, his face awash with confusion. "Audition? What audition?"

"For the movie, dear." She laughed. "Do you think you got the part?"

Morris turned bright red. It was all starting to make sense now. "Are you telling me I was up for a part in a movie?" he exploded. "A real live movie?"

"It's some sort of scary movie, they said on the phone. I was a bit worried that you're too sensitive to handle that sort of thing, but they said not to worry. It all just feels like playacting, and kids normally have a good time."

Mounting rage made Morris feel like his head was about to explode. "A movie?"

"Isn't it exciting? I think it's a pretty big one too, with real stars and everything. Apparently you were recommended as being perfect for one of the main parts!"

"Why didn't you tell me that?" Morris demanded, his voice cracking with frustration. "Why didn't you tell me anything?"

"Isn't it obvious?" asked Mrs. Mealey. "I didn't want you to get nervous."

"So you just decided to lie to me about it?"

"I didn't lie to you," insisted Mrs. Mealey. "I just didn't mention it. There's a big difference."

"Mother!" the boy shouted. "I made a complete fool out of myself in there!"

"I'm sure you were fantastic, dear. You're just being hard

on yourself. Who couldn't love you? You're handsome, you're smart, and you're just a natural actor."

"I didn't even know what the lady was talking about! She started reading out all these weird lines and telling me to repeat them. I thought she was crazy!"

The elevator doors opened. "Oh."

"Why do you do things like that?" Morris shouted, his voice echoing as they entered the lobby.

"Do things like what, sweetie?"

"Like always ruin everything for me!"

At the sight of his mother's crumpling face, Morris regretted the outburst. He hated upsetting her in public, and enduring the hideous display that always resulted. Morris watched in horror as instead of hailing a cab his mother literally wailed one down by stumbling, sobbing, into its path. With screeching brakes still ringing in his ears, he climbed into the back of the taxi after her, where she then moaned all the way home, mercilessly stabbing at her eyes with a tissue.

Still, she had blown his one big chance, Morris thought angrily. Acting. Why had he never thought of it before? After all, it was something he had been doing his entire life.

And with that he finally understood what the pretty lady from the audition had meant about the advantages of being able to play younger. Of course! He was the perfect choice for those roles, so long as his father's gigantism didn't kick in anytime soon.

It seemed like the ideal career for him, especially now that his plans to join the city administration seemed out of the question. He had seen firsthand how that environment had torn up his mentor, Mr. Phipps, and there was no way he was made of equally strong stuff. Municipal politics, it turned out, was a real meat grinder.

No, becoming a huge movie star was about the only realistic option left open to him, he realized.

"You've got to tell them!" he shouted, seizing his mother by the shoulders. "When we get home, phone them and explain that I didn't know it was an audition. That I need another chance! Beg them if you have to. Okay, Mother? Please!"

His mother turned, her swollen face streaked with tears. "Okay," she choked out.

However, by the time they returned home and hung up their jackets, the phone was already ringing.

"It's a callback!" cried Mrs. Mealey, hanging up the receiver. "Morris, they want to see you again!"

"Are you kidding me?"

"No, dear!" she assured him. "Now that's it, Morris— not a word about this to anyone! In fact, I'm pulling you out of school as soon as you land this thing!"

"Mom!" cried Morris, rushing toward his mother with open arms. "Mom, I love you!"

CHAPTER 12

The sonorous doorbell of Number 9 Ravenwood Avenue rang out, startling each and every member of the Wells family from their positions scattered throughout the house. The Wellses remained unaccustomed to receiving unannounced visitors, despite the increased number over the past few months. So it happened that the entire family gathered in the foyer, staring at the front door in silence.

"Well?" Joy asked finally after it rang for the third time. "Don't you think someone should answer it?"

Everyone turned to Mr. Wells, whose bleary eyes suggested he had just been roused from a nap on his office couch.

"Oh, all right, then," he snapped irritably. He tiptoed forward. First turning the inside key, he opened the door, catching a pair of retreating individuals as they made their way down the path. "Hello there!" he called after the man and woman before deciding they must be door-to-door salespeople. After all, who else rang doorbells in the middle of a Sunday afternoon?

Mr. Wells suddenly thought of a couple of even less pleasant possibilities and wished he had quietly shut the door. But it was too late. The visitors had turned and were already heading back up the path.

"Ah, you are in," said the man. Wearing a suit jacket over a turtleneck and a pair of tight-fitting black jeans, he had a pair of sporty-looking sunglasses perched on the brim of his tattered old baseball cap. It was a look that served only to further confuse and alarm Mr. Wells as the man's companion joined him, a beautiful dark-haired woman wearing a designer pantsuit.

"Is this the Wells household?" the man then asked.

"Why, yes," confirmed Mr. Wells suspiciously. "Can I help you with anything?"

I certainly hope so," said the man in the baseball cap. "Templeton Cray," he said, offering his hand. "I'm the director of *Blackthorne Inn*, the movie we're shooting in your wonderfully quaint little town. And this is my associate, Miss Audrey Parker, our casting director."

The introduction was enough to draw the children and their mother instantly into the entranceway, where they fought for a glimpse of the pair through the narrow gap surrounding Mr. Wells.

And had Joy heard correctly? She could have sworn she heard the man mention "Blackthorne Inn," one of Peugeot's most famous stories.

"We're sorry to intrude on your weekend, but we were wondering if we could come in and have a word with you. We tried calling, but your phone appears to be out of order."

"Oh, for heaven's sake. Is the line down again?" cried Mr. Wells.

This would make it the third time a nest of squirrels had disconnected the Wells family from the world. Unfortunately, it usually took them two weeks to notice the lack of both phone calls and a dial tone.

Nevertheless, the news made Mr. Wells no more comfortable about the unexpected intrusion. However, despite his tremendous urge to slam the door and close the curtains, he found himself inviting the pair inside. Ahead of the strangers, the rest of the family scattered like frightened rats.

"Right this way," Mr. Wells said, directing them to the sitting room.

Peeking around the doorway, Joy watched with her brother as the pair took their seats on the same two antique wing chairs where her parents relaxed every evening. Noticing how dingy and uncomfortable the furniture looked in the full light of day, she found herself feeling somewhat embarrassed at the sight.

But the director and his associate took no notice. Instead they stood up as Mrs. Wells strode in to introduce herself.

"A pleasure, madam," said the director.

"Would either of you like a cup of tea?" interrupted Mr. Wells. "Or some coffee, perhaps?"

"No, no, I'm quite all right," replied Mr. Cray.

"I'm fine too," Miss Parker agreed, brushing her hair out of her face. Joy admired how long and black it was. Miss Parker reminded her a bit of what her mother's sister might have looked like if she'd had one.

"How might we be of service?" Mr. Wells inquired as

if the pair were a couple of potential clients who had just walked into his legal firm.

Mr. Cray did not answer, his attention drawn elsewhere around the drawing room. "Say, this sure is a beautiful house you've got here," he enthused. "Have you lived here long?"

"Oh, just about ten years or so. Is that right, Helen?"

"Eleven. We moved in when our daughter was still a baby."

"And we've been slowly renovating ever since," explained Mr. Wells.

"*Very* slowly," added Mrs. Wells icily.

"Hey, why rush things?" asked Mr. Cray. "Anyway, I can't see anything you should change. Just look at all the character! Audrey, did you notice the wonderful crown molding?"

"It's very beautiful," Miss Parker marveled.

"Do you know if that fireplace is original, Mrs. Wells?"

"I suppose it is," she answered, looking over at the mantel. "If only it weren't hidden under twenty layers of paint."

"It must be pretty cozy in here in the wintertime."

Listening in, Joy turned, wide-eyed, to her brother. She had worked it out, she was certain. "Byron, they want to shoot the movie here!" she whispered excitedly. "In our house! I'm sure of it!"

"How do you know?"

"Well, just listen to them. They can't stop going on about it!"

"So?" Byron asked. "What does that have to do with anything?"

"Shh!"

The two children continued listening intently as the

adults talked about the various architectural features of what Mr. Cray described as a clearly historical property. The conversation went so painfully overlong that eventually even Mr. and Mrs. Wells began shifting around uncomfortably on the love seat.

"So anyway, I suppose I should come to the point," Mr. Cray finally said. "As I said, we're shooting a movie nearby."

"I had heard a few people at work talking about it," confirmed Mr. Wells. "What is it about, anyway?"

"Well, it's a horror flick, to be honest—but an old-fashioned one. The emphasis is not on blood and gore, but rather on suspense."

"I see," said Mr. Wells.

"Set in Victorian times, the story is about a family who take over running an inn in the country. But then creepy things start happening around the place, and the father slowly becomes possessed by a slumbering evil. Finally all hell breaks loose as he goes on a murderous rampage."

"It sounds good," said Mrs. Wells. "I like scary stories."

"Since when, Helen?" Mr. Wells demanded.

"I don't know, since recently. If you must know, I've been staying up in the library working my way through our daughter's precious E. A. Peugeot compendium. It's quite entertaining, actually."

"Ethan Alvin Peugeot!" Mr. Cray exclaimed. "Well isn't that a coincidence? Our movie is actually an adaptation of one of his stories."

From the hallway Joy let out a strangled cry of delight.

"Did you know he is rumored to have lived in these

parts?" the director asked. "Perhaps in the Steadford Mines area, I'm told, where an important discovery was recently made. But that's why we're shooting here, to get a really authentic feel for the movie."

That was it. Joy leaped forward, her objections already on her lips. But her brother grabbed her arm and held her back.

"Mom and Dad will kill you," he whispered in warning.

He was right, Joy knew. So instead, chewing her fist like it was a candy apple, she stood listening intently.

"Unfortunately, something's come up that has stalled the production at the moment," the director continued. "And if you know anything about the movie business, every hour lost means part of our budget dollars lost, so we've got to get things back on schedule and moving forward."

Mr. and Mrs. Wells nodded knowingly, as if they were a pair of veteran producers. "I can well imagine," Mr. Wells insisted. "Time is money, as they say."

"It certainly is," agreed Mr. Cray. "Anyway, not to waste your time, then. That's where your family comes in. A local contact suggested that you might be able to help us out. Now, I'm not promising anything just yet, but if things work out, it could be a great opportunity. With a nice fee."

Mr. and Mrs. Wells shot each other looks of disbelief.

"Wow, how exciting!" replied Mr. Wells finally, grinning uncontrollably. "So can we assume it's our house you are interested in?"

"Actually, no." It was Miss Parker who now spoke, leaning forward in her seat. "It's your daughter."

CHAPTER 13

Joy still couldn't believe what she was hearing. They were considering *her* to be in a movie based on a story by E. A. Peugeot!

And not only that, the part was one of the leads.

It turned out that Penny Farthing, the well-known starlet originally cast in the role, had gone missing a month earlier. She was widely known as a temperamental young woman—a "wild child," as newspapers less graciously called her—and her parents at first had believed that she had only run away.

It wasn't the first time, after all. On the previous occasion Penny had turned up a few days later, safe and sound at a hotel, where she'd spent the time sobbing down one phone to her best friend, Rachel, and ordering room service on another. The incident, however, had received a lot of attention in the press and had very nearly gotten her fired from her last movie.

Fearing the top-earning actress would be replaced this time, Penny's parents and agent had initially conspired to hide her disappearance. Instead they'd waited, hoping she would phone, and had hired a private detective to locate her. In the meantime they had seen no reason to worry the studio.

But Penny had never called, and even her friend Rachel had hysterically insisted she'd never heard from her. The private detective—presumably the man who had approached Joy and shown her Penny's picture in the street—had located no trace of her so far.

So it happened that it was only on the first scheduled day of the shoot that the producers had finally discovered they were missing someone to play the role of Mr. Blackthorne's adolescent daughter, Agnes.

Which was where Joy came in. Her name had been suggested to the casting director, Miss Parker, who had visited Winsome and watched Joy for an entire lunch hour. Joy seemed perfect for the part, she'd decided.

"Isn't Penny Farthing, like, sixteen years old or something?" Joy asked in a panic as she sat squished between her parents on the love seat.

"Actually, Ms. Farthing just turned seventeen," Miss Parker corrected. "But with her youthful looks, she tends to play younger parts."

"According to the script, the character of Agnes is not much older than you, Joy," the director assured her. "And she's supposed to be a blond-haired girl. Penny was going to wear a wig because she refuses to dye her hair."

"You know, come to think of it," Miss Parker said, "don't you think there's a bit of a resemblance between the two of them?"

Joy frowned. Was she supposed to be flattered to hear that

she looked like a spoiled little runaway? Then again, no one had ever compared her to anyone well-known, unless the bride of Frankenstein counted.

"But I'm not sure if I can act," Joy blurted out nervously. "Ow!" she screamed, feeling a pinch from her mother.

"Joy is just being modest," Mrs. Wells declared. "She's a great little actress, believe me," she insisted.

Seeing her mother's sidelong glance, Joy was pretty sure it wasn't meant entirely as a compliment.

"Well, we'll need to do a screen test, of course," Miss Parker explained. "But don't worry. If you get the part, you'll have plenty of acting coaches and elocution experts helping you. The important thing is to just be natural."

"Anyway, I'm not worried. You've got the perfect look and intensity," said Mr. Cray. "She's exactly like your friend promised," he added to his colleague.

The remark made Joy sit forward. "Wait a second. Exactly like who promised?"

"What was your friend's name again? The special municipal consultant."

The casting agent answered, "Octavio Phipps."

"*Mr.* Phipps?" Joy shrieked.

"That's him," said Mr. Cray. "He was the one who suggested you might fit the bill. Audrey knew him growing up around here."

"He said a lot of very nice things about you," added Miss Parker. "That you were smart, pretty, and very mature for your age. And best of all, that you were completely fearless—not afraid of anything or anyone."

Mr. Phipps said that? Joy shivered. What was he up to now? It had to be some sort of trap.

"You actually knew Mr. Phipps?" Joy asked. "You mean you grew up in Spooking too?"

"I sure did. I was raised on Cliffside Crescent at the other end of town." It was the ritziest street in town, Joy knew, and one of the few that were still completely occupied. "I don't get back often to see my parents, though. They usually come to see me."

"And how do you know Mr. Phipps?" Joy demanded, her forthrightness earning a sly glare from her mother.

"Octavio and I were tennis partners. I guess he was my best friend, really."

Mr. Phipps was her best friend? What kind of secret monster could the pretty woman be? Filled with dread, Joy felt just about ready to regretfully decline the incredible opportunity, when they began discussing the upcoming shooting schedule.

"Now, would it be possible for Joy to miss the rest of the school year?" Mr. Cray asked.

"We realize this is a lot to ask," Miss Parker continued. "However, we could bring in a dedicated tutor if you're worried about her falling behind academically."

Joy had heard enough—she was sold. "That's it! I'm in! Let's do it!" she shouted, leaping to her feet.

"Sit down please, dear," said Mr. Wells sternly. "We will have to discuss it. But I think it could be a possibility."

"And I don't need a tutor. It's not like we're doing

anything in class anyway. Plus, I'm about to graduate. It's totally okay!" Joy insisted.

"I said that we'll have to discuss it," her father said.

"Anyway, let's not get too far ahead of ourselves," said Mr. Cray. "There's still the screen test to get through. But I have a lot of confidence that you'll be great."

"Now, if you'll excuse us, we've got to get back to the set. Can we make an appointment to see Joy tomorrow morning, perhaps? We really would like to get moving on this."

Joy turned to her father and mother, her hands clasped together. "I think Joy could miss the first half of school tomorrow," Mr. Wells agreed.

Miss Parker scribbled down an address and a time on the back of her business card. The pair then made their way to the door.

"Good afternoon then," said the director. "It was really nice meeting you all."

Joy stood in the doorway, stunned.

"Good afternoon, Mr. Cray, Miss Parker," said Mr. Wells, squeezing his daughter's shoulders.

"Umm, yeah, bye," said Joy.

They closed the door behind the departing guests.

"See?" Byron said. "I told you they didn't want to use our house."

That evening the Wellses ordered in a pizza. It arrived about an hour and a half later, borne by a particularly sullen deliveryman who, upon being paid, walked off without offering any change.

"What nerve," Mr. Wells grumbled as he carried the box into the kitchen. "I think seven dollars is a pretty generous tip to simply assume."

"Oh, Edward, shush," Mrs. Wells scolded. "At least he actually made it up to Spooking."

"For that we are supposed to be grateful?"

But Mr. Wells had to agree. Too often lately their food never showed up at all, and when he would call to complain, the restaurant would deny any knowledge of the order.

The pizza turned out to be stone cold, however, requiring a blast in the microwave before it could be served.

The starving family finally sat down around the dining room table and began eating. It was only when Joy looked up from her third slice that she noticed everyone staring at her.

"What?" she asked, detaching herself from a strand of cheese.

"Nothing," replied Mrs. Wells. "Are you enjoying your dinner, sweetie?"

"You sure drained your glass," declared Mr. Wells. "Do you need a refill?"

"Yes, and yes," she answered suspiciously.

But it was Byron who finally broached the topic on everyone's mind. "So what's going on, anyway?" he demanded. "Is Joy going to be famous?"

It was a question Joy hadn't even begun to consider. Her parents, however, burst out with nervous laughter.

"There's no point in obsessing over that sort of thing," said Mr. Wells. "Your sister has to get the part first."

Mrs. Wells glared at her husband. "Oh, she'll get the part," she insisted forcibly.

"I'm not saying otherwise," agreed Mr. Wells. "Nevertheless, it remains to be seen if she will become famous."

"Why shouldn't she?" Mrs. Wells objected. "She's twice as beautiful as that Penny Farthing girl, and not even half the screwup."

"Pardon me?" cried Joy.

"That was badly put. I meant to say you're not a screwup at all."

Byron then asked the second question on everyone's mind. "Are we going to be rich, then?"

All eyes turned to Joy again.

"What?" she said. "How I am supposed to know?"

"We'll just have to wait and see," said Mr. Wells, gazing with peculiar intensity at his daughter.

"You'll just have to try your best," replied her mother, who wore an identical expression. "But whatever you do, you must blow them away at that screen test."

"It's imperative," her father agreed. "Just don't think about the pressure. Remember to act natural."

After dinner Joy excused herself and retired to her room. She wanted to be alone, away from the weird attention of her family. It seemed like everything suddenly depended on her, she thought, changing into her pajamas.

She took Fizz out of his aquarium and let him hop around for a while. If she did become rich and famous, what would become of him? She supposed she would build him a big pond, with real lily pads to frolic around on. But then she imagined herself flying around in private jets, attending premieres and parties around the world. It wouldn't leave a lot of time for pets.

And it definitely wouldn't leave a lot of time for solving the mysteries of Spooking, she suddenly realized. And there was so much yet to uncover! For example, she had never even figured out what Melody Huxley had been doing in town, nor her connection to E. A. Peugeot. Could it be just a coincidence that his personal letters had turned up in her cottage in Steadford Mines?

Joy thought about Ms. Huxley's diary again, still packed away in the dark cellar. With everything about to possibly change, she had no more time to waste. She had to get answers now. Perhaps then, if she did become famous, people would start taking her theories more seriously.

Joy retrieved her adventuring bag from the post of her bed. After fishing around, she pulled out her trusty flashlight. It had been a while since she had last probed any dark and uncertain terrors, so, getting down on all fours, she gave the flashlight a quick test by shining it under her bed.

The batteries were pretty weak, but they would have to do. Joy put on some slippers and her housecoat. Sneaking downstairs, she could overhear her parents talking in the sitting room. Bursts of delighted laughter punctuated their conversation.

"You know, I always thought Joy had a real flare for the dramatic. This could be her calling."

"It could change everything, you know."

"How exciting!"

Blocking her ears, Joy slipped down the hall. Quietly she undid the bolt on the cellar door.

With a final pop the last of the cellar lights died as Joy flipped on the light switch. "Great," she muttered. After closing the door behind her, she descended into the black abyss.

The cellar felt colder than normal to Joy, even with her slippers and housecoat on. From some unknown source an icy draft blew. Shining the flashlight ahead of her, Joy pushed on toward the stack of trunks. Out of the darkness something unexpected appeared, lit by the weak yellow beam.

It was bits of shredded cardboard, she saw, strewn across the floor. Squatting down, Joy was able to make out a few words.

"Deep-pan deluxe."

It was the pizza she had dropped. Something had chewed right through the box and eaten it.

It was probably just the mice, Joy told herself. They had made just as big a mess upstairs in the pantry, where they'd even managed to eat all of the marshmallow bits out of Byron's favorite cereal. Still feeling uneasy however, Joy pushed onward.

Shining the flashlight ahead of her, Joy approached the shelves where the old residents' possessions were stacked. She then screeched in horror.

Where Melody Huxley's trunk had once stood was a gaping black hole.

CHAPTER 14

With lunch over, Winsome Elementary was once again locked up tightly, so Joy discovered. Having shaken the front door, she turned shrugging to her mother, who sat idling in the station wagon.

"Try the intercom!" Mrs. Wells shouted.

Joy pressed the button and waited.

It had been a stressful morning. Having not slept a wink, Joy had felt exhausted at the screen test. She had been given a script and had then stood in front of the biggest camera she'd ever seen. She'd read lines while Miss Parker, Mr. Cray, and a couple of other people watched. Most of the lines had been short, but with each she had been coached to portray some sort of emotion—happiness, sadness, anger, and fright—which she had then dutifully tried to fake. Standing there in front of the camera, she supposed that's all acting really was—faking things on command.

They had then asked her to give them her best scream.

For this, Joy had only to think back to the moment when she'd discovered Melody Huxley's chest was missing. Everyone had seemed pretty impressed when she'd delivered the same piercing shriek she'd let loose in the cellar the previous night.

Joy's parents had been less impressed the night before. They had leaped from their seats at the sound and raced around the house trying to find their clearly distressed daughter. Finally Joy had emerged from the cellar.

"What on earth were you doing down there at this time of night?" Mrs. Wells had demanded.

"Where is it?" Joy had snapped back, ignoring her.

"Joy Wells, I do not like your tone!" her mother had scolded. "Where is what?"

"Melody Huxley's chest, that's what!"

It had turned out that her mother had taken it down to Wiskatempic University, with a plan to show the contents to a professor she was friendly with in the history department.

"I showed your mother," Mr. Wells had told her. "And like you said, those photos do bear quite an uncanny resemblance to the famous Melody Huxley. Don't you want to show them to an expert and find out for sure?"

"Yes. But you should have asked me first!"

"Perhaps we should have, but the woman's things are perfectly safe in my office," Mrs. Wells had assured her daughter. "So I don't see the need for all this shouting and drama."

"*Because*," Joy had said between gritted teeth, "I *need* something in it!"

"And what exactly would that be?" Mrs. Wells had asked crossly. "What exactly do you need at ten thirty the night before your big audition?"

"Oh, just forget it!" Joy had replied. "It's too late now anyway."

Standing in front of the door at Winsome, Joy wondered why she had been so upset. Wasn't that what she'd always wanted, for her parents to take her seriously and get an actual expert to look at the contents? But those contents were her discovery. She wanted to uncover their secrets personally.

"Hello?" said a voice as the intercom crackled to life.

"Yeah, hi. It's Joy Wells. I'm a student here."

The door buzzed. Yanking it wide, Joy gave a quick wave to her mother.

"Bye, dear!" Mrs. Wells shouted cheerfully through the open window before peeling away.

Inside the school the halls were deserted, and only the distant sound of thudding basketballs broke the hush. Holding the note excusing her morning absence, Joy headed along to the office.

A boy sat outside, his head buried in the crook of his elbow.

"Byron?" Joy asked, recognizing his thick dark hair.

"Huh?" he cried, startled.

"It's just me," whispered Joy. "What are you doing here? Are you in trouble?"

"No, I'm the hall monitor today," he said, yawning. "And they keep sending me up to the top floor with messages. So I'm really tired! I just need a nap!"

Joy watched as without a further word her brother settled back into a comfortable position. Didn't he even remember about her audition? From the snoring that quickly followed, apparently not.

Joy knocked on the door and then entered the office.

"Hello there!" the school secretary said, beaming at her.

"I'm Joy Wells," she explained. "I was absent this morning and was supposed to bring in a note."

The secretary put on the glasses dangling by a chain around her neck. "Everybody knows who you are!" she cried, barely glancing at the note. "You're Winsome's very first movie star!"

"Huh?" Joy craned her neck to see exactly what her mother had written, but the secretary clutched the note like she had a winning lottery ticket in her grip.

"Quick, everybody. Lock down the school!" cried Principal Crawley, rushing out of his office. Wearing a big grin and a green sweater pulled tightly across his belly, he made Joy think of a giant sprinting pea pod. "Don't let the paparazzi know there's a star in our midst!"

What was going on? she wondered. Then Joy remembered Miss Parker saying how she had come to Winsome on a casting stake-out.

Which meant the whole staff probably knew about her business now.

Just then Grayson, a well-known fifth-grade troublemaker poked his pinched, freckle-splattered face out of the principal's office. "A star?" he demanded, sneering. "Where?"

"Why, Joy Wells here. She has a big part in that movie they are making here in Darlington!"

"She isn't a star. She's just one of the chicks who takes the Spooky Express," the boy said, using the unflattering but nonetheless popular name for her bus. "Big deal."

"It is a big deal," Principal Crawley answered crossly.

"Especially when you consider that they've never made a movie in Darlington before."

"Actually, they're making the movie up in Spooking," Joy corrected irritably. "But it was just a screen test," she admitted. "So I don't know if I'm even getting the part yet."

"Oh, I wouldn't worry," said the principal, not noticing as Grayson then slunk out of the office and escaped into the hall. "I was with the casting lady when she was watching you over the lunch hour, and she said you were perfect! So you're going to get it, all right. Unless you can't act, of course. You can act, can't you?"

Joy shrugged, feeling a bit creeped-out by the thought of being spied on like that. "I guess that's what the screen test will tell us."

"Well, I for one still can't believe it," said the secretary. "That a real live star got her start right here at Winsome! It's amazing!"

Joy could hardly believe it either. She had gone to the school for almost seven full years now, and this was the first time the principal or the secretary had ever acknowledged her existence. And now they were staring at her with the kind of expectation usually reserved for people about to start throwing free money into the air.

"Hey, hold on a second!" Principal Crawley said, slapping a pile of parental permission slips. "This is exactly the kind of news that calls for a special announcement!"

"No!" Joy shrieked as Principal Crawley's pudgy index finger homed like a heat-seeking missile to a big green plastic button on the public-address system.

"Attention, Winsome students!" he bellowed into the microphone. "Good afternoon. This is your principal here. I'd like to interrupt your studies for a moment to share some exciting news. It seems we have a movie star in our midst! Joy Wells, one of our own grade six pupils, is going to be starring in the major motion picture currently filming in Darlington!"

Joy stood by helplessly as Principal Crawley went on to tell the whole school about how a casting agent had visited the school and how she had been specially picked out from among the entire student body. And knowing talent when he sees it, the principal couldn't have endorsed a better candidate.

"Anyway, a big congratulations is in order. Let's just hope that when she's rich and famous she doesn't forget all the friends she made here at Winsome," he finished.

It was not something worth worrying about, Joy thought.

"Great announcement," said the secretary.

"Thank you, Gladys. This could be very good for our school, you know," the principal then remarked. "I've read before about big stars coming back to their old schools and pumping some money into the library or the school yard as a way of saying thanks," he said. "It's something to think about, huh, Joy?"

"Umm, yeah," Joy agreed. "Except I don't even have the part for sure yet," she pointed out again.

"Like I said, it sounded like a done deal to me. Oh, and don't worry about Miss Keener," Principal Crawley told her. "She has been informed that this is probably your last week and not to give you any more homework."

Hmm, maybe she was wrong, Joy thought. Maybe celebrity did have its perks.

At that moment Mr. Star, the music teacher, arrived breathlessly at the office. "Is this her?" His look of excitement waned as he registered Joy's face. "Congratulations," he said, unable to cover his disappointment. Woefully tone-deaf, Joy had dragged down her entire grade for the past seven Christmas concerts. "You know it's a shame you didn't apply yourself more in music class," he nonetheless added. "You could have been a triple threat."

"A triple what?"

"A triple threat," Mr. Star repeated, looking startled at such a display of ignorance. "Somebody who can not only act, but sing and dance as well."

"Oh. Sorry." Joy shrugged, unsure why she'd apologized. The truth was that she wasn't even sure if she was any sort of threat at this point.

Finally excused, Joy headed off to class. On the way she passed a large poster pinned up on the announcement board. Stopping, she gawked at the grotesque three-humped camel drawn on it, under which AN ARABIAN NIGHT NEVER TO FORGET had been written.

The graduation dance, Joy remembered, suddenly picturing herself busting a move. No, she was definitely a single threat at best.

Passing by the washroom, Joy decided to slip in and cool her flushed face with a few handfuls of icy water. Drying off with a scratchy brown paper towel, she looked at the blond girl in the mirror, the one whom everyone had always made fun of. Was this really happening? Was her face really going to be projected onto giant screens across the country? Shuddering, she dried herself off and headed upstairs to class.

Entering the classroom, Joy was met by stares and stony silence. She took her seat.

"So Miss Wells," said Miss Keener finally from her desk. "I hear you're leaving us."

Joy looked up. "Umm, maybe."

"Maybe," Miss Keener repeated. "While we all sit here in this stifling classroom, you're going to be off making a movie, *maybe*. How nice is that for you?" she asked with an eerie grin.

"Really, I don't know yet," Joy said. "I'm still waiting to hear."

"Well, for now you can join the rest of the class in some silent reading."

Joy sunk down in her chair. Hoping not to catch anyone's eye, she drew a book from her desk and began reading. Surely for this she would get hit in the head with an elastic band, she thought. But no missiles were incoming.

After the bell rang, Louden caught up to Joy in the hall. "Hey, so you're going to be a movie star! That's awesome!"

Hoping to dispel the certainty, Joy explained the whole process of the screen test.

"But you felt good about it at least?"

"I don't know," Joy said. "I guess so. I just stood in front of the camera and read out a bunch of lines."

Louden nodded. "Hey, what did Miss Keener mean about leaving us early?" he then asked.

"Shooting starts right away. So if I get the part, this will be my last week at school," Joy explained.

"Really?" Louden replied with an unhappy look. "But what about the graduation dance? Are you going to miss it, too?"

"I guess that depends," Joy told him. "But I probably won't be able to go."

Louden's face fell further before his impossibly wide smile returned. "Well, it's just a stupid dance," he said. "I'm sure you won't be missing much."

"Yeah," Joy agreed.

"Well, I guess I'll see you tomorrow, then," Louden said.

"See you," Joy replied, turning to collect her things from her locker.

Joy had forgotten about the dance, which she had been so hoping to get out of. And being in a movie was a pretty good excuse to use on her mother, she supposed. Joy wondered if there was any chance they could take the dress back, but then she reconsidered, thinking she might need it for a movie premiere or something. The blue would certainly pop against a red carpet, she imagined.

But then she thought about Louden, and the landslide of disappointment that had tumbled down his face. He hadn't been going to ask her to go as his date, had he? Surely not. But, then, why bring it up?

Joy turned, looking down the hall for any sign of Louden. Resolving to ask him outright, she hurried downstairs, but by the time she reached the stop for the Spooking bus, he was gone.

✿ ✿ ✿

Morris arrived panting at the front door of his home. It had been perhaps the longest day of school ever, and what was worse, his teacher Mrs. Whipple had kept him for a few minutes after school as punishment for reading during class. Could the woman not make an exception? He was up for a role in a major movie and had to prepare!

But his mother had ordered that he keep things a secret.

The school library had only produced two titles of any use to him—*Acting: The Bliss and Business Behind Make-Believe*, and *Let's Make a Movie! A Modern Guide to Film Production*. Morris had been completely engrossed in the former when Mrs. Whipple had caught him.

Since he'd been running late, he had sprinted home. "Mom!" he called, bursting in.

The bungalow was completely silent, with the tracks of a vacuum cleaner on the butterscotch carpet the only thing betraying recent occupancy.

"Mom, are you home?" Morris shouted again in mounting panic.

"I'm in the living room," came her low, monotone reply.

Dumping his bag, Morris hopped around, careening against the closet as he desperately tried to claw off his tightly laced shoes. Finally free of them, he tore down the hall, his heels raw and burning.

"Well? Did you hear anything?" he asked.

His mother's swollen face looked as if she'd spent the day inspecting the inside of a beehive. She'd been sobbing again, and hard.

He gasped. *Oh no*, he thought as his legs turned to jelly. He didn't get the part. From the depths of the well of personal misery into which he usually only lowered a bucket, a great geyser now arose, gushing high into the air before raining down despair and hopelessness.

But maybe he was wrong. Maybe his mother had only been freaking out because he'd been late getting home. She did that sometimes, such as when Mr. Phipps took him places as a Caring Chum—a program his mentor had sadly had to withdraw from after losing his job.

Maybe that was it, he hoped. Maybe she'd just thought he was murdered again, or perhaps run over by a car or hit by space junk as were her usual fears.

But before he could ask, his mother sprung to her feet, exploding in a hysterical expression of glee the likes of which he had never witnessed—her arms flailing, her legs jigging, her lungs giving wind to the loudest squeal of excitement ever to resound in their modest living room.

"You got it, Morris!" she shrieked. "You got it!"

"Really?" he cried. "Are you serious?"

"Yes! Yes! Yes!"

Morris stood motionless as his mother continued dancing around the room. He finally walked to the window and stood there, staring out at the street, the passing cars, and the neighbors opposite.

Seeing himself in the reflection, he straightened his screwy-looking bow tie. "I am going to be a movie star," he announced, his eyes shining like a pair of polished pebbles. "Suck on it, suckers!"

CHAPTER 15

At home after school Joy found waiting around for such life-changing news to be an unbelievably agonizing activity. If she got the part, would they get in touch today, she wondered, or wait for tomorrow? Could the movie people leave her to wait an entire week feeling like this? The possibility was too much to bear.

Then again, maybe they weren't calling because she'd bombed out. Because really, except for the scream, she didn't feel like she'd exactly nailed the screen test. She'd been fidgety in front of the camera, and unsure of what to do with her hands, and her constricted voice had often quavered noticeably while delivering a line.

But sitting around her room wasn't helping, she decided. So, securing Fizz into her side bag, she headed off to the park to get a bit of fresh air.

It had rained a bit since she'd been home, and the leaves dripped icy water down the back of Joy's neck. She walked to the center of the park, heading to the island where the bent old willow grew. There, she removed Fizz from his leather prison.

Having been cooped up all day, the frog was happy to get

out, splashing gleefully in the waterway for a while and then lounging in the shallows with only his two eyes showing. Joy watched him, delighting in his every move. If she got the part, she would be too busy to take him out like this, she guessed. Joy wondered if she could trust Byron to take him for walks and not lose him down a storm drain. If so, maybe she would pay him to do it for her.

Passing by the play area, Joy stopped to gaze at the merry-go-round. After about a minute it began revolving, slowly round and round. She looked around to see if anyone was near.

"Hi, Poppy," Joy then said to the empty ride. "Did you hear? They're making a movie in Spooking. And guess what? I tried out for it today."

The rusty old merry-go-round creaked in congratulations.

"Thanks! I'll let you know how things turn out," she said.

Heading back along the Boulevard, Joy inhaled deeply, enjoying the smell of puddles evaporating on the warm pavement. Approaching the Happy Fates Retirement Estates, Joy spotted Madame Portia out front. It had been a while since she had seen her friend, she realized. In fact, they hadn't spoken since Joy's birthday dinner.

Beside her now, however, was a familiar-looking man in a baseball cap. Getting closer, Joy confirmed that it was Templeton Cray, the movie director. In their wake a small entourage followed, feverishly scribbling notes as they cast their eyes around the property.

Dressed head to toe in black velvet, the old gypsy wore

an unusually thick application of makeup that rendered her face bright orange. "By the way," Joy heard the woman say as they reached the sidewalk. "Tell me, is there anybody famous in the movie? Some hunky young actor, perchance?"

"Hmm, I don't know about hunky young actors," Mr. Cray apologized. "But look, here comes one of our beautiful stars now."

"Hello, Mr. Cray," Joy said, blushing as she drew up to the pair.

"Call me Templeton, please. We're workmates, after all."

"Joy!" cried Madame Portia, her makeup cracking like a bed of sunbaked mud. "Is this true, bambina? Are you really going to be in the movie?"

Joy felt suddenly hot with renewed embarrassment. "I don't know." She shrugged.

"You don't know?" repeated Mr. Cray, turning to Madame Portia with a laugh. "Why, our young friend here only has one of the starring roles in our production!"

"Did I get the part?"

"Oh, sorry. Didn't Miss Parker call you? Of course not. I just remembered, your phone isn't working. Well, I'm sorry to spoil the surprise, but yes, you've got the part."

Joy's jaw dropped open.

"How exciting!" Madame Portia cried, carefully hugging her young friend so as not to squish her frog. The old gypsy then glowered comically at the girl. "But you never told me you wanted to be an actress! Why would you keep such secrets from me, young lady? Is it because I am a shifty old gypsy?"

"No," Joy replied, still stunned from the news. "I don't know. This just came up."

"We lost our original actress at the last minute," the director explained. "And Joy kindly agreed to step into her role. What she lacks in experience she makes up for with natural talent. Plus, she looks amazing on camera, let me tell you."

"I don't doubt it! Joy is the most beautiful and talented girl in the whole town!"

Joy blushed even more. She then found herself wondering if Madame Portia meant just Spooking or the entire metropolitan area of Darlington itself. Because if she meant just around Spooking, the competition was not exactly stiff.

"But tell me," whispered the gypsy conspiratorially, "who is she replacing? Anyone famous?"

The director shrugged. "Keep it quiet, but we had previously cast Penny Farthing for the part," he admitted.

"Blech!" Madame Portia spat, making the kind of face usually reserved for scraping slime from a shoe. "Oh, I've read about her—the late-night partying, the catfights with her costars. . . . I'm not surprised she didn't work out. What a spoiled brat! Honestly, you are much better off with our sweet bambina, Joy, even if she is a bit of a nobody right now."

"Well, I can't really comment other than to say we are excited about her replacement and what she will bring to the role," said Mr. Cray. "Speaking of which, young lady, we're sending over a script by courier. So start memorizing your lines as soon it arrives," he told Joy, smiling.

"Yes, sir," Joy answered.

"And thank you again," the director said to the old woman. "We'll be in touch about the schedule. And hopefully the shoot won't cause too much disruption for your residents."

"Bah, I'm sure they'll be fine," Madame Portia replied, waving her hand dismissively. "A bit of disruption is good for the very old, you know. If they get too comfortable, they forget to keep breathing!"

Mr. Cray gave the old gypsy an uncertain look. "Yes, well, let's just hope nothing like that happens." He then turned to the large black SUV parked on the street, where the rest of the crew sat waiting.

"What's going on?" Joy asked when the movie people finally drove away.

"They're shooting a movie in my house!" exclaimed Madame Portia. "Can you believe it? My decorating tastes are finally getting honored! I don't mean to sound conceited, but I always thought they were underappreciated."

"They're using your place?" Joy asked, feeling excited for the woman.

"Well, just the inside, as far as I know. I think they will mostly be using the parlor, in fact. Mr. Cray said they often use a lot of different locations and then make it look like it's the same house."

"Oh."

"Anyway, it's all very exciting." Madame Portia beamed, but then her face turned serious. "Oh, wait, bambina. I have to apologize to you!" she burst.

"What for?"

"For ruining your birthday meal, of course! I was feeling

a bit, um, unwell by the end of it, and those waiters and their off-key wailing were simply the last straw. My word, your parents must think I'm a mad old bat!"

"Not at all," Joy replied lightly. "They liked you."

But the truth was that her parents had openly wondered why their daughter couldn't find a single friend her own age to bring along but instead had invited some geriatric soothsayer with a weakness for wine. Joy even found herself regretting making the invitation, once the old woman began telling her parents about the night she'd nearly drowned with the Wells children when her submarine house had sunk in the swamp. Luckily, Mr. and Mrs. Wells had simply assumed she was suffering from some form of dementia, and had disregarded every word.

Not wanting to hurt the old gypsy's feelings, Joy thought that a change of subject was a good idea. "By the way, I forgot to ask. How did your new groundskeeper work out?"

"Do you mean old Al?" the gypsy asked. "I'm afraid he isn't working for me anymore."

"You fired him?" Joy was surprised to hear the news. She remembered how wonderful the grounds of the asylum had looked before the calamity, with its beautiful lawns and gardens. She had been certain he would do a good job for Madame Portia.

"Oh, no, bambina. I would never fire someone. I'm too softhearted! No, I'm afraid his health took a bit of a turn for the worse."

"What happened?" said Joy.

"Dear old Al has become rather ill these past few months.

You know, it is the strangest thing to say out loud, but sometimes I'm sure he is literally aging right before my eyes! I've had the doctor around to see him, of course, and he says everything appears normal, and that there is nothing wrong with the man beyond his age."

"How old is he anyway?" Joy asked.

"You know, I really have no idea," the gypsy replied. "When the doctor asked him, he said he was a hundred and fifty! The dear old gentleman. It appears he's losing not just his hair but his marbles as well. Quite honestly I don't think he'll see the end of the year if he keeps going like this."

"Really? That's awful." Joy felt sick to her stomach. This didn't sound like the same man she had met only a couple of months earlier, picnicking by the bent old willow in Spooking Park. Later that same day he had helped Joy, Byron, and Poppy rescue Fizz from the asylum, an hour before it had been swallowed up by what the authorities believed was an enormous sinkhole in the center of Spooking Hill.

Joy knew better, however. Having been there that night, she had witnessed firsthand the cause of the catastrophe. She had seen those terrible Hessian soldiers from the Peugeot story "The Legend of the Ghost Cannons" rising from the earth with their evil artillery.

Apart from the children and Mr. Phipps, the groundskeeper was the only other person who had survived.

Joy's attention was suddenly drawn across the street. "Hey, would you look at that funny old puppy!" she said, pointing.

Across from them a black dog stood watching. He was

a stout, barrel-chested creature, with a low flat forehead tinged with gray. His ears looked notched, and out of his wide tooth-lined maw, a large red tongue lolled, dripping globs of white saliva onto the concrete.

It was then that Joy noticed something peculiar about the animal —that he had only three legs, with a terrible scar marking where the front right limb had once been.

"Well, I've never seen him around before," Joy remarked. She then saw that Madame Portia had completely blanched and was now visibly shaking. "Hey, what's wrong?"

"That creature," she breathed. "I know it."

"Do you know his owners? Because he really should be on a leash, especially with all the traffic lately. He's going to get run over!"

"No one owns it," the old woman declared without removing her eyes from the creature. "It is a harbinger."

"A harbin-what?" asked Joy.

"A harbinger," the gypsy repeated, hardly able to expel the words. "A sign that bad things are about to come."

"What? That three-legged old dog?" She laughed.

In the single second before Joy turned back, the dog disappeared. "Where did he go?" she exclaimed.

But the old gypsy didn't answer. Instead she took off, bolting back up the path to the safety of her building. Joy called after her, but the woman's replies were only a stream of panicky-sounding gibberish.

Joy stood on the pavement, feeling annoyed with the woman. It was one thing to be superstitious, which did seem a bit of a forgivable quality in a gypsy. But it was quite another to run off and abandon a kid to whatever unnamed horror was supposedly approaching.

Sighing, Joy headed back home. Just as she turned onto Ravenwood Avenue, an out-of-breath bicycle courier arrived at Number 9. After dropping his bike on their lawn, he walked up the path to the porch.

"Excuse me," Joy called while jogging after him. "Is that for me?"

After confirming Joy's name against the one on the thick yellow envelope, the sweaty-faced young man handed it over. "I never had a drop-off here before," he told her breathlessly. "The road up is seriously hairy!"

"Yeah, sorry about that," Joy replied. Out of politeness, she waited until he set off again on his bike. "Be careful going down!" she shouted cheerfully after him, but she received no reply.

Clutching what could only be the *Blackthorne Inn* script, Joy then rushed inside, where her excited squeals drew the entire family into the foyer.

"I got the part! I got the part!"

"That's terrific news!" Mrs. Wells declared. "Oh Edward, isn't this the most exciting thing ever to happen to our family?"

"Other than the births of our beloved children, it certainly is, my dear."

"Nice," said Byron. "Sweet," he then added in a display of extra enthusiasm.

Joy raced upstairs to her room. After dumping Fizz back in his aquarium, she tore open the padded envelope. Inside she found a sheaf of paper punched and bound with three brass paper fasteners. Flinging herself onto her bed, she began reading.

Blackthorne Inn the movie would be in the proper period, Joy quickly learned to her delight. Set just before the turn of the twentieth century, the plot centered around a young family who take over a rundown hostelry. Enjoying the idyllic countryside, things go well for the stuffy Blackthornes at first, as they both renovate and reconcile after a few trying years.

But their newfound peace does not last. Having been the site of a terrible tragedy years earlier, the inn soon proves host to a lingering evil. Falling under its supernatural influence, Mr. Blackthorne slowly degenerates into a rampaging axe murderer. By the end of the story his young daughter, Agnes—to be played by Joy—and her brother, Alfred, are the only survivors of the bloodbath.

Joy already knew the story well, having read it at least ten or so times in *The Compleat and Collected Works*. However, having finished the script, she had mixed feelings. On the one hand she felt excited to see all the scenes in which her character appeared. And there was a call for a lot of screaming, she saw, which was probably why she'd gotten the part.

But the problem was that the script just didn't seem that scary to her—not as terrifying as the Peugeot original anyway. But maybe that was because she knew what was coming, she considered. Still, the whole thing had way too much talking and not enough action.

And whenever there *was* action, the script contained only

the barest description of what was going on. For example, replacing the carefully crafted tension and horror of the story were such passages:

INT. HALLWAY—MOVING CAMERA

Blackthorne stalks down the hall, dragging the axe behind him. Looking back, terrified, the bloodied guest runs out the front door.

> BLACKTHORNE:
> "Where are you going, traveler?
> I haven't even fared thee well!"

EXT. GARDENS—WIDE SHOT.

> GUEST:
> "Please, I beg you! No!"

The guest rushes outside, running into the gardens. Blackthorne gives chase.

EXT. GARDENS—CLOSE-UP SHOT

The guest tries hiding in a bush but shouts out when a thorn pricks him. He looks at a trickle of blood on his thumb. Blackthorne leaps out and sticks the axe into the man's head.

Joy stared at the script. It all seemed a little off to her. Checking her copy of *The Compleat and Collected Works*, she found the "fared thee well" line wasn't even in there.

But then again this was a movie, not the E. A. Peugeot story, she reminded herself. She guessed that the scariness would probably come from lots of moody visuals and an ominous sound track. And an axe in the head, she thought, probably would look a lot more impressive on the screen than it currently did on the page.

Standing in front of her bedroom mirror, Joy decided to try reading out a few of her lines, which someone had gone through and painstakingly highlighted in pink for her.

The process proved too painful, however. No matter how hard she tried, she just couldn't get started. She kept imagining her face, projected forty feet high on a gigantic movie screen. What about that pockmark on the end of her nose, the remnants of her terrible bout with chicken pox? It was going to look bigger than a hubcap!

Tossing the script onto the bed, she gave up.

Cursing the brightest moon he'd ever known, Phipps entered the cemetery gates, a large duffel bag over his shoulder. Despite his black clothes, he was sure he would be easily spotted slipping among the headstones if that detective were here, lying in wait for the inevitable return of the criminal to the scene.

Except he wasn't the criminal, he reminded himself. Or at least not the one in question, if indeed there had been any sort of foul play behind the disappearance of the actress Penny Farthing. And though he'd spent the past week telling himself not to panic over the detective's remarks, he had become increasingly certain that a thorough search of the cemetery was imminent. Which meant that Phipps could no longer relax until he had removed and properly disposed of the effects of Felix and Vince.

It would be a ghoulish business. Using a crowbar, Phipps would first have to pry open the heavy tomb door and then grope around the dank interior, all the while holding his breath so as to not inhale whatever sepulchral stenches might still linger in the ancient burial chamber. But worse than even this would be confronting the memories of his old bandmates and the terrible ends he had brought upon them. And for what—a couple of development projects, both failed and forgotten?

Because despite Felix's betrayal in joining Teddy's band, he had once been an irreplaceable friend. Even the thuggish Vince had not been entirely bad, although fairly close.

Though he felt wracked with renewed guilt, Phipps could not let their disappearances come to light.

After having come face-to-face with Teddy, Phipps had returned home, seething with the bitterness that had consumed his life. This was the fool who had outright stolen his sound and his riffs, remaking them into a thin gruel that was nonetheless slurped up by mankind. This was the wannabe who'd become a somebody, and in doing so had not only deprived Phipps of his due but had somehow made *him* look like the talentless copycat.

It made Phipps want to kill him. And truly, he would never get a better opportunity.

But after spending a few nights plotting what unfortunate accidents could befall "the ultimate rebel," as Teddy had once been called, Phipps had begun thinking about Audrey. He thought again about her story, how she had tried to kiss him while sheltering at the gingerbread house. And he began imagining all the ways things would have been different had he simply returned her affection. Could they be married now, living here in the town of their birth?

Happily, with a brood of little tennis champions?

There would have been no Black Tongs. No Teddy Danger. And no tragic ends for Felix or Vince, or even Madame Portia's husband Ludwig.

All of it hinged upon a single kiss.

But the curse on his family would have remained. And what greater pain could there be than passing such an affliction on to a child of his own? No wonder his father had been plagued by such black moods and had tried so hard to keep him from ever leaving Spooking. He cringed to imagine relaying the same preposterous ghost story, and delivering the same words of warning:

Son, you can never leave Spooking. . . .

Just as in his own case, the plea would certainly have been ignored.

Which meant he could never have been with Audrey, he realized. Not without cursing her, too, to the horror of watching her husband vanish, and then the agony of knowing her own sons would follow. He remembered his own mother, whom he had not even returned to once since she'd become widowed, and he shuddered to imagine what she must have endured during those final years.

No, he had been right to let Audrey slip through his fingers.

Still, his parents hadn't thought so. And yet they had known better than anyone else the awful burden to be carried! But why? How could they have been so cruel?

Had they perhaps seen such a match, of two young lovers from the same small town, as the only chance of keeping their son from vanishing?

If so, he had failed there, too. Instead vanishing had somehow become his life's central activity. Octavio had vanished from Spooking, then vanished from the music scene, and finally vanished as a person with any aspirations greater than the pursuit of power and the wreaking of vengeance.

And this is what it had gotten him, he thought, jamming the crowbar into the narrow gap between the door and the stone of the old Egyptian-style tomb. A life of skulking around at night, full of fear and regret. A life that no one would even notice as it passed.

The heavy door groaned open.

The air inside was stale and musty but nonetheless free of the deathly scents he could still vividly recall from his teenage career as a grave-digger. Pulling a flashlight out of his bag, he peered inside.

In the center of the room were two stone sarcophagi. One of them contained the remains of a rich old fellow who'd once lived in a mansion on Weredale, young Octavio had been told. The man had ordered the tomb built for himself, vainly thinking how much he'd been like a sort of local pharaoh, or so the story went. His ethereally beautiful young wife would join him later, he had most certainly planned. But judging from the empty sarcophagus beside him, the self-styled king was spending eternity alone for some reason.

Phipps would not end up like him, at least, because he would never have fame, nor riches, nor the simple company of a wife, he knew. But he would at least make his confession to Audrey before he vanished. He would do it so that if he were destined to be forgotten, at least some small part of him might remain in someone's heart.

Holding the flashlight, Phipps leaned over the open vessel. It was here that he'd stashed the possessions of his dead friends. But as the beam illuminated its contents, he found himself gasping in surprise.

The items were there, he saw, just as he'd left them. But now a new object lay atop them—a cell phone in a pink leather case.

Feeling unsettled, Phipps picked it up and turned it on. The phone beeped, its battery flashing an alarm as it loaded wallpaper of a moronic-looking young man flexing his abs for the camera. Standing closer to the open door, Phipps pressed redial.

After a few rings an answering service picked up.

"You've reached the office of Marty Newman & Partners, Artist Management Company. We're not available to take your call at the moment. However—"

Out of charge, the phone then went dead.

Phipps felt a chill claw up his back. He stepped into the doorway and looked out at the gravestones lit pale white. Could someone have planted this and be out there watching him right now? That private detective, maybe? Peering into the shadows, he saw no sign of anyone stirring among the avenues of the dead.

Phipps put the phone into his pocket and stepped back into the tomb. There he began loading up the duffel bag with Vince's and Lix's modest possessions. A leather jacket. Some cheap sunglasses and ancient cassette tapes. Dingy socks, torn jeans, and a pile of worn old T-shirts emblazoned with long-forgotten bands.

Why had he not just put these things out in the trash, he now wondered, to be carried off to a landfill? Meanwhile he'd just left Vince's guitar and Lix's amp sitting out in the old shop.

Some master criminal he would make. . . .

Once done, Phipps turned to go. His flashlight, however, caught a dark square on the floor behind the two coffins. Moving over to it, he discovered to his surprise that a heavy stone tile had been removed and a large opening revealed. Shining the flashlight in, he saw with a start a ladder leading down into a dank tunnel and what looked almost like a hairy creature lying at the bottom.

Wait a second—wasn't it just a blond wig somebody had dropped? Looking closely, he became sure of it.

At that moment Phipps heard a noise outside. Something was moving out there. Turning off the flashlight, he quickly shouldered his bag and slipped outside. Despite his best effort to close the door quietly, the heavy iron portal clanged shut behind him. Panicked, he hurried off, heading back toward the cemetery gates.

But before long he heard the noise again. He stopped and listened. They were footfalls, he had no doubt, but strange clomping ones that possessed an awkward rhythm he could not identify.

Whatever it was, the thing was coming for him. Struggling under the weight of the full duffel bag, Phipps turned and began running as fast as he could, leaping over head stones and dodging around monuments. All the while, his pursuer kept pace, now clearly panting with what sounded like animal bloodlust.

It was only when he got through the cemetery gates that Phipps finally glanced back, desperately hoping not to find some mind-boggling beast close on his heels.

And though he was relieved to see there was not, and that the thing had already given up chase, what he did see standing in the moonlight nevertheless gave him a chill.

For though it was only a dog, it was an unbelievably brutish-looking specimen, broad and black, standing hideously upon just three legs.

That much Phipps could see distinctly in the clear light of the moon before he raced back to the safety of the old music shop across the street.

CHAPTER 16

The street in front of Madame Portia's was jammed with white trucks and trailers that morning, stretching right along the Boulevard all the way to the park. Marveling at the unprecedented scene, Byron walked along the opposite side of the street, holding a walkie-talkie in each hand.

"Psst. Hey, kid. Over here," came a hoarse yet girlish voice unmistakably directed at him. "Do you want to come in for a soda pop?"

Terrified, Byron stopped, looking around for the source.

"It's just me," said Joy, grinning from a little window set in one of the parked trailers. "Come around and check it out."

Still feeling uneasy, Byron crossed the street and slipped through a narrow gap between two of the parked vehicles. On the other side he found Joy hanging out of an open door.

"What is this place?" he asked, his eyes opening with wonder as he regarded the large mobile structure. "Is it a bathroom?"

"No, it's not a bathroom, Byron," Joy replied, miffed. "It's actually my own personal trailer. The honeywagon"—as Joy had just learned they called the bathrooms—"is down at the other end."

"Your own trailer?" he repeated in disbelief. "What do you need that for? Our house is, like, only two blocks away."

Joy sighed, shaking her head. "Byron, don't you know anything about the movie business?" she asked. "All the lead actors get their very own trailers. It's just how things work around here."

Byron examined the open door. "Okay, so isn't there suppose to be a star with your name on it outside?"

Her brother did raise a good question, Joy had to agree. Craning around to the other side of the door, she confirmed that there was indeed no star. Maybe it was just an oversight. Should she get in touch with someone? she wondered.

But on second thought, maybe they left it off on purpose. "Actually, real stars don't like to advertise what trailer they are in," she told Byron, deciding it was the most likely explanation. "Movie stars are private people, you know, and it gets pretty tiring to have people hanging around, constantly hounding you for your autograph. That's why they prefer to be anonymous and hide out in their trailers until everybody's gone."

"Okay," Byron answered, a hurt look crossing his face. "So does that mean you want me to go away now too?"

"Of course not!" Joy exclaimed. "You're family! Come in and have a look."

Byron climbed up the steep steps, slipping under Joy's arm. "So where's this bunny wagon? Because I really, really need to go."

"Honeywagon," she repeated, closing the door behind him. "Us stars have our own private bathrooms, of course. But you can hold it long enough to have a quick look around first, can't you?"

Frowning, Byron followed his sister down the cramped hallway.

"Now, this is the kitchen area," Joy said, gesturing to the fridge, stove, and cabinetry as if each were a prize on a game show. "Over here is the lounge, where I get to hang around and entertain guests, which sometimes may include some famous people. And back there, that's the dressing room, and the place where they do all of my makeup," she finished. "It takes a lot of time to do my hair and makeup, you know, even longer than it takes Mom."

"Really?" asked Byron, suddenly noticing how his sister's face was the weirdest color he had ever seen, like she had been replaced with a life-size porcelain doll or something. Her hair, held back with a black velvet ribbon, looked unbelievably straight and silky, like something that would hang off the back end of one of those little ponies a few girls at school collected.

"Oh yeah, really. It actually takes, like, three times as long," Joy remarked proudly. "And that's with a professional doing it."

"What's up with your clothes?" her brother then asked, noticing that Joy was wearing a black dome-shaped dress with puffed sleeves that made her look like a human bell.

"Don't you like it?"

"It's weird," he said, remembering how she could barely squeeze down the hall in the outfit.

"It's called a crinoline, and it's very period," Joy informed him wearily. "I'll have you know our costume designer has won three major industry awards," she added.

"Whatever." Byron turned, snooping around the lounge. "Hey, can you eat any of that fruit?" he asked, pointing to a large bowl of apples, oranges, bananas, and grapes in the lounge.

"Yeah. It's all for me—and my guests, of course. So help yourself. And like I said, there's even soda pop in the fridge. Do you want one?"

"In a minute," Byron replied, putting the walkie-talkies down on the table. He then rushed down the hall back to the door leading to the tiny lavatory.

Sighing contentedly, Joy sat down in the lounge to wait for him. The couch was incredibly comfortable, she thought, much more so than any of the lumpy old eyesores they had at home. It even folded out into a bed, a nice assistant had explained to her, if she ever wanted to take a nap. There was also a stereo system, a TV, and two video game consoles at her disposal, each with a stack of what seemed like the latest games.

But so far it just didn't seem like she had time to enjoy any of her trailer's many distractions, what with the endless stream of people constantly consulting with her. Between assistant directors, makeup artists, and acting coaches, it seemed like she was never alone, even for a couple of minutes.

"Brrrr," said Byron, emerging from the lavatory. "It's totally freezing in here."

"I know. I don't know where the controls for the air conditioner are. And when I asked, they said it was better if I kept it cold so my makeup doesn't run down my face."

"Oh."

"Anyway, in this getup I could probably cross Antarctica and not care," Joy declared, scratching under the itchy fabric she was told contained actual horsehair. "Hey, feel free to grab yourself something while you're in the kitchen."

Byron opened the fridge and peered inside.

"Yuck. They're all diet drinks."

"Yeah, well, this is show business, remember. You really have to watch your weight a lot more closely than regular people, I'm told."

A banging noise interrupted the two siblings.

"What was that?" cried Byron, jumping up.

"It's just someone knocking at the door. Hold on."

Joy squeezed down the hall and answered it. Retrieving a diet cola, Byron listened as from outside a woman spoke to his sister. Unfortunately, he could not make out what she was saying.

"Okay, sure," he heard Joy answer. "Except I've got my little brother in here. I'll just get rid of him and then I'm ready."

Get rid of him. The words echoed in Byron's ears. He pressed himself against the counter, holding his unopened can as Joy joined him again in the kitchenette.

"Did you pick a drink?" she asked. "Good. Because you've got to go now."

"How come?"

"I've got someone coming in to double-check my wardrobe for the scene and touch up my makeup. We're going to shoot our very first scene in a few minutes! Isn't that exciting?"

"For you, maybe."

Joy sighed as her brother stood dejectedly in the middle of the tiny kitchen. Didn't he realize that she was doing this as much for him as for herself? "Oh, come on, Byron. Don't be like that. If everything works out, our family will be rolling in dough! Don't you want to be rich?"

Her brother shrugged. "I don't know. What's so great about being rich anyway?"

"What's so great about being rich?" Joy laughed. "Well, for one, we can fix up our house."

"But what's wrong with it?" Byron asked.

"Well, does it have a pool, or tennis courts, or a private movie theater? Oh, and what about finally fixing up one of the bigger rooms for you? Wouldn't that be nice?"

In their entire house there was only one room smaller than her brother's bedroom, and that was the pantry. At the idea of getting something a bit more spacious, Byron's eyes went wide with delight. "Really? Which one?"

"How about the one that looks over the backyard? It's big enough for a Ping-Pong table. And bunk beds, so you can have friends sleep over."

"And a pool?"

"In your room? Be serious."

"I meant in the backyard!"

"Of course! And it will even be a heated pool so you can

swim in winter. Or maybe an indoor pool! Which one do you want?"

"I guess I'd rather have an indoor pool in case of thunderstorms," Byron decided. "But I still want it to be heated."

"Done."

There came a few impatient knocks on the door.

"Okay, great. But you've really got to go. I can't keep the director waiting any longer."

Joy hustled her brother down the hall and opened the door. Out on the curb a frizzy-haired woman laden with beauty gear stood waiting.

"Sorry!" Joy called over her brother's shoulder as he descended the trailer steps. "Come right in."

The woman disappeared inside. Joy went to close the door.

"Hey, what do I do now?" Byron called up from the street.

"I don't know. Go to the park or something. Or better yet, go home and start thinking about what you want in your room. Look, I've really got to go!"

The door closed. Byron stood there for a moment, looking at the exterior of the trailer. He then noticed a printout in a plastic sleeve taped to the outside. JOY WELLS, the sheet said. Underneath the name was a large black star.

Staring, he opened his drink and took a sip.

"Blech!" he cried. "I hate diet!" Putting the full can on top of a nearby aluminum equipment case, he watched as one of the film crew began talking into a large black walkie-talkie.

"Darn it!" cried Byron, looking up at the closed trailer door. Empty-handed, he then slunk back down the street toward home.

A forest of metal light stands had sprung up in Madame Portia's dusty front room, flooding its dark corners with thousands upon thousands of lumens. Moving deftly around them, a gang of gnarly-looking grips and gaffers taped cables and hung reflectors as a few pale young women fussed over the set and props.

Feeling as ready as ever for her close-up, Joy stood gawping at the scene.

"Quite something, isn't it?" Madame Portia remarked, appearing behind her so suddenly that Joy jumped in alarm. "Look at those handsome tattooed young men over there, working up a sweat in my humble lounge. I wish I had a video camera!"

Joy looked at the sea of burly hairy guys and wondered who exactly she was talking about.

"How are your residents doing?" Joy asked, changing the subject. "With all the noise down here, I mean."

"Oh, they're fine, I suspect. They all jumped on a bus and are off playing bingo or visiting the Mega Mall or something for the day. Everyone except Al, of course, but with his medication I think he'll sleep right through it all."

"He's still sick, huh," said Joy, who could still not believe how the asylum groundskeeper could have become so suddenly ill. He was a man who had seemed almost abnormally vigorous, she recalled, clearly remembering the sight of him swimming like an athlete to coax Fizz from the depths of the facility's unpleasant pool.

Joy had also not forgotten what the groundskeeper had said about the pool's sulfurous crimson waters. He had explained how the water had bubbled up from a mysterious source deep in the ground, and had special healing powers that had not only restored Joy's frog to his physical prime but had made the groundskeeper himself outlive all of his friends.

At the thought an almost electric jolt racked Joy's body. "The Crimson Pool"! It was the title of the last unpublished story of E. A. Peugeot! She had been so shocked reading about the Melody Huxley connection that she'd never put the two together!

Unfortunately, the mysterious pool to which the groundskeeper credited his good health had also vanished that same night when the asylum had sunk into the earth. Which left the poor ailing fellow the last person who could testify to its existence.

Joy was just about to ask if she might visit the man the old gypsy called Al, when a booming voice drew everyone's attention.

"Good morning, everybody!" cried Templeton Cray, arriving on set. His cowboy boots clomping on the hardwood floor, he strode past them into the center of the room, cupping his hands around his mouth to fashion a makeshift megaphone.

"Thanks once again for all your hard work so far. We're just going to have a quick meeting with the talent and then get down to shooting this baby. So let's get everyone cleared out of here so the director of photography can get in and start working on the first setup."

As the crew members followed the instruction, the director turned back to the entranceway.

"Hello there, Madame Portia," Mr. Cray said. "Thanks again for letting us use all of your furniture. It's going to look so great on camera."

"You are most welcome, young man." The old woman beamed. "I guess if I can't be the star of the show myself, at least I can let my sofa set enjoy the limelight."

"Yeah, for sure," Mr. Cray replied. "Ah, there you are, Joy," he said, finally noticing the girl standing beside the old gypsy. "Could you come with me? I want to introduce you to your costars."

Finally she was going to meet some real celebrities! Fists clenched in anticipation, Joy followed the director outside onto the veranda. There her eyes fell immediately upon a gorgeous woman and an older man standing together in full makeup.

"Guys, I would like you to meet your costar, Joy Wells," Mr. Cray said. "Joy, meet your new family."

"Hi," Joy said shyly.

"This is Viola Renfrew, whom you may recognize from such films as *Specimen 9* and *Soldiers of Misfortune.*"

The pretty redhead smiled at Joy, who was obviously drawing a blank. "I also do a lot of voice-over work. I was the rich, snobby cat in *Kitty-Kitty-Bang-Bang.*"

"Oh yeah!" said Joy excitedly. "I saw that!"

"And this here is Teddy Danger, who has been rocking our butts off for the past twenty years."

"Has it really been that long?" The music icon laughed. "Hello there, young lady," he purred. "So lovely to meet you."

Joy tried not to stare at the man. While he still bore a resemblance to Mr. Phipps, his face seemed almost waxen in comparison, like he had been carved out of a candle. Gone were his many trademarks: his colorfully spiked hair, studded leather jacket, and bondage pants, replaced by an oily haircut parted down the middle, as well as a dark old-fashioned suit and a laced cravat. Joy shook his offered hand, and only the grip of her own father had ever felt quite as wet, limp, and soft.

"So, Joy, have you been in the business long?" he asked.

"Umm, not really," Joy answered. "In fact, this is the first time I have ever been in a movie."

The musician leaned in close. "Me too," he said. "Just don't tell anyone," he added with a wink.

"Now, Joy, normally when you make movies, you get time to meet your costars and rehearse," explained Mr. Cray. "But since we're running terribly behind schedule, we're going to have to just start shooting. I'm so sorry that we're working this way. But fortunately, Agnes and Alfred don't have any lines today, so you can just relax and start getting comfortable with your characters."

That's right, Joy thought. She had a brother.

"Where is our Alfred, by the way?" the director asked as if reading her mind.

"Sorry. I'm right here," said the boy in a little black and

gray striped vest, appearing from inside. "I had to go pop some allergy medication."

Joy's eyes fixed instantly upon him as she gasped.

"Oh no. You've got to be kidding me," Morris M. Mealey groaned. "*Spooky* is my costar?"

CHAPTER 17

"So how was your first day in the movie business?" Mrs. Wells asked her daughter when she finally staggered through the door that night.

"Umm, pretty good. It was long." Joy could hardly keep her eyes open. Trying to kick off her shoes, she stumbled and had to sit down to complete the task.

"Do you want something to eat?" Mr. Wells inquired, looking at his watch with concern.

"No, thanks. I already got something from the canteen."

"From the what?"

"The canteen," Joy repeated. "It's this truck where they serve food."

"Oh wow," said Mr. Wells. "Now, that is fancy treatment!"

"Did you bring home my walkie-talkies?" Byron demanded from where he sat up on the stairs.

"Huh? What?" Joy asked impatiently.

"My walkie-talkies. I left them on the table in your trailer."

"You have your very own trailer?" her father exclaimed. "Surely you can't be serious."

At the insistence of her parents, Joy was then forced to relay in full detail each and every feature of her trailer. "Oh yeah, and there's a fruit basket and a stocked fridge," she finished, yawning widely.

"Except all the drinks are diet," Byron grumbled.

"Joy has to watch her sugar intake, Byron," Mrs. Wells interjected. "She is an actress now. If she doesn't stay slim, she won't get any more movie offers. Oh, wait—did you get to meet Teddy Danger today?" her mother asked excitedly.

"Yeah," Joy answered flatly. "We shot a few scenes together."

"And?"

"And what?"

"Well, what was he like?"

"He seemed nice enough, I guess," Joy replied with a shrug. "He seemed like just a regular guy."

In truth Joy thought Teddy was probably one of the most boring and annoying people she had ever met. However, she decided to keep these feelings from her mother to put the conversation to an end.

"And what did you think? Is he a good actor?" Mrs. Wells asked.

Joy found this answer a bit harder to conceal. Instantly looking pained, she thought back to the countless takes caused by the man's repeatedly flubbing his lines. And when he did get them right, he seemed about as natural as a cardboard cutout. The director had looked particularly infuriated, often calling "cut" with his head hanging between his own knees.

"He's pretty bad, actually," Joy confessed.

But though this was the truth, it was not what her mother wanted to hear, apparently. "Well, remember this is just a silly horror movie, not some fancy drama," Mrs. Wells explained. "And remember this is Teddy's first movie, after all. I'm sure he'll get better once he feels comfortable."

"Boy, I sure hope he does," Joy said.

"More important, what did everyone seem to think about your acting, darling?" Mr. Wells asked.

"They seemed happy enough with it," Joy reported, although as the director had promised, she hadn't had any lines of her own to deliver yet. "And that Morris kid was pretty good, I have to admit."

It hadn't taken Joy long to work out that Mr. Phipps must have also had a hand in the casting of his little friend Morris, the miniature politician who worshipped the ground the mayor's former assistant walked on. But fortunately, after his initial outburst the boy had composed himself and acted professionally for the remainder of the day.

"Wait a second. Morris who?" Byron demanded, standing up on the stairs.

"The freaky kid from your class. You know, the one with the bow ties."

"Morris Mealey is in the movie?" Byron exploded. "How did that jerk get in?"

"I don't know," Joy answered, her head throbbing from the shouting. "Somehow he got an audition and got the part, I guess. Look, it's not like I'm happy about it. I even have to do a scene where I hug him and kiss him and every-thing," she relayed, feeling nauseated even at the thought.

"But that's stupid!" Byron shouted. "*I'm* your real brother!" His face bright red, he turned and stormed upstairs.

"Byron!" Mr. Wells called up crossly after the boy. "Really, there's no need to be so silly!"

From above, the door to Byron's diminutive bedroom could be heard slamming shut. Even the sound of it was somehow puny, Joy felt ashamed to notice.

"Never mind him, dear," Mrs. Wells told her daughter. "He's just feeling a bit jealous. And who can blame him? Now, I have to ask: Do you think Teddy would be open to signing a few old records of mine? I mean, just if he has a spare moment. . . ."

Desperate to get to bed, Joy agreed to ask him tomorrow. She then headed upstairs. On the way to the bathroom, she paused at her brother's door and raised a hand to knock. Working hard all day, she hadn't even noticed his walkie-talkies, she wanted to tell him. But she was just too tired, she realized.

She quickly brushed her teeth and then slipped off to her bedroom to get into her pajamas.

"Do you have another early start tomorrow, honey?" Mrs. Wells asked, poking her head in.

"The call is for five thirty," Joy relayed, climbing under her covers. Five thirty? Had she really heard that correctly? It was insane. She had never been up at that hour in her life.

"Well, I'll set the alarm for five, then," her mother said. Just then the curtains blew in, snapping like whips. "I'd better close your window, though. It looks like bad weather is on its way."

Bad weather, Joy thought, her eyelids fluttering shut.

It was on the way.

A storm blew into Spooking that night, lashing the lifeless town. Outside the set, trees shook as the tarpaulins strung over the expensive movie equipment cracked mightily against their ropes. Sitting in a rocking chair on Madame Portia's porch, a lone security guard watched over the front yard sleepily, stirring only for a moment when a black dog hopped across the yard.

Meanwhile, a few minutes away on Weredale Avenue, Teddy Danger was still awake. Restless, he had tangled himself up in his bed linen, a set of black silken sheets and matching comforter that Molly had ordered shipped to the address from Italy.

Replaying the first day of shooting, Teddy sighed to himself. He was worried about this project. In his opinion the director was pretty uptight and way too stuck on the script. He hadn't been forgetting his lines. He'd just been trying to loosen things up a bit, make the scene feel a bit more natural. It was called ad-libbing. Most great actors did it, as far as he knew from the book he'd just recently read on the subject.

But this director seemed to think everything had to be done exactly as it was written down. Well, that wasn't the way they'd worked when he'd made his last award-winning music video, Teddy would have the man know.

But worst of all was the call time. Why so early? Was the director purposely punishing him?

Well, there was no way he was getting to sleep now, not with the infernal pounding on the tin shingles above his head adding to his discomfort. How could anyone be expected to be ready to perform, staying in a hellhole like this? He thought fondly of home and the gentle crashing of waves he could hear every night from the patio mere steps from his king-size bed, and of the salty air that made his face feel wonderfully tight each morning.

Now, that was a place where a person could get a good night's sleep.

What he needed was a cup of milk, he decided—warm milk, perhaps with a hunk of Belgian chocolate melted into it, assuming it was at least 70 percent cocoa. The thought, however, made him pinch his midsection, where he found a depressing growth of paunch developing. This, he thought grimly, is what happens to you when you don't have a swimming pool at home.

No, he would have to skip the chocolate and just go with the warm milk.

"Molly!" he called out.

There was no response from across the hall.

Rolling over, Teddy glared toward the door. It was so dark in the room, he realized, that he couldn't even see his hand in front of his face. Was this what it felt like to be dead? he wondered with a shudder. Feeling panicky, he shouted out a few more times but was only answered by the howling wind.

Where was Molly?

Throwing back his bed coverings, he stood up.

"Cripes!" he shouted as his bare feet contacted the frigid floorboards.

Jumping back onto the bed, he then remembered that Molly usually left some slippers out for him at the foot of the bed. Fishing around for them, he discovered he was in luck. He slipped them on and went to switch on the lamp.

It didn't work.

There must have been a power failure, Teddy realized, seeing that the clock radio was also dead. "This place is a joke," he cursed. He then felt his way toward the door. "Molly!"

The hall was just as black, he discovered, the carpeted floor creaking underfoot. Did she have her headphones on or something? He felt around for her door, which he then opened slowly. "Molly?" he whispered inside, again receiving no reply.

Perhaps it wasn't a good idea to surprise her, Teddy decided. He remembered how the last time he'd startled the little woman at her bedside like that, he'd soon learned about the semester of self-defense courses she had taken in college, and what amazing skills of incapacitation she had acquired.

No, he couldn't risk showing up on set tomorrow injured, especially not with a funny walk, that was for sure. He would just have to go down to the kitchen himself, he decided. Feeling his way along the hallway, he knocked against several paintings and even sent one crashing to the floor before eventually finding the banister at the top of the stairs.

About halfway down Teddy realized that he had no idea where the kitchen actually was, thanks to the previously dutiful efforts of his assistant. Doubting his chances of locating even the room itself much less the fridge and a glass, he was about to turn back when the warm glow of candlelight caught his eye.

Teddy continued on, soon arriving at the bottom of the stairs without disrupting any more picture frames. To the right was the large dining room, where he'd recently eaten some mediocre Chinese takeout. Sitting at the center of the long table was a silver candelabra, now burning brightly.

"Hello?" he called uncertainly. "Is anybody there?"

The nearby windows rattled madly in their frames.

Wasn't the kitchen usually located just off the dining room? Teddy was sure this was the case. He began to think longingly back to his own beachfront home, where the ultramodern kitchen and dining room occupied the same space—a hangarlike room with thirty-foot windows facing the sea. Teddy sighed, thinking about how much he liked to just stand there, watching the crashing waves as he shouted obscenities to echo off the high vaulted ceiling.

Plucking a candle, Teddy continued on, lighting his way toward the set of doors he could just make out on the other side of the room.

His instincts were right. Pushing open the pair of swinging doors, he found himself in the kitchen. It was a huge old-fashioned-looking kitchen, with wooden countertops and gleaming copper pots on the walls. Teddy held up the candle and examined a cluster of terrifying-looking knives and cleavers hung from small hooks by the stove, their metal blades ringing out like wind chimes as he prodded them.

"Aha!" he cried, finally spotting the refrigerator.

The light was off inside. Teddy thrust the candle inside, searching for the milk. He then stood back, leaning against a butcher's block and guzzling directly from the carton. So what if the unsanitary habit made Molly queasy? He was thirsty, and she wasn't doing her job.

"Teeeeddyyyyy . . ."

Teddy spat milk down his silken pajama top. He listened again.

"Teeeeeeeeeeddyyyyyyyyy . . ."

It was unmistakably the sound of a woman's voice, he thought, whispered and raspy. It was coming from the other room.

"Molly?" he called out. "Is that you?"

"TEEEEEEEDDYYYYYYYY . . ."

The carton hit the floor, gushing milk.

The dining room was completely black now, Teddy saw with horror as he threw open the double doors. In the air, however, the smell of extinguished candles still lingered thickly. The flame of his own candle shone weakly in the dark as he shivered to feel an unseen presence nearby.

"Stop fooling around, Molly." His voice was now low, strangled with fear. "This isn't funny, you know."

But as much as Teddy hoped it was true, that this was some sort of silly prank, he knew it was impossible. Even on her best days Molly did not care for jokes. She would no more ambush him in the middle of the night in a spooky old house than she would allow him to drive or make dinner reservations or use her cell phone. No, this was not Molly's style.

He inched forward, the outstretched flame now sputtering uncertainly. Once again his name rang out from somewhere nearby. Even as he struggled to resist, the eerie and unearthly voice drew him, pulling him forward, step after step, toward a flickering light.

Teddy emerged in the foyer in a trance. The room was now bright with what seemed like hundreds of burning candles, each dripping great quantities of hot wax as they fizzled and popped angrily.

His eyes, however, did not linger even on this incredible sight. Nor did they stop for more than a moment at the hearth, where an enormous blue fire was licking the very bricks and mantel with wisps of eerie flame. Instead his eyes were drawn immediately above the fire, to the portrait of the beautiful gypsy in its now glittering frame.

And his gaze was instantly returned.

"TEEEEEDDYYYYYY . . . ," she said.

CHAPTER 18

Through the black veil of slumber, the disembodied voice gradually pierced, echoing over and over as if shouted from a distant mountaintop:

"Breakfast, kids, *kids, kids, kids* . . ."

Joy groaned as her bedroom came slowly into focus. What time was it anyway? She couldn't even remember getting home, much less lying down. Rolling over, she checked her bedside table.

However, in the place of her normal clock, she found only Ms. Melody Huxley's trusty pocket watch. And something was wrong with it. Peering, she saw that the antique watch had somehow partially melted down the side of the table, with its hands now hanging like two strands of black licorice.

Now, that was weird, Joy decided at once. Hearing her mother's call again, however, she got out of bed without further considering it. The floor had never felt colder, it seemed, like a frozen lake under her bare feet. She whimpered, looking around for her slippers.

It was at that moment she noticed something else: She was still in her costume.

Uh-oh, Joy thought. The wardrobe lady—what was her name again? She was going to be mad. Really mad! How could Joy have left the set dressed like that? Or possibly gotten under her covers still wearing that stiff crinoline skirt?

"Breakfast, kids!" came her mother's echoing voice once again.

Feeling panicked, Joy rushed from her room. Could they throw her off the movie for this? Her giant skirt scraping noisily against the walls, she hurried along the hall and downstairs.

As she entered the kitchen, the glorious smell of delicious pancakes immediately soothed her frazzled nerves. She was starving, she realized, as there came the sizzle of batter hitting the hot grill. In front of the counter Joy spotted the familiar knot of her father's apron tied tightly around the back of the busy figure.

"Good morning, sleepy head," Mrs. Wells said, appearing from behind the fridge door with a big smile. Decked out in what appeared to be Joy's blue graduation dance dress, she looked utterly beautiful. Her hair had never looked so black, her lips never so red, nor her teeth ever so radiantly white. Her slender alabaster arms barely supported the weight of a huge glass pitcher containing what Joy somehow knew could only be freshly squeezed orange juice.

"What's going on?" Joy asked, blinking at her. "What time is it?"

"It's pancake time!" declared Mr. Phipps, turning to face her. Wearing her father's apron, he stood there grinning—his face almost obscured by a towering plate of perfect-looking flapjacks.

Joy stumbled back in alarm. "What are *you* doing here?" she demanded to know. "In *our* house?"

"Now, Joy," Mrs. Wells chided. "That's no way to speak to your father, especially after he's slaved over the stove all morning," she added, placing the pitcher on the table. She walked over and kissed him sweetly on the mouth.

"Mom!" Joy screamed in outrage.

"What on earth has gotten into you, dear?"

But Joy just ignored her. Instead she pointed an accusing finger at Phipps. "What have you done with my father?"

"You mean the wimpy little fellow with the beard?" Phipps asked with a cackle. "Oh, he's gone now. Vanished, into thin air, as it happened. Isn't that just the craziest thing?"

Joy stood openmouthed in fear as a short figure shuffled up beside her.

"Good morning, Byron," said Mrs. Wells. "You sure slept in."

"I was so tired," replied the boy, who not only looked absolutely nothing like Joy's little brother but was also wearing a bow tie. Yawning, he looked up at Joy.

"Hey, what the heck is this?" Morris Mealey shouted. "Is Spooky here supposed to be playing my sister?"

At that moment Joy awoke in her trailer, a stream of sunlight in her face. With her scream still clawing its way out of her throat, she realized it was just another night terror. Except now they were coming in the daytime. Was that even possible?

Apparently so.

An urgent knock on the trailer door quickly followed.

"Is everything okay in there?" It was one of the assistant directors.

"Uh, yeah," Joy called back cheerfully. "A spider just landed on me, that's all."

It was a skillful demonstration, Joy thought proudly, of what as a kid she would have called lying, but as an actor now knew as ad-libbing.

"It happens," came the relieved reply.

When Joy was left alone again, events began coming back to the budding starlet. She remembered how, dizzy with exhaustion, she'd arrived on set that morning for her five-thirty call. Once laced into her stiff and itchy costume again, she'd had her hair and makeup done, the stylist tutting at every nod of her sleepy head.

But then, as a result of some important equipment having been damaged in the overnight storm, there had been a delay in shooting. All dressed up but with nothing to do, Joy had been dismissed from the set. She'd wandered off back to her trailer, folded out the couch bed, and carefully stretched out like a corpse in a casket in the hope of disturbing her costume and makeup as little as possible.

The shouting of the crew and the thrum of a nearby generator had kept her in a frustrating netherworld between sleep and consciousness, however. Other than the usual cawing crows, Spooking had never been that noisy in the morning. But after a while fatigue must have overcome her, because Joy had finally passed out completely.

Now fully awake, she looked at the old vinyl records in their giant jackets on the table, sitting beside Byron's walkie-talkies. She couldn't forget about either promise to her mother or brother today or she would never hear the end of it. Tucking the records under her arm, she headed outside.

Teddy's trailer was at the end of the property, shaded by Spooking's tallest poplar. Worrying he might also be trying to fit in a nap, Joy listened at the door for signs of life. Soon she heard the clattering of some dishes inside and the rush of water from a tap, so she decided to knock.

"Hold on," called a woman's voice.

The door opened. It was a pink-haired woman. Joy had seen her wandering around but not been introduced yet.

"Oh, hi," she said. "You're Teddy's costar. Joy, isn't it?"

"Yes," the girl answered, thinking once again how weird it was to meet people who knew her name before she knew theirs. "I've seen you on set."

"I guess I'm hard to miss," she said, sweeping back her pink hair. "My name's Molly. I'm Teddy's personal assistant. Come in. It's starting to rain again."

Joy climbed the stairs and entered the trailer. Looking around, she saw that the layout was pretty much identical to her own, although the interior was a bit more swanky, with upholstered leather seating and fancy-looking wood veneer surfaces. Everywhere silk cushions lay, tossed as if in the aftermath of a high-class pillow fight.

"Are those Teddy's records?"

"Yeah," said Joy shyly.

"Let me guess: Your parents want them signed."

Joy nodded. "They're for my mom. My father doesn't really like that kind of music," she found herself admitting. Joy suddenly could not even remember what music her father liked, or if he even liked music at all, which seemed a bit weird.

"Yeah, well, Teddy has a lot more female fans for some reason," Molly told her. "It's one of the world's greatest mysteries, if you ask me," she added in a lowered voice, "on the scale of Bigfoot and Easter Island."

Joy laughed. She was starting to like this young woman, with her fuchsia hair and jangling collection of bracelets. Joy even found herself wondering if she would ever one day have a personal assistant of her own. If so, she hoped she would find one just like Molly. It would be fun having a full-time friend—even one that you paid for, presumably.

"Anyway, Teddy's not around at the moment. He went to the park to do some yoga or tai chi or Pilates or something. I never know which, to be honest, even when I'm witness to them."

"Really?" Joy asked, surprised. "I didn't picture a punk rock type like Teddy being into that kind of stuff."

"Are you kidding me?" Molly asked. "Don't tell anyone I said it, but really, Teddy is way, way, *way* more New Age hippy than punk rock, believe me. Look here," she said, pointing to her laptop. "I was just searching for someone to do a tarot card reading for him. Now, you tell me. How punk is that?"

"A tarot reading?" Joy replied, surprised. "Really? Wow."

"Unfortunately, all that magic and mysticism stuff doesn't

seem too big here in Darlington. Oh well. I guess I'm going to have to disappoint him. Which means I'm going to have to hear about it for the rest of my life."

"Hey, maybe that stuff isn't big in Darlington," Joy agreed, "but this is Spooking," she reminded her.

"Which means?"

"Which means I could hook him up with a full-on gypsy in, like, two minutes."

Wearing the black pajamas of a kung fu acolyte, the rock star Teddy Danger finally returned to his trailer. Slightly damp from the drizzle, he grabbed a towel and began drying his hair. He then turned in shock at the gathering in his living room—his little blond costar, his assistant, and another woman—an old woman—wearing a red kerchief and black shawl.

"Teddy, I would like you to meet Madame Portia," Molly said.

Examining the wrinkly creature, Teddy stiffened noticeably. "How do you do?" he inquired nonetheless.

"I am doing quite fine," Madame Portia replied. "But I hear you are in need of my services. . . ."

Teddy looked at her quizzically for a moment before shooting a glare at his assistant. "Actually, my back is feeling much better at the moment. No tightness at all," he said. As proof he did a few windmills with his arms, banging his knuckles against the low ceiling in the process. "Ow! Yeah, so I guess it was just a minor strain and nothing more."

Madame Portia stared at the man as if he'd lost his mind. "Excuse me?"

"Teddy," Molly interrupted. "Madame Portia is a fortune-teller. I thought you said you wanted your cards read."

"Oh, I'm sorry," said Teddy, slapping himself in the forehead. "I thought you were a massage therapist!" he explained.

Madame Portia, however, looked entirely unamused at the suggestion. "I, sir, am a Romany," she declared humorlessly. "I was taught the ancient art of soothsaying by my mother, who was taught by her mother, who was taught by her mother before, who was taught by her mother before—"

"Okay, okay. I get it," Teddy interjected.

"And yet you are asking for some kind of a rubdown for your pathetic aches and pains?"

"I really didn't mean to cause offense—"

"I am a gypsy!" the old woman bellowed. "I offer windows into the future, into the very netherworlds of possibility themselves! I do not offer Swedish massage, nor Thai, nor hot rock, nor deep-tissue therapy!"

"That's perfectly fine," Teddy insisted, holding up his hands. "But do you take credit cards?"

"Of course," Madame Portia answered with a shrug.

A few minutes later Teddy joined the gypsy at the table as Molly and Joy sat at a discreet distance.

"He doesn't like getting readings done alone," Molly whispered. "He gets too freaked-out."

Stifling a giggle, Joy pulled her chair closer to her new buddy.

After lighting a few candles, Madame Portia drew the blinds and killed the lights. In the center of the table, she placed a crystal ball, which appeared to boil with a strange blue supernatural-looking fog.

"Hold on," Madame Portia said, turning to Joy. "You asked for tarot, no?"

The girl nodded.

"How annoying! I hate lugging this thing along," she grumbled, zipping the mysterious sphere back into a baby blue bowling bag. Putting the heavy bag down at her feet, she then thumped a worn pack of cards onto the table in front of her. "The name of the game is twenty-one," she declared.

"I'm sorry?" Teddy asked.

"It's just a joke," she told him, snapping off the elastic band holding them together, which then went flying off into a dark corner of the trailer. "But being of good humor almost always improves one's fortunes, I've found."

"Oh."

Madame Portia sat forward in her seat. "Now I want you to take this deck, shuffle it, and place the cards exactly as I tell you."

"I should let you know I've done this before," Teddy advised. "What kind of reading do you have in mind? The Ellipse, the Mandala, or the Celtic Cross?"

"I was thinking five-card stud. I mean *spread*—five-card spread."

"Oh," said Teddy, sounding disappointed. Nevertheless, under Madame Portia's instructions he laid out five cards in a star shape on the table.

"Now, I will not touch these cards again with my hands," Madame Portia told him seriously. "You must do all of the handling. Understood?"

"Sure," answered Teddy.

Molly leaned over to Joy. "I'll bet you ten bucks the Fool pops up," she said into her ear. "It always does."

Joy playfully elbowed Molly in the hopes she'd knock it off.

"This card tells of the past," the gypsy said after Teddy turned it over on her instruction. "And it is the Ace of Wands. I sense you were very fortunate once upon a time. Wildly fortunate beyond anyone's dreams, even your own."

"Well, that's no secret," Teddy said, smiling smugly. "I'm Teddy Danger, aren't I?"

"Yet I sense a hidden guilt here," she continued, ignoring him. Her veiny hand hovered an inch above the card, free of even the slightest tremble. "You have a secret shame about your success, as if your fortune were in fact someone else's. That somehow you drained someone of their creative energy and took it as your own."

Listening to the gypsy, Teddy's face darkened at the suggestion.

"And for that you were tormented, weren't you, my famous friend? Oh, you tried to soothe these feelings, with superficial spirituality, bogus mystical explorations, and endless subscriptions to self-help shams on late-night television. But none of it worked. Nothing ever filled that void. The feeling of being a charlatan, and a thief."

Teddy laughed derisively. "Really?" he said.

"I am only telling you what I see, Mr. Danger. As a client it is your choice to find value in my vision or to discard my gift. But anyway, that was the past, I should add. For a more important insight, we must see the present. Flip this card now, please."

The leering face of the Devil appeared.

Molly and Joy shot each other worried looks as Teddy sat bolt upright in his chair. Madame Portia, however, didn't appear the slightest bit concerned or perturbed.

"Fear not this card, which speaks in this case of egotism, conceit, and materialism. Of covetousness, self-obsession, and self-doubt. This card is in fact too easy, all too obvious. For isn't the Devil the steward of unwarranted fame, the guardian of outrageous fortune? The granter of wishes that exact a greater toll than bestow a benefit?"

This time Teddy remained silent. Nevertheless the thinnest of smiles began crossing his face as he listened.

"The Devil tells us nothing that one can't easily presume as a trapping of celebrity, so let's move on to something more revealing. Please turn this card."

Slowly Teddy leaned forward and extended his hand.

"Hidden Aspects," she declared as he flipped the card.

Without even glancing at the result, Teddy looked over his shoulder at Joy and Molly. In the candlelight his face suddenly looked weirdly distorted, Joy thought, like a hideous mask of innumerable hatreds. His liquid eyes shone with a flickering flame, but were otherwise jet black. He smiled, his teeth reminding Joy of broken yellowed piano keys.

At the same moment Madame Portia inhaled sharply.

Teddy turned back to the gypsy, his face now the very portrait of delight. "What do you see?" he asked her.

"The Tower," she said.

At that Teddy began laughing. Except it was not the laugh of the man who yesterday had held up filming with his canned jokes and inappropriate banter. It was the laughter of someone gone mad, the sound that might drift up through the grates of some terrible medieval dungeon.

"Do you see chaos?" he asked. "Ruination?"

But the gypsy did not answer. Instead her eyes focused on the face in front of her, the grinning man whose cards lay before her.

"Is there something awful coming, madam?" he asked.

A thunderous banging interrupted them. Everyone except Teddy leaped from their seats.

"Who is it?" Teddy shouted toward the door.

"Mr. Cray would like to see you on set, Mr. Danger," came a man's voice from outside.

"Okay. I'll be right there," Teddy replied in a loud voice. "I'm afraid I will have to abandon this reading," he said, standing up. "But I must say, I've enjoyed it nonetheless. Your theatrics have been most entertaining, my good woman, even if your fortune-telling has been inaccurate." He then turned to his assistant. "Molly, can you handle the woman's fee for me, and add on a generous tip? Thanks. Well, folks, I mustn't keep the big man waiting."

Whistling tunelessly to himself, Teddy then exited the trailer.

Once the man's affront to melody had trailed off, Madame Portia finally stirred in her seat. She looked visibly shaken, not to mention uncharacteristically old and frail. "Are you okay?" Joy asked as the old woman shivered, pulling her ratty black shawl tightly around her shoulders.

"I'm not sure I am, dear," she said gravely, her voice quivering slightly.

"What's wrong?"

"There have been too many bad omens, bambina. First that beast, that three-legged animal—the harbinger of doom—and now the Tower, immediately following the appearance of the Devil! This is bad, I tell you—very, very bad! In fact, I have not felt the presence of such evil in this town for forty years. We must prepare, and remain on our guard!" she shouted, trying to get to her feet. "We must stay by our loved ones for the coming of the black hour!"

Gasping, the old woman then slumped back down into her seat.

"Madame Portia!" Joy cried.

Joy rushed to the old woman, who quickly regained consciousness in her arms. Startled, Molly stood looking on for a moment before rushing over to the windows and opening the blinds. The light of the late Spooking morning leaked in, casting everything in a solemn blue.

"Thank you, bambina. I'm fine," said Madame Portia after a few minutes. "I'm sorry to have scared you."

Molly put on a few lights and snuffed the candles. "I'll put on some tea. How does that sound?" she asked, stepping into the kitchenette.

"That would be lovely," the old gypsy replied.

"Hey, I wanted to mention," Molly said, filling the kettle. "Teddy and I are staying over at a house on Weredale Avenue that has an old portrait of a gypsy in the entranceway. Are you a relative of hers, by any chance?"

Madame Portia's head snapped back toward Molly as one of her eyes enlarged, looking for all the world like a goose egg that someone had drawn an iris on in marker.

"A house, you say, on Weredale Avenue?"

"Yes. Right at the end," Molly said, placing the kettle onto the hot plate.

"That's it!" Madame Portia cried. "That is what I am sensing! You can't stay in that house, my dear. You can't!"

"Why not?" asked Molly, a shiver running up her back. "What's wrong?"

"The Witch of Weredale!" the old gypsy shouted. "She has returned!"

CHAPTER 19

"Okay. Great job, everyone. That's a wrap for today!" the director called out from his folding chair. At these words the crew flew into action, packing up the equipment as if they had a bus to catch.

"Thank you, Templeton!" Morris bellowed from his position on the floor. Much like Joy's own real-life brother, he had been on the floor playing in front of the roaring fire. Joy had been sat on the couch beside Viola, directly across from Teddy, who sat in a leather club chair.

The whole room had been lit to resemble nighttime, with Madame Portia's tall front windows carefully blacked out from the outside. Inside the windows they had rigged up something to make it look like a thunderstorm was raging outside. The thunderclaps themselves would be added later in the sound mix, it was explained to Joy.

The scene was quite dramatic, it turned out, and rich with tension-building dialogue as the family slowly began noticing the subtle but sinister changes in their once-sweet father's personality.

The director had seemed particularly impressed with Teddy's performance.

"You are nailing it today, my man!" Mr. Cray said, approaching the legendary rock star, who despite the wrap had still not budged even an inch from his seat.

Noticing he was being addressed, Teddy looked up, wild-eyed.

"I'm just loving it!" the director cried with a laugh, slapping a hand on Teddy's shoulder. "You are so capturing the essence of someone losing his mind, I've got to tell you."

"Am I?" asked Teddy, fixing the man in a searing gaze. "Really?"

"Oh yeah. You're giving the crew actual chills. Keep it up!"

Joy looked across the room at the musician. He was giving her chills too. Even between takes he didn't seem like the same guy, now sitting in deadly silence instead of chattering incessantly.

Meanwhile the terrifying scene in Teddy's trailer kept playing over and over in her mind. Joy had never witnessed an actual tarot card reading before, or any other sort of fortune-telling, for that matter, other than the quick palm read the old gypsy had performed back when they had first met in the bog. And now Joy felt in no great hurry to repeat the experience.

But even more chilling was the history that Madame Portia had relayed about the Witch of Weredale.

The story involved a witch who had come to town posing as a wandering gypsy. Because of her striking looks, she had been immediately admired and courted by dozens of suitors. Before long she'd surprised everyone by marrying an affluent gentleman who'd been rapidly approaching the end of his years. Taking up permanent residence in his house on Weredale, the witch had installed herself as a fixture in the town, and had worked her way into its most exclusive clubs and social circles.

The sorceress, reveling in devilry, then began wreaking all sorts of havoc on the town. Upstanding citizens began lying, cheating, stealing, and generally running riot. Under her spell the entire town descended into darkness, becoming a playground for her evil whims.

But then something entirely unexpected happened, and a secret lover captured her black heart. So transforming was their romance that the witch ceased her wicked meddling, becoming instead a besotted servant to her paramour, a mysterious man who scratched out eerie tales by candlelight.

The town found itself once again at peace. Or at least as much at peace as was possible in the terrible town on the hideous hill.

This peace and their love, however, did not endure, and the man resolved to leave both his lover and the town. But the sorceress found out about his plans. Wounded and betrayed, she became determined to prevent his escape at all costs.

And so she created a monster.

Casting a spell over Oswald, the town's simpleton, she unleashed an unstoppable maniac who hacked his way through eight poor souls in pursuit of the witch's former lover. But then, with a cunning trick, the man trapped her and her homicidal creation in the cemetery and set them both ablaze.

But even this was not enough to secure his freedom. Spitting flame, the witch cursed the man for all eternity. He could never, ever leave the town of Spooking again. And neither could his sons, nor their sons onward. For to leave would be to bring on a terrible curse that would make them turn to smoke and disappear.

This part of the story, Joy knew immediately, was incredibly familiar.

"Nicely done," Morris congratulated his costar, coming over to the couch where Joy was stretching. "You had a couple of great moments there—really great. I loved that part when you ask where the little barn kittens went and you give Dad that suspicious look. It was beat perfect!"

"Thanks," replied Joy, feeling embarrassed to recall her own acting. "You did a great job too," she quickly added.

A frown crossed the boy's face. "You're sure?" he asked. "You don't think I overplayed it at all?"

"Not at all. You looked exactly like a kid playing on the carpet," Joy assured him.

"Good. Because to be honest I never had toy soldiers or anything like that growing up. So I was pretty much just totally winging it the whole time."

"Well, it looked pretty realistic to me," Joy said, and then yawned.

"Did I look up at the right moments? And did you see how whenever Dad came to the line where he snapped at Mom, I dropped a toy soldier in shock? I made that part up!"

Joy thought it was kind of creepy the way Morris called their two costars Mom and Dad. It was a trick, Morris had explained, to keep in character.

"Yeah, it looked good, all right," she told him.

"Phew. I hope Templeton thought so," he said. "I wouldn't mind getting a look at the dailies to see if I was really in the shot," he mumbled to himself, finally wandering off.

Joy had to admit to missing the days when Morris used to hate her, hissing names at her and making faces. It had been kind of fun, she realized, cutting him back down to his actual size.

But now she had to work with him, and it was getting exhausting. Even at lunch he wouldn't leave her alone, banging on her trailer door to try to fit in some extra rehearsal. He was like the annoying little brother she always dreaded having. She made a mental note to buy Byron something in thanks for his restraint as soon as she got her first paycheck.

Joy pulled out her hair band, the ends of which had been digging into her scalp for the past hour. Holding it in her fist, she left the set to make room for the crew.

Looking out the front door of the rest home, she was surprised to see it was almost dark. How many hours had they been shooting? It seemed like only an hour ago that they had led a trembling Madame Portia from Teddy's trailer. Without another word the terrified old woman had headed straight to her private quarters and had not emerged since.

Standing in the entranceway, Joy turned and looked up at the stairwell. With Madame Portia out of the way, she considered sneaking upstairs to see Al the groundskeeper.

But it was pretty late and the man was gravely ill, after all. Fortunately, there were a few more days shooting still scheduled at Madame Portia's. Perhaps she would still get another chance to talk to him before the production moved on to its next location.

As she stood there, Joy suddenly detected a presence behind her. "Why, hello there," purred a familiar voice.

Shuddering as if an ice cube had been run down her spine, Joy spun around. The sight of Mr. Phipps made her instantly recall the nightmare image of the man standing in her father's apron as her mother kissed him square on the lips. Would she even be able to smell a pancake now without wanting to hurl?

Instead of an apron he wore his usual costume, however—a dark suit with a somber-colored tie tightly cinched beneath a stark white collar. But his hair now had a thick streak of white starting from the left side of his forehead and angling back imperiously.

"Are you okay?" he asked upon registering the girl's horrified expression.

"I don't think you're allowed to be here," Joy told him, her lip curling. "This is a movie set. It's not open to the public."

At this, Phipps laughed. "I'm on the job, young lady. Look, I'm the special municipal consultant for Darlington," he explained, holding out the laminated pass hanging around his neck.

Examining his credentials, Joy felt instantly stupid. Who did she think she was, a security guard? Phipps and his sudden appearances always made her uneasy, and after that awful dream in her trailer, she now found herself positively squirming.

Joy thought back to the tarot reading and its portentous ending. Was it possible that the approaching evil had something to do with Mr. Phipps? If so, Joy had no idea how. While the man was always up to something, riding around on a broomstick probably wasn't one of them.

"I don't know why you're always so prickly around me," Phipps remarked as Joy held her disdainful expression. "You know, I've tried pretty hard to be your friend. How is your big break working out, for example? Because I had a big part in getting it for you."

So that was it, Joy figured out. He was fishing for thanks! But what would he expect from her in return? For her to betray Spooking in either words or deed? There had to be a catch. There just had to be when it came to Mr. Phipps.

"I already know you got me the audition," Joy admitted. "The thing I don't know is why."

But instead of looking offended, Phipps just laughed. "The reason is nowhere near as sinister as you presume, young lady. My old friend Audrey said they were looking for a local girl with blond hair, about twelve years of age. Believe it or not, you were the only one I knew."

Joy frowned. She hated reasonable explanations, especially when they came from someone entirely unreasonable.

"Besides, I thought you'd enjoy being part of all this," Phipps continued. "To have a starring role in Spooking's transformation? That must feel pretty special."

"Spooking's transformation?" Joy repeated. "Transformation into what?"

Phipps looked at the girl in disbelief. He then gestured toward the scurrying crew members. "Why, into the world's biggest movie lot, of course! Can't you see it? Once this film hits screens, the studios will be lining up to start shooting here. Ghost stories, slasher flicks, monster movies . . ."

As if a budding director himself, Phipps began drawing the scenes in the air. The man looked positively crazed, Joy thought. She recoiled as he bent over and breathed directly into her face.

"I'll admit it," he murmured. "You were right all along. There is some value to this old eyesore of ours! Because we're not living in a town. We're living in a fantasy world! A fantasy world that has immense value to the most booming business of them all—the entertainment industry!"

Joy stepped back. One thing was certain. She didn't like this vision any better than his others. Reducing Spooking to nothing more than a stage set? How was that any different from making it into an amusement park, really?

"Well, I think it's a stupid idea," she told him.

Phipps glared at the girl. Sighing in frustration, he began rubbing his temples. "You think it's stupid," he said. "And pray tell, why would that be, exactly?"

"Because Spooking is too important," she insisted.

At this remark Phipps shook his head in surprise. "Too important? Please elaborate."

"Because of its historical significance," she told him,

recycling a phrase she had used to masterful effect on a history assignment only last month.

"Its historical significance?" Phipps scoffed. "Like what? Name one important event that has transpired here, or a single notable person who ever called it home."

Joy became gripped by cold fury. She was tired of the exchanges with this tie-wearing loser. "How about the great author E. A. Peugeot?" she declared, putting her hands on her hips. "And the famous aviator Melody Huxley? That's two people right there!"

Joy swallowed hard. Now she'd done it. She'd blurted out her most precious conviction to Spooking's number one enemy.

She instantly regretted it.

But instead of laughing, instead of once again making her feel like a silly little dreamer, Phipps froze. Eyes wide, he stared back at the girl for what felt like an eternity.

"Where did you hear that?" he demanded in a lowered voice.

And while Joy could not understand the look of horror at her statement, she did immediately see that, unlike everyone else, Mr. Phipps required no convincing.

"You're not surprised—at all!" Joy cried with delight. "Because you already knew!" She pointed an accusing finger. "Just like you knew about everything else: Spooking Bog, the asylum, Poppy . . ."

"I have no idea what you are talking about," Phipps replied smoothly. But Joy knew otherwise. Because despite all of his scheming and plotting, the man was probably about the crummiest liar she had ever set eyes upon.

"And what about the Witch of Weredale?" she probed. "Why do I have a feeling you know something about her returning too?"

But if Joy thought she might finally get some answers, she was wrong. Because, flapping like a black bird, the mayor's former assistant immediately fled the premises.

CHAPTER 20

There was something fishy about this place, Leon Loveday knew at once. As a veteran private detective with more than thirty years' experience, he could sense things other people just couldn't. Like a car following too closely, a gun hidden under a raincoat, or a guy pretending to pick out pantyhose.

He could practically smell when something was wrong.

And while this whole town stunk pretty much to high heaven as far as Leon was concerned, there was something about that last house on Weredale Avenue that really wasn't right. Maybe it was the freshly mowed front lawn, the first he'd seen after walking the entire length and breadth of the weird old town. Or maybe it was the crazed cackle he was sure he heard as he was walking up the path.

But something was definitely wrong with it. Waiting on the porch after ringing the doorbell, Leon peered in through a window and saw a glowing laptop computer sitting out on a table beside a half-eaten lunch. Black forest ham on olive loaf, if he wasn't mistaken. With mustard and arugula.

"Bingo," Leon said to himself. He had recently played

the game of the very same name in a bid to win cash and meet ladies. But he'd had little luck with either. Alone and empty-handed, he'd filed out of the bingo hall dejectedly.

But somebody lived here all right, Leon now knew, and not only did they have good taste in sandwiches, they were probably home. But despite the detective's repeated rings, no one answered.

The computer, he thought. These days the juiciest clues were always left on them. He'd already taken a few notes as to Penny Farthing's favorite websites, so if the little lady had logged on here, he'd likely know about it. All he needed was a couple minutes of access.

However, just as he was removing his lock pick from his jacket, Leon heard a sound. Having spent his tender years on a farm, he knew it instantly. The sudden *thunk*, the satisfying clatter. Somebody was splitting wood out back.

Maybe it was better not to break in, he decided, pocketing the lock pick. People with secrets didn't like surprises, in his experience. Touching the butt of his revolver—a reassuring habit ever since the day he had forgotten it on a motel side table and taken a bullet as a result—Leon headed around to investigate. Avoiding the noisy pebble path, he slipped around the side to scope things out.

There he found his chopper, a wiry-looking guy in an undershirt, with expensive-looking tattoos and dyed brown hair. He was standing by a thick tree stump, busily working away on sections of log that he retrieved from a woodpile. And from the heap nearby, apparently he'd been at it for a while.

Thunk. Clatter. Thunk. Clatter.

"Excuse me, sir," called the private detective as he approached. "Do you live here?"

The man did not respond. He just kept on chopping.

Thunk. Clatter. Thunk. Clatter.

"Excuse me," Leon repeated, raising his voice. "I'm a private detective, going around the neighborhood doing a routine inquiry. I'd like to ask you a few questions."

Thunk. Clatter. Thunk. Clatter. Thunk. Clatter.

Was the guy deaf or something? Leon wondered. "Sir?" he called again, coming up behind the man. "Hello?" He touched his shoulder. "Do you mind if I ask you a few questions?"

Thunk.

Little would Leon ever know, this time there came a *thump* rather than a clatter.

After struggling through a slow morning of shooting in Madame Portia's front room, the crew had finally broken for lunch. The particular scene had included only Joy and Viola, however, with Teddy and Morris not called until later. Joy had had a lot of lines, and she'd found herself struggling to remember them, much less perform them as the director requested. At least Mr. Cray was nice and patient with her, simply making suggestions and asking Joy to try them over and over again.

Walking out of the room, Joy yawned. Last night she had gotten home after midnight and had been lifted into bed like a coma patient by her mother and father. Nevertheless, she'd slept badly, visited once again by another night terror.

Fortunately, this one didn't involve Mr. Phipps. Instead she'd once again been the aviatrix.

This time she had not been climbing up into a plane, however, waving good-bye to her admirers. In this dream she'd been in a house, a large one, with the brass door handle feeling queerly familiar in her palm as she'd exited.

It was Number 9 Ravenwood Avenue, Joy had realized with a start.

As she'd stepped out, the house had looked different, however. It had been freshly painted, with a carpetlike lawn and a beautiful flowering garden out front. Wearing an oil-skin coat and a long white scarf, she'd carried a leather suit-case in each hand as she'd headed out to a gleaming roadster parked in the driveway.

But in this dream she'd felt upset. Angry. She'd turned to glare at an indistinct figure standing, unmoving, out on the porch.

"You are being ridiculous," she'd told the figure—a man with a mustache—as she'd flung the suitcases into the trunk. Her voice had then softened. "Please come with me, Alvin. Please. I'm begging you."

"I can't," the man had replied, his features still lost in a haze. "I already told you so. I'm sorry."

A consuming rage had once again taken hold of her. "You are a coward!" she'd shouted at him. "A fearful little man who cringes at the sight of his own shadow! I'm going now, and I can't promise I will return!"

The figure had lowered his head, but had not responded.

Without another word she'd started up the mighty roadster and peeled away.

Joy thought about this dream as she joined the crowd of people lining up in front of the canteen truck. While the substance of it seemed nowhere near as scary as the dream where she'd crashed into the sea, Joy had awoken screaming in her bed, not stopping until her parents had finally rushed in to calm her.

Even today the murky image of the man standing on the porch sent chills up her spine.

"Hi, Joy. Great work this morning," another of the seemingly endless number of assistant directors told her. "Hey, you shouldn't have to stand in line. You're one of the stars!"

"It's okay. I'm not really feeling hungry, come to think of it. I just need to lie down for a bit."

"Well, don't forget to eat something, because it's going to be a long one."

"I promise I won't."

Feeling exhausted, Joy headed back toward her trailer. With a night shoot scheduled at the inn on the other street, it was indeed going to be a long day. What was worse, she had arranged for her parents and Byron to watch tonight and was worried about them embarrassing her. More specifically, she was worried about her mother, who was dying to meet Teddy.

Approaching the trailer, she groaned to discover Morris sitting perched outside on her steps. Cramming a sandwich into his mouth, he was thumbing his way through his completely massacred copy of the script.

Spotting his costar, the boy called out to her. "Hey, Spooky!" he said, sending crumbs flying. "Let's use this break to run some lines, okay? There's some stuff I want to try out on you."

Joy stopped in her tracks. There was no way she was wasting another lunch hour rehearsing with Morris, especially when she so desperately needed a nap. But given her previous experience, she knew the boy would not take no for an answer.

"Actually, I can't," she lied. "I've got a meeting with Templeton on set."

"The director wants to see you? Maybe I should come too."

"No, no. He said just me. It's about a scene you aren't in anyway."

"Well, okay," the boy said dejectedly, turning back to the script.

Joy turned around and headed back to the house. Well, that was great, she thought. Now she had trapped herself for the whole lunch hour.

The set had completely cleared out, Joy saw. She wandered around the ground floor, careful not to disturb any props or equipment. Finally she found herself at the door leading to the old gypsy's downstairs apartment.

"Madame Portia?" she called, knocking. There was no answer.

Joy then had an idea. Checking around to make sure no one saw her, she headed upstairs.

With the residents sent off on another day trip, the

second floor of the Happy Fates Retirement Estates was deserted. Joy began working her way down the hall, peeking through doors of bedrooms as she went. Each contained a huge four-poster bed, hulking furniture, and decrepit rugs and throws. The residents' rooms struck her as rather dangerously dark and cluttered for the safety of fragile old people. Nevertheless they seemed cheery enough places and smelled lovely, with an abundance of freshly cut flowers sitting out in vases.

Still, Joy felt too creeped-out to have a nap among all the weird personal items and photos of loved ones. There had to be at least one unoccupied room, she thought, with a bed she could curl up on. Having come to the end of the hallway, Joy gently pushed open the last door.

The room was even darker than its neighbors, with its heavy curtains drawn and a single lamp casting an orangey pool of light over the slumbering figure.

Even from beneath the thick pile of blankets, the motionless form on the bed struck Joy as uncommonly slight for a fully grown adult. The person's length, however, remained considerable, with a pair of pale feet poking out from under the covers at the end of the mattress. Joy stared at them, noticing how veined they were, and how they almost glowed blue.

It was the groundskeeper, she knew.

Joy approached the bedside on her tiptoes. From there she saw with horror how the man's always narrow face now looked positively gaunt, his cheeks sunken and his wrinkled flesh looking painfully tight. With his mouth hanging open, he wheezed awfully as his parched-looking tongue lolled between his few remaining teeth.

It was too late to speak to him, Joy decided, feeling a pang of guilt for even thinking of disturbing him. As anyone could plainly see, the poor man was barely alive, much less able to answer a child's pestering questions. Which meant that whatever answers might be locked inside his disturbingly visible skull would remain there forever. She became overcome by a feeling of regret. Why had she not come sooner?

Backing away, Joy heard a noise—a rattle from the chest of the prone man. And then his eyes snapped open, two glittering points of light deep within their shadowy sockets.

It was like seeing a shriveled corpse in a morgue suddenly come to life. Joy almost cried out in shock.

"Hello there, young lady," breathed a reedy voice. "I was hoping you might visit."

"Hi," Joy replied, forcing herself to smile despite the considerable horror of looking into the man's tortured face.

The groundskeeper nonetheless detected her discomfort. "Do I really look that bad?" he asked her. "I guess it's a good thing my thoughtful host covered up the mirror for me."

Following the man's gaze, Joy saw that a black cloth had been thrown over the mirror above a broad old dresser.

"Did you ever hear how if you die in sight of a mirror, your soul may get trapped inside?" the man asked. "That's what the gypsy downstairs believes, anyway. She pretended she hid it for good luck, but I know what she was really up to. After all, I once made a living off such superstitions, I must confess."

"I really didn't mean to wake you," Joy apologized, turning with a shiver from the covered mirror.

"There's no need to apologize, young lady. I sleep all day and all night these days, and it's a pleasure just to have a visitor. What was your name again?"

"Joy."

"Ah yes, Joy, with the lost frog. How is your little green friend doing, by the way? That was quite a chase he led me on."

Startled at the wasting man's crystal clear recognition of her, Joy stood dumbstruck for a moment. "He's fine," she reported. "He's got a lot of energy now."

"What did I tell you?" he said. "That pool was very powerful. But it's good that it's gone now, and has remained a secret. It is still a secret, isn't it? You didn't tell anyone?"

"Umm, no," she answered. "Not yet, at least."

"You must never tell anyone about that pool," the groundskeeper said, his voice becoming urgent as he tried to sit up. Failing, he fell heavily back against his pillow. "I beg you, girl, never to speak of it."

"But why not?" Joy asked. "You said yourself it's powerful. Couldn't it help a lot of sick people? Couldn't it help you?"

"Yes, it could help me, and others. But how many? And at what cost? You saw how mad it drove the asylum doctor and his staff, trying to keep the pool all to themselves.

"Imagine what savagery men would commit in order to

possess such a thing—to control the power over life and death itself. Such a discovery would plunge humankind into a war that would never end, causing more hurt than a thousand pools could remedy.

"No, this miracle was never meant to be found, young lady," he insisted, his voice rising. "It is an abomination of nature and only curses those who meddle with it!"

Joy drew back, frightened by the sudden intensity of the fading man's words. Still, she persisted. "But you said it could help you at least," she reminded him. "Maybe there's a bit of the water left somewhere on the asylum grounds. I could sneak back and see if I could find some . . ."

"You are sweet, my child. Do you think I didn't search for myself, in the days following the disaster? That I didn't stay up nights, crawling around the ruins like a sad little ant over the remains of a picnic spread? The waters are all gone now. Which means my time is over.

"But there's no need to grieve for me, little girl," he said, growing weak again. "I have lived a long life, and a storied one at that."

A storied life, Joy thought.

"I wanted to ask you something . . . ," she began hesitantly.

"Ask anything. I'm not in any hurry."

"There's this story," she began. "A lost story called 'The Crimson Pool.' I was wondering if you knew anything about it."

At the mention of the title, the man's eyes opened wide. He then stared at Joy with absolute focus.

"Did you say 'The Crimson Pool'?"

"Yes. Have you heard of it?" Joy asked hopefully.

"Yes. Of course."

"Really?" Joy cried in excitement. "What do you know about it?"

"Why, everything," the man admitted. "I am its author."

CHAPTER 21

"You're trying to tell me that you are Ethan Alvin Peugeot?" Joy cried for what might have been the third time. She was no longer sure anymore. The gloomy room had begun spinning, and she had been forced to take a seat by the bed to avoid falling down completely.

"Actually, I was never fond of the name Ethan, and never used it other than in my work," the man explained. "Ethan was my father's name, you see. He was a terrible brute. My mother, his dear wife, died in childbirth, something for which he endeavored to punish me accordingly. His all-consuming anger finally drove me from home at age twelve, and I narrowly escaped with my life, whereupon I began wandering the country. Later, when I became an author, I began using his name in the hopes that it would irk him to see how his hated son had nonetheless thrived and made a name for himself despite his father's efforts to destroy him.

"After years of drifting, I settled in Spooking, calling myself by my middle name, Alvin. It was here that I began writing. Perhaps thanks to my experience with my father, the elder Ethan, I found myself constantly drawn toward darkness. And the town, handily, offered no shortage of strange and murky events to inspire me.

"I chronicled these stories in secret so that no one would ever fear in confiding in me and so staunch the flow of uncanny anecdotes. You see, I could never have dreamed up the outlandish accounts on my own, nor the eerie scenes I would subsequently witness. It became a simple case of dutifully recording them as well as I could, and then sneaking off to a publisher to sell them. These narratives, which I told through the viewpoint of Dr. Ingram, proved quickly popular, I soon learned.

"However, I eventually found myself caught up in a supernatural saga of my own. I became entangled with a beautiful woman who nonetheless proved to be a vindictive sorceress. I finally made a desperate bid to escape her. So scorned, she unleashed unbelievable horror upon everyone in her path. To save the town, I was forced to destroy her.

"But even in death she lost little of her considerable power. With her last words she cast a powerful hex over me: that if I ever left Spooking—left her—I would turn ghostly and vanish from the earth. So she cursed me and my unborn progeny alike.

"At first I dismissed her threat. Even by Spooking's peculiar standards the possibility seemed just too incredible. But the next time I ventured from Spooking Hill to hunt down in the woods, I felt the immediate and powerful onset of her curse. I was lucky to even make it back.

"And so it happened that I never left the town again. Unable to visit my publishers, I could no longer find an outlet for my work. I did not even correspond with them, out of an irrational fear it could somehow alert my barbaric father to my whereabouts. Living simply and quietly by means of my existing fortune, I carried on my life under my pseudonym.

"Then I met Melody.

"On the occasion I was having an extended stay at the asylum, which had began functioning as a sanitarium catering to the well-to-do. It was about twenty-five years after the author Ethan Alvin Peugeot had mysteriously disappeared from the world. I had been convalescing there for years, enjoying the famed healing waters that attracted custom far and wide.

"In fact, it was sitting poolside in a pair of deck chairs that we first fell in love. Thanks to my repeated visits over the years, I had hardly aged a day, and she was no wiser as to how much older I was than her. She was beautiful, with a crooked smile and an intrepid spirit unlike any other woman I had ever met.

"But soon she went away again, off to explore the world and make history, as was her bread and butter. And I sent letter upon letter in pursuit of her, calling out to her heart, drawing her back to Spooking with whatever spells my words could cast over her.

"And they worked, apparently. We soon moved into a house she purchased on Ravenwood Avenue. And we lived happily for a number of years. But despite her oft-stated desire, I refused to marry her.

"Because to Melody life was an adventure, I knew. She

wanted to travel, to see every inch of our glittering planet, view it from every angle imaginable. The thought of being stuck here forever in Spooking filled her with the kind of horror I had built my considerable but secret fame upon.

"I, on the other hand, could never leave. That's what she could never understand. I finally confessed who I was, and told her that I had trifled with a dangerous person's heart, and that I was cursed for it, that I could never go outside the town's limits without bringing a terrible fate upon myself.

"Of course she thought I was lying, or more likely insane. She called me a coward, and accused me of making up stories to hide from the world. She refused to believe anything I said. And finally she left in anger, to spend some time on her own, to travel and to think.

"She took away my letters, along with a new story I had written to prove to her that I was in fact Ethan Alvin Peugeot, chronicling my years convalescing at the asylum. And again I assailed her with loving notes, beseeching her to return.

"But I heard back from her only a few times, the letters written from a summer house she kept in Steadford Mines. Informing me that she had secured some financing, she said she was off to break yet more aviation records on the other side of the earth. Did I want to come? she asked. She wrote in great detail about the glorious white beaches and emerald jungles that abounded there, about the coconut trees and the turquoise surf and a thousand other things I had never seen in all my life. And yes, I did want to go. All were sights I burned to see even once with my own eyes.

"Yet I could not. And again I told her so. Again I begged her to understand that it was not me but the curse that kept me here, and that I would do anything to be there, by her side, cheering her on as she soared off into that great blue sky she so dearly loved.

"But instead, without a word of good-bye, she set off by herself. On a sunny June third, she took off from a faraway airstrip, flying solo above the ocean. It was the same ocean she had so beautifully described to me in her letters—how the sea and sky would become one, twinkling off into infinity, so beautiful that it was almost painful to behold.

"Into that infinity she then vanished.

"My grief was absolute, a white-hot fire that has burned in my heart forevermore. For it was she who vanished, not I. It was as if I had cursed her with my own sickness, my own cowardice. It should have been me who vanished in her stead, disappearing like a ghost among her many well-wishers.

"I resolved at once to leave Spooking. To get on a plane and fly off myself, and let myself dissolve into nothingness. But I could not do it. I stood at the crest of Spooking Hill, shaking with fear. Ethan Alvin Peugeot, the author who had lived his entire life mining mountains of terror, was too afraid.

"And so I returned to the asylum. After selling all my worldly possessions, I installed myself there permanently, making myself useful to the mad doctor so he would not take my brains away, as he had with the others. I grew their food and tended to the grounds for scores and scores of years, kept alive by the pool.

"And so it went until the terrible events you witnessed."

The old author exhaled. His story at an end, he seemed drained. Joy sat there, quietly staring at his ravaged old face. All of a sudden he reminded her of someone. Teddy Danger, perhaps? No, that wasn't it at all, she decided. It was someone else.

Mr. Phipps.

It was unmistakable.

"So you never had any children?" Joy asked.

The old author turned his head wearily toward her. "Melody and I did have a son together," he whispered, shame written plainly across his features. "But we were not married, you must understand. And Melody was a very public person.

"So we had to give him up to be raised at the local orphanage in the hopes that we might at least see him growing up. It was run by the Zotts, a local family who were thankfully beyond making the judgments that were so prevalent in that day."

Joy trembled to hear it. "Do you know what his name was?"

"Yes, of course," the legendary author replied. "We had to provide one when we admitted him. We called him Lorenzo Phipps, using one of the names I sometimes adopted to hide my identity. And I left him with my last compendium of stories, *The Compleat and Collected Works*, trusting that one day he might recognize his father in them."

Joy gasped. This could mean only one thing.

Mr. Phipps was the grandson of E. A. Peugeot.

Before she could speak, there was a rap on the door.

"Joy, what are you doing in here?" asked Madame Portia, entering with a tray of mushy-looking food and a glass of milk. "You are wanted on set, or so I keep hearing them calling through those walker-and-talkers."

The movie shoot! Joy had forgotten all about it. With lunch long over everyone was no doubt looking for her in a panic. Not that she much cared.

"Uh, I have to go," Joy said, getting up.

"It was very nice talking to you, young lady," the man said, managing a warm smile.

Feeling dazed, Joy paused, looking at the person whom she now knew was her favorite author, who had somehow lived on from another era. She hadn't even told him how much she loved his work! What had she been thinking?

But it was too late. Madame Portia took Joy by the arm and began hustling her out of the room. She resisted, pulling away from the old gypsy. She had so many things to ask this man, so many things to say to him!

"Are you going deaf, bambina?" Madame Portia snapped as she ushered the girl into the hall. "They are waiting for you downstairs. Now leave poor old Al alone to eat his lunch in peace!"

"But wait!" Joy shouted. "You don't understand who that is in there!"

Delivering a terrible stink-eye, the old gypsy slammed the door in her face.

Desperate to get back in, Joy began pounding on the door. "Hey! Open up!" There was a sharp click as the lock was turned, followed by what Joy guessed was likely another Italian profanity.

Groaning with frustration, Joy turned and stomped off down the hallway. She stopped, seeing a man standing in silhouette at the top of the stairs.

"We've been everywhere looking for you," said Teddy.

"Sorry," Joy told him. "Something came up."

Joy tried to move past him, but the rock star threw his arms out wide, blocking the stairs.

"So who is it?" he asked, smiling with a frightening display of teeth.

"Pardon me?"

"Who is it in there?"

"Just a resident," Joy answered. "He's sick."

"Yes, but what's his name?" Teddy asked.

"Al," Joy told him, noticing how his eyes were pinched into slits.

"Al what?" he probed.

"Just Al," Joy said, exasperated. "Look, can I get by or what?"

But instead of letting her pass, the man suddenly snatched her arm and squeezed it painfully. "Tell me," Teddy growled, "his name!"

Joy yelped.

"Oh, good, Teddy. You found her!" Templeton Cray called from the entranceway below. "Joy, where have you been? We've been looking everywhere for you."

"She's been visiting a sick resident," Teddy reported as he released her arm. "Isn't she a real sweetheart?" he added before turning to Joy with a frightening glare.

"Well, that's great, but everybody's waiting to get started," Templeton scolded. "Now come on, kiddo. Let's get things rolling again."

Swiftly ducking under one of Teddy's arms, Joy made a break down the stairs.

"Wait for Daddy, Agnes," the towering man called after her. "Wait for Daddy."

CHAPTER 22

Mr. Phipps had spent the afternoon consulting with the film's production manager. They were hoping to shoot one of the movie's gruesome axe murders in Spooking Park, using the cascading waterway that wound through it. Having stumbled across the interconnecting series of pools and channels during his lunch hour, the director was now envisioning a dramatic scene where Mr. Blackthorne would thrash through the water in pursuit of a victim.

"It will look amazing!" Mr. Cray had told them. "We'll turn the whole stream bloodred and film it flowing all the way down to that cool old tree at the end."

Unfortunately, the waterway was dry, relying on a large storm drain at the top for its supply. It meant that Mr. Phipps would need to get the fire department's permission to pipe the water in using a couple of hydrants up on the Boulevard.

"It shouldn't be a problem," Mr. Phipps had assured the production manager, adding that the fire department already had somewhat of a disinterest in Spooking, having to drive their large trucks up such a dangerous incline whenever they were called to a fire.

Phipps considered this as they returned to the set at Madame Portia's. Perhaps that was what Spooking needed, a cleansing by fire. He imagined the hill burning brightly against the night sky, with all of its secrets and memories turning to ash and floating away.

After thanking the special municipal consultant for his help, the production manager disappeared into his trailer office. Phipps stood on the curb, looking at his watch. Did he have time to head down to the fire station? He wasn't sure. Then again, perhaps a phone call would suffice for something so trivial.

Turning, he saw a nearby trailer bearing the name of Spooking's first starlet. He shuddered to remember the young woman's accusation, that he somehow knew something about E. A. Peugeot. And the Witch of Weredale? He'd not heard that name since his father had breathed it during what Octavio had thought was just another ghost story.

How could Joy have heard of such things?

Phipps jumped as he caught sight of Audrey again, strolling toward him down the Boulevard. She must have been staying with her parents on Cliffside Crescent, he realized. For some reason he had pictured her staying at a hotel like the director.

But then why would she? She was clearly a sophisticated woman now, and the hotels in Darlington were little better than drive-in motels turned on their end. And as she'd said, she didn't get back often to visit her parents.

Mr. and Mrs. Parker had always been pleasant enough to young Octo. Then again, their friendliness had seemed somewhat reserved compared to the constant fawning and doting of his own family over Audrey. But the Parkers were rich, Phipps had always known, and he'd been just some punk—a grave digger with poor prospects.

Since Phipps had moved back to Spooking, he had even crossed paths with the Parkers. They hadn't recognized him. Oblivious to his glares, the happy-looking old couple had continued on right past him, holding hands as they'd dragged a hulking black mutt behind them.

Phipps could only imagine how much they must have secretly hated his guts, and how relieved they had surely felt when Audrey had finally moved on from their teenage flirtation. Because to these sort of people, breeding and background were everything, he believed. A man's own deeds and actions counted for nothing.

What would they have thought, he wondered, had they known that their daughter's companion in fact traced his bloodline to one of the country's most celebrated authors? Probably little. After all, Phipps had in no way benefited from the man's standing nor his fortune, both of which had vanished just like the author himself. No, the author's only legacy had been his curse, which Phipps's father had so dolefully explained to him.

"Hello, Octavio!" Audrey said, drawing up with a smile.

"Miss Parker," he replied formally.

Audrey cocked her head, unsure whether he was joking. "Actually, I was just talking about you," she told him. "My parents and I were wondering if you were free for dinner this week."

Phipps looked over her shoulder at some crew members loudly rolling large aluminum flight cases along the pavement. "I don't know," he replied, raising his voice. He then paused, waiting until the noise had passed. "I don't think so, actually. I'm very busy at the moment."

"Oh," Audrey said, a look of disappointment crossing her face. "It's just that I'll be leaving soon, and we haven't had a chance to catch up yet."

"That is a shame," Phipps said dully. "But perhaps your parents would enjoy an evening with Teddy Danger instead. He is delightful company, I recall."

Audrey frowned at the remark. "I don't think so," she replied. "They were really hoping to see you again."

"Oh well. Maybe next time." Phipps looked at his watch anxiously. "Now if you'll excuse me, I really must go."

"Okay, Octavio."

Looking perturbed, Audrey watched as the special municipal consultant then hurried off, leaving her standing alone on the curb.

Listening in from her trailer, Joy stayed out of sight until Mr. Phipps and Miss Parker went their separate ways. This was the same person Madame Portia had once told her was the love of the man's life? If so, he seemed pretty much over her now.

Peering nervously out the window, she then caught sight of a pink head wandering by.

"Hey," she whispered through one of the small windows on the side. "Molly!"

The woman stopped. "Oh, hi there," she replied, noticing

the girl's uncertain-looking face. "Is everything all right?"

"Not really," Joy told her frankly. "Do you have a minute?"

"Of course," she answered.

Joy pulled Molly into the trailer and shut the door. Sitting the woman down in the lounge, she then made her urgent observation.

"Teddy's been acting really weird."

"Welcome to my world," the personal assistant muttered wearily. "Just be thankful you're only visiting it."

"No, I mean it. Have you not noticed that he's acting funny? I mean, not just weird but scary-weird?"

"I don't know. I guess he has been a bit withdrawn and quiet. To be honest, it was a nice change for me, so I didn't ask any questions." Molly frowned. "Actually, one thing was pretty odd," she then remembered. "He'd arranged a couple of weeks ago for a few of his idiotic friends to come stay with him at the mansion, but when they arrived, he wouldn't even let them inside. It was quite awkward. I had to stand outside and call them a cab to take them back to the airport. They were pretty mad. But again, I was pretty happy. . . ."

Joy told the assistant how after the tarot reading, when Madame Portia had foretold of some terrible catastrophe, Teddy had begun behaving differently, and how even his acting abilities had suddenly changed, in this case for the better. She then relayed how he had grabbed her upstairs and insisted she tell him the name of one of the residents.

"Okay, now you are freaking me out," Molly said. "What do you think is going on?"

"If I had to put money on it, I would say he's possessed

by an evil spirit. And you heard what Madame Portia said about the Witch of Weredale being back."

Molly looked at the girl, trying to determine if she was playing some sort of joke on her. Seeing Joy's serious face, she shivered. "I don't know. I don't usually believe in that kind of stuff."

"I know it's a weird thing to ask," Joy continued, "but I was wondering if you could take me to the house. I've actually read quite a bit about witches, and I thought if I could have a look around, maybe I could get a better idea of what is possessing him."

"Oh, I guess so," Molly agreed. "But wait—what if Teddy is there?"

"According to the schedule, he's supposed to be in makeup for the next couple of hours having his face melted."

"Considering all the plastic surgery he's had, that could make quite a bad smell," Molly joked.

"All right, let's go," said Joy, laughing.

A few minutes later, Joy and Molly drew up to the imposing Gothic mansion.

"Well, this is it," Molly said. "Quaint, huh?"

Joy knew the house well. It was always for rent, she'd noticed, rather than for sale, which in Spooking was quite rare. She'd once briefly known a couple of kids who'd lived there whose wealthy parents had moved them into the fully furnished home while shopping for a permanent home in the neighborhood.

They had left very suddenly, however—both from the house and the area.

Joy waited as Molly retrieved the key from under the mat. "Teddy doesn't like carrying things in his pockets, and I'm sick of coming running every time he gets locked out." She then unlocked the front door, which opened inward with an unnerving creak. They stepped into the large entranceway as Molly flipped on the lights.

"Gosh, half the bulbs have blown now. What's with that?" Molly demanded as they stood in the half-light. "Anyway, have a look around. I don't know what you're going to find other than a whole lot of creepy stuff, but knock yourself out."

"Okay, thanks," said Joy. With Molly at her heels, she peeked around the dining room, the kitchen, and the sitting room. Each indeed shared the same dreadful atmosphere but offered no particular clues to the girl. At least nothing she could recall from *The Compleat and Collected Works.*

Joy thought back to her meeting with the author only a few hours before. Had he not just confirmed everything she had always believed? His stories were true! A strange feeling of pleasure had filled her ever since, combined with a deep sense of relief. She wasn't crazy, it had turned out. She had been right the whole time.

But if his stories were true, she realized, that meant they were in considerable danger.

Finding nothing of interest on the first floor, Joy returned to the entranceway, where the sweeping stairwell headed to the bedrooms. She paused on the first step, noticing the many pictures hanging on the wall. Then her eyes were drawn to the portrait of the beautiful gypsy above the large hearth.

A cold fear suddenly swept over Joy. There was something in the subject's shifting gaze that turned more and more malevolent with each passing second.

So this was her, the witch herself, thought Joy.

Looking to the right, Joy then noticed a door tucked under the stairs.

"Where does that go?" she asked.

"The basement, I think," Molly answered. "I've never gone down there."

"I think we should have a look," Joy said.

"Are you sure? I'm feeling scared."

At Joy's insistence Molly unlatched the door and swung it wide, revealing a rickety set of stairs leading down into profound blackness.

"Maybe there's a light," the pink-haired young woman said, stepping in. "Yuck. The floor is all sticky—"

Just then they were interrupted by a loud bang. The pair spun around, both screaming in fright.

"Who's there?" boomed the hideously deformed creature standing at the open front door.

"Teddy!" cried his assistant. Stepping out of the shadows into the entranceway, she closed the door to the basement behind her. "You're back. I thought you were supposed to be in makeup."

The rock star stared back at her, his eyes flashing out of a latex mask made to look like torched flesh. "As you can see, they've finished me up early."

"Then, shouldn't you be on set?" Molly asked.

"There's something I have to do here first," he said. He

peered at the woman suspiciously. "Hey, what were you doing back there? Is someone with you?"

"It's just your costar," Molly said, leading Joy out into the light. "She was bored, so I brought her back for a quick tour of our pad."

Through the mask Teddy's eyes burned. "I thought I made myself clear," he growled. "No visitors!"

"It was just for a minute," Molly replied meekly.

"Did you go into the basement?" Teddy demanded.

"No. I just opened the door, but it's too dark down there. Anyway, we were just leaving."

"Yes, you are, Molly Sinclair," agreed Teddy. "Because you are fired."

"What?" The pink-haired woman reeled in surprise.

"Go and get your things. I want you out. Now."

"But, Teddy—"

"NOW!" he bellowed.

Breaking into tears, Molly tore across the entranceway and headed upstairs. She left a trail of red boot prints behind her.

"And you," Teddy said as he followed Joy's horrified gaze to one of the glistening prints. "I think you should leave. Now!"

Trembling with fear, Joy ran out the open door.

CHAPTER 23

L it up by powerful lights, the gingerbread exterior of the Shew Inn looked almost fresh out of the oven. Blazing against a blue-black night sky, the building looked even more ominous and off-putting than before.

Sitting in a lawn chair, Mrs. Wells excitedly pointed to a man about a hundred yards away. "Do you think that's him there?" she asked.

"Helen, I don't think Teddy Danger would be carrying a boom mike around," Mr. Wells replied from beside her.

"I suppose you're right," Mrs. Wells conceded. "But look, there's Joy! She looks like she's getting ready to do something. Isn't this exciting, Edward? I'm so glad she got us permission to come along and watch."

"It is pretty interesting to watch the process in person," her husband granted. "I just wish there weren't so many darned mosquitoes."

Sitting on the damp ground and hardly able to see above the grass, Byron was of two minds. While he agreed about the mosquitoes, he most certainly disagreed about the interest. Making movies was boring, he'd already decided an hour before, and now it was becoming painfully boring.

He wished he was at home, or better yet sleeping over at Gustave's. But then he would have really wanted his walkie-talkies, which were still stuck in Joy's stupid trailer.

Then he had a thought. Maybe he could sneak back and get them himself.

"I need to go for a walk," Byron told his parents. "My legs are getting sore."

"Oh, you poor thing," said Mrs. Wells, patting his head. "We really didn't know that chair was broken, dear, or we would never have brought it."

Byron grunted. His parents had sure laughed hard enough when the chair had suddenly folded in two beneath him.

"Don't go too far, though, because it's a bit dark," Mr. Wells called as his son headed off down the drive.

The streets were dead, Byron soon discovered. He hurried down and along the Boulevard to where the trailers were parked. After looking around for a security guard first, he then tried the door.

It was unlocked, he discovered with a smile. Moving quickly, he slipped inside.

The inside of the trailer was dimly lit. Not wishing to draw any attention to himself, Byron decided to fumble around instead of putting on a light. Feeling like an international jewel thief skulking around some heartless billionaire's mansion, he crept down the hall in search of his prize.

Luckily the walkie-talkies had not been moved, he soon learned after bumping into the table. Stuffing them into his pockets like they were a pair of gold bricks, he turned to leave. He felt thirsty, though, and stopped at the fridge, where he managed to extract a bottle of water from behind the diet drinks. Imagining it as a sort of stubby diamond scepter, he then helped himself to a plum—or rather, the world's largest ruby.

Feeling satisfied that he was now set for life, Byron the international jewel thief went to make his escape.

Back at the Shew Inn, the crew signaled its readiness. Standing just behind them were Mr. Phipps and three individuals: a man in a suit and two women.

"C'mon, let's get this show on the road!" the mayor yelled loudly enough that he received a scowl from the director himself.

Phipps decided to ignore them both. After all, it was no longer his job to worry about the mayor's behavior. "So how have you been doing, Mrs. MacBrayne?" he instead asked the woman in pearls standing to his right.

"Quite wonderful, Mr. Phipps, quite wonderful," the mayor's wife replied. "And thank you again for the kind invitation tonight—how glamorous to see an actual movie being made!"

"You're most welcome," said Phipps. About Mrs. Mac-Brayne's true feelings on the matter, however, he could not even begin to guess. With her aging skin pulled even more tightly across her face than ever, the mayor's wife now appeared completely incapable of rendering even the slightest expression of joy or misery.

Hiding a shiver, Phipps turned to his left toward the pretty woman who was all smiles upon meeting him. "Have you ever been on a film set before, Miss Sparks?"

"It's my first time," she confessed. "But I must say, I'm really quite excited about it!"

"Well, they should be starting soon," Phipps assured her. Putting a hand in his pocket, he then remembered something. "I'm sorry, but would you three mind excusing me for a few minutes? I have a small but very important errand to run."

"Absolutely, dear," Mrs. MacBrayne replied.

"Hurry back, Phipps, or you'll miss all the action!" the mayor shouted after him.

"QUIET ON THE SET!" the director shouted through an actual megaphone for once. From his position in a folding chair with his name on the back, Mr. Cray irritably swatted at a cloud of bugs. "Okay, let's get things rolling before it's morning. Ready? Everyone into first position."

Standing on the long front porch, Joy and Morris waited at their marks. For safety the porch cover of the collapsing inn had now been fortified by means of cleverly hidden steel scaffolding, as had the reception area that Teddy was supposed to emerge from. Looking up, Joy could see the wooden cover hanging at an unnerving angle, as the porch itself remained so inclined that Joy found it hard to even stand comfortably.

"Now, kids, when I say "action," Teddy is going to kick open that door. Remember, he's not your father anymore. He's a monster who wants to kill you. So I want you to scream like you're really scared and run down the stairs toward that tree over there. Got it?"

"Reading you loud and clear, Templeton," Morris confirmed from the porch.

Joy nodded, thinking this performance would be easy. After the incident at the house on Weredale, she now felt motivated to run from Teddy given the slightest opportunity. Terrified for her friend's safety afterward, Joy had hidden in some bushes until she'd seen Molly emerge unharmed from the house carrying a suitcase. A taxi had then drawn up.

It was only then that Joy had raced back to her trailer where she'd waited for her call at the night shoot.

"Great, guys. Okay, Bob. We're ready to go. Copy that?" the director said into his walkie-talkie.

"We're not in position. Over," came the tinny reply from the assistant director inside.

"How come? What's your twenty?"

"I'm here by the door, but Teddy's taken off. Over."

"Where is he?" the director asked. "Taking a ten-one-hundred?"

Standing on the porch, Joy made a mental note to relay some of this official walkie-talkie lingo to Byron—starting with ten-one-hundred, which he would get a kick out of knowing meant "going to the bathroom."

Behind the door she heard what sounded like a short cry and then the heavy thump of something hitting the floor.

"Did you hear that?" she asked Morris.

"Don't talk to me," he snapped, his eyes staring forward. "I'm getting into character. . . ."

"Hello?" the director said, clicking the walkie-talkie.

"Bob, did Teddy go to the honeywagon or something? Over."

Again there was no answer.

"Templeton for Bob, come in," Mr. Cray tried again. He sighed impatiently, turning to Marcus, another of the assistant directors running around set. "Do you think maybe his walkie ran out of juice?"

"Could be. I'll go and check."

Joy watched as the fellow bounded up toward them. Flashing a smile at the children, he squeezed past and opened the door.

"Hello?" he called out, entering the building. "Bob? Teddy? Hello?"

The door swung shut behind him.

Still feeling spooked by the strange noise, Joy looked out at the director, who was holding up a hand to shield his eyes from a gust of wind that suddenly blew up.

That's when Joy saw it, standing right behind Mr. Cray's chair. It was the three-legged dog again, the harbinger, and it stood panting heavily beside the unknowing director, the inside of its mouth shining red against its white teeth.

There was a general cry of alarm from the crew as the wind picked up strength, howling across the property and sending production notes and paper plates flying everywhere. Reflectors fell down as the lights started swaying, before crashing to the ground and exploding with frightening pops.

Plunged into darkness, Joy and Morris clung to the railing.

"AND ACTION!"

The earsplitting shout came not from the director but from behind Joy, as with a crack, the door flew open. Joy turned and saw Teddy. Backlit by a blazing light, he stood there in silhouette, his hair now standing up in terrifying spikes.

"IT'S SHOWTIME, FOLKS!" he shouted before swinging the dripping axe in his hands.

CHAPTER 24

Gasping in horror, Joy ducked. The blade whooshed above her head, clanging off the supporting scaffolding.

The impact proved incredibly destructive. Steel pipes clattered to the ground as the boards of the porch roof began groaning. Trapped against the railing, the children stood screaming as the structure tore free from the building.

"Okay. Take two!" cried the madman as he wound up to swing at them again.

But then a section of falling pipe struck Teddy in the head. Stumbling to the side, he swung the axe wildly, its momentum spinning him in the opposite direction.

Grabbing Morris by the arm, Joy leaped forward into the building as the porch covering collapsed. The two of them landed hard on the wooden floor of the lobby. From behind came a great roar of falling boards and a whoosh as a cloud of dust was driven inside. Choking on the acrid particles, Joy crawled on all fours, dragging her costar behind her.

When the noise finally stopped, she rolled over and peered back toward the entranceway.

The doorway was now completely blocked with debris. Just inside, an injured figure struggled to get up.

It was Teddy.

"Run, Morris! Run!" Joy cried.

But the boy was immovable. "Oh, for heaven's sake," he cried. "I'm Alfred. Remember?"

"What?"

"For crying out loud, I'm working with a complete amateur! That was supposed to be a single take. How long do you think it's going to take to reset that mess out there?"

Teddy was now on his hands and knees, his latex face hanging off. From a gash in his forehead a stream of blood flowed, obscuring his vision as he groped for the axe lying only a foot and a half ahead of him.

"You blew the whole scene," Morris said, and sighed. "And that was so perfect! Man, did you hear me scream? I thought I brought some real intensity to it."

At that moment the crawling rock star's fingers finally found the end of the axe handle. The blade began scraping noisily across the hardwood floor.

"Morris, are you completely out of your mind? This is real! Teddy wants to kill us!"

"Listen, Spooky, now you're really losing the plot, if you know what I mean."

Teddy had now gotten to his feet, Joy saw. Yanking off his shredded face, he blinked away dust and looked for the source of the two children's voices. She had to do something—and quick.

"All right, Morris," Joy said, slumping her head forward in shame. "You're right. I was just embarrassed that I blew my line."

"Hey, don't sweat it," Morris said kindly. "It happens to the best of us. And I'm sure they can fix your audio loop in postproduction later. I'm telling you, they can do just about anything these days."

"The thing is, the director said he was going to keep rolling, no matter what," Joy said. "They've got cameras mounted all over this place. So come on. Let's keep doing the scene!"

"I don't know," Morris said as the girl yanked on his arm. "I'm pretty sure we've stopped shooting."

"Did you hear the director yell cut?" Joy shrieked desperately. "No!" She pointed at the crazed-looking man now lurching toward them. "And look, Teddy's still acting!"

"Bwahahahahaha!" Teddy cackled.

At the sight, Morris's face lit up with delight. He then twisted his features with convincing horror.

"No, Daddy, no!" he shouted at the killer limping toward them. "Daddy, please stop!"

"That's not our father anymore, Alfred! Run! RUN!"

With nowhere else to go, Joy and Morris ran up the large sweeping stairwell of the inn. At least the climb would slow Teddy down, Joy hoped, while she tried to find another way out. But when they reached the top, she glanced over her shoulder to see Teddy taking the stairs two at a time.

"This way!" Joy ordered, quickly pushing the dark-haired

boy through the nearest door and closing it behind them.

Inside, the floor crunched oddly underfoot. Even though the room was pitch-black, Joy could tell from bumping into a rotted old bed set that it was a guest room, which meant there were likely no other exits.

They were trapped in there.

"Get under the bed!" she whispered urgently.

It was then, hiding under the ancient box spring, that Joy began hearing a strange noise overhead—like the irritable squeaking and shuffling of a thousand tiny creatures.

"Oh, you think you can run, do you?" they heard Teddy muttering out in the hall. "Oh, you think you can hide?"

The floorboards creaked ominously close by.

"Aha!" Teddy shouted, booting the door in. Startled, Joy and Morris abandoned any attempts at stealth and shrieked at the top of their lungs.

But even more terrified than the children were the bats above, who took immediate flight toward the open door. In a great rush of leathery wings and greasy fur, they roared over Teddy, who screamed and staggered back across the balustrade. With a crack the upper banister gave way as with a cry the man fell backward, landing a moment later in the lobby with a grotesque thud.

Scrambling out from under the bed, Joy rushed out and looked down at the unmoving man.

"He's down!" she called to Morris. "Come on! Let's find a way out of here!"

The children descended the stairs, keeping a watchful

eye on Teddy. Lying on the wrecked banister, his eyes were clamped shut, and in addition to the oozing wound on his head, there was now a trickle of blood coming out of his nose. Beside him his axe stood, its blade stuck in the floor.

Was he dead? Joy couldn't tell. Trembling, she stepped around his stricken form toward a hall leading off the lobby.

"GAAAAAAAA!"

With a yell Teddy grabbed her ankle, his eyes rolled way back in his head. Joy screamed. Morris gave the man a sharp kick in the hand, and he released her.

"Come on!" Morris shouted.

The two children sprinted down the hall, hurrying on through large empty rooms where water-spotted wallpaper hung off the walls in tattered rolls. Looking for an exit, Joy found only shard-lined windows too dangerous to attempt.

"Keep going!" she shouted. "There must be a back door somewhere."

Finally they found one leading off a wrecked kitchen lined with huge old sinks and a giant woodstove. Finding that the door held fast, Joy began frantically undoing a series of latches and bolts.

"Hurry!" Morris urged as maniacal cackling drifted toward them.

As the hulking outline of their pursuer reappeared, Joy managed to unlock the door. She threw herself bodily against it and tumbled out into the cool night air, as Morris followed closely behind.

Joy slammed the door behind them. They then raced across the back lawn toward a wall of blackness that turned out to be a thick line of bushes.

"Ow!" Joy cried, cutting herself on a thorn. "Careful. It's spiky!"

"Base to walkie-talkie," they both heard. "Come in, walkie-talkie. Where are you, walkie-talkie?"

It was coming from a few feet away.

Joy picked up the yellow walkie-talkie, one of a set of two she had personally picked out at Electronica Veronica. Pressing the button, she replied in a whisper:

"Byron?"

"Joy?" came the full-volume response. "Is that you, Joy?"

"Shhh, keep it down!" she hissed into the radio device. "Where are you?"

"I'm in Spooking Cemetery. Over," he said. "Behind the house, on the other side of the bushes."

"How did you get over there?" she asked, probing the dense vegetation. "It's full of thorns!"

"I found a sort of a tunnel going through it. But I must have dropped one of my walkie-talkies as I was crawling through. Do you have it?"

"Of course I have it!" Joy replied. "How else would we be talking?"

"Oh yeah," came Byron's crackling reply.

"What's up with the modern props?" Morris demanded. "There were no such gizmos back then! Oh, they're going to have a field day with all these gaffes on the Internet."

Just then there was an explosion of glass as the axe came smashing through the back door window. A twisted face appeared, glowing in the moonlight.

"Here's Teddy!" he cried madly. "Oh, you don't know how long I've waited to say that!"

"Alfred!" Joy called under her breath as she got down on all fours. "Come here! There's a tunnel through the bushes!"

Not wasting a second, Morris crawled after Joy. Before long they emerged on the other side. Standing in the old pauper's burial ground was Byron.

"Oh, good. You found it," said Byron, taking the walkie-talkie off her. "We need to get back. Mom and Dad said not to go far in the dark."

"Byron!" Joy said, seizing her brother by the shoulders. "Teddy Danger has gone berserk. He's on the other side of those bushes, and he's coming to kill us!"

Her brother smirked. "Are you sure you aren't taking this whole movie thing a bit too seriously?"

"Or not seriously enough?" Morris suggested.

The sound, however, of Teddy cursing and swearing as he flailed through the thorn bush was nevertheless frightening. The three children ran off.

The cemetery soon became thick with swirling mist. Around them headstones poked up like blackened teeth, as sorrowful monuments loomed above.

"I hope you're happy, Spooky," snarled Morris, glancing around with distaste. "Now we're totally lost!"

"We're not lost," Joy assured him. Joy knew almost every stone in the cemetery and could always easily find her way out. But looking around, she saw with a start that none of the stones nor the names etched upon them looked familiar.

"This is a just great," Morris continued. "I'm sure Mr. Danger will get us both fired now, thanks to you."

"Morris, don't you get it?" Joy snapped at the little boy whose head floated above the mist beside her. "He's not Teddy Danger anymore. He's possessed by something and is a mindless killer!"

"Oh, please," replied Morris. "You obviously don't know anything about method acting."

"Method what?"

"Method acting. It's a technique where you completely become your character. Look it up. All the great actors do it."

Joy scoffed. "I don't know if you've noticed, Morris, but Teddy isn't exactly the greatest actor. He isn't even a particularly great musician, come to think of it."

"Now, hold on right there, missy!" Morris shouted. "My father was a huge Teddy Danger fan!"

"Okay. What about the fall, into the lobby? How did he do that?"

"That wasn't Teddy," Morris said confidently. "That was a stuntman in a Teddy mask."

"Would you both be quiet?" whispered Byron. "Listen . . ."

At first Joy and Morris heard nothing. Then, above the deathly silence of the cemetery, rose the sound of panting.

"Is that you, Mr. Danger?" called Morris. "Listen, we're sorry. How can we make things up to you?"

Joy clamped a hand over the boy's mouth.

"Look!" cried Byron, pointing.

Just ahead, atop a large stone crypt, the three-legged dog stood, bathed in moonlight. With its black coat shining damply and a thick loop of white spittle hanging from its maw, the creature stared with unblinking eyes at the children.

"Oh no," Joy said. "That dog is a harbinger," she explained, remembering the word Madame Portia had used.

"It's a what?"

"A harbinger. It appears when something bad is about to happen. I saw it just before Teddy jumped out with the axe."

"Oh no," Morris moaned. "I knew it! We're both going to be fired!"

Just then the dog began growling as behind them came a hideous scraping sound.

"Hello, kiddies," a voice breathed evilly. "I was wondering where you'd run off to. . . ."

Whirling around, the children saw a figure standing behind them.

It was Teddy. Now bleeding with countless cuts to his hands and face, he stood there, one eye madly wide and the other pinched into a lizardlike slit. Grinning, he began grinding his axe against the top of a headstone with such force that it sent sparks flying.

"Mr. Danger!" Morris laughed jovially. "We've been looking all over for you! I guess they want us back on set?"

"Morris, no!" Joy screamed as the boy took a step forward, bringing himself within range of the maniac's weapon.

With a look of crazed delight, Teddy drew back the gleaming axe.

"Hold it!" someone shouted.

Surprised, Teddy stopped midswing just as a figure jumped between him and the children.

"Back off, Ted," the shadowy man growled, "or I'll bust your nose just like Vince did that night you threw up on his jacket."

Despite the reference to this old incident, it wasn't Teddy but rather Morris who recognized the man first. "Mr. Phipps! What are you doing in the shot?" he asked. "Wait, are you an actor too? Of course you are! You know, I always thought you had a whiff of the thespian about you!"

Phipps turned, looking down at the boy. "What?" he asked quizzically.

"Look out!" Joy shouted.

But it was too late. Teddy butted Phipps in the head with the axe handle. With a sickening thud the lead singer of the Black Tongs landed in a heap.

"Why, hello, Octo!" Teddy exclaimed at the man at his feet. "You've come to the party early! No matter. I don't mind. In fact, it was thoughtful of you to save me the hunt."

With a moan Phipps roused and clutched at his head.

Morris shrieked in horror as Teddy kicked his former Caring Chum hard in the stomach.

"Stop it!" Joy shouted. "Leave him alone!"

Teddy looked at the girl, the axe heavy in his hands. "Whatever for?" he demanded. "Do you have any idea who this is?"

Joy was no longer sure she did.

She had once seen Mr. Phipps as a simple villain, the dark son of Spooking, a traitor to her beloved town. But since then she had learned a lot more about him. About his broken heart. His family, his ancestor, and his curse. Was it any wonder he hated this place?

Nevertheless, Joy did not know quite everything about him, she realized, as Teddy continued.

"This is the once great Octavio Phipps lying here at my feet," he declared. "Did you know what a talent he once was? Or the far-reaching influence of his band, the Black Tongs? No?

"Oh, I'm surprised. Just listen to him. He'll tell you! What brave new ground he broke, what avenues he opened. And then he'll no doubt tell you how I stole his licks, his sound—and how I even stole his bass player out from under him!

"And yes, it's all true. But the truth is equally that he wasn't doing anything with it all anyway. The truth is that he was a loser who squandered every opportunity that ever came his way. But not me! Because I am Teddy Danger, a winner, a star!"

Writhing on the ground, Phipps tried to speak, to say something, but only a horrible noise escaped him.

"You know, you should have thanked me, Octo. You should have thanked me for taking your muddled, pretentious creations and paring them down. You should have thanked me for bringing them to the world to be properly enjoyed, instead of consigned to the dustbin of obscurity. But no. Instead you mock me still.

"Do you know how long I've waited to see you crawling around in the dirt like this?" Teddy asked the man struggling onto all fours. "Crawling around like the little worm you used to tell me I was?"

"I never called you a worm," Phipps croaked. "I called you an insect." Staggering, he nonetheless managed to stand and then point a finger directly at Teddy. "But what you really were—and still are—is a pathetic talentless poseur."

"And YOU!" Teddy shouted, his voice suddenly becoming strangled and disembodied, the screeching voice of a spiteful witch. "YOU ARE THE LAST OF THE PEUGEOTS, AND NOW YOU WILL DIE!"

The blood-soaked monster raised the axe high.

"Run, children, run!" Phipps yelled.

The old son of Spooking didn't even flinch. He just stared at the steel blade glimmering in the moonlight.

But the blow never fell. Instead something black leaped from the shadows.

It was the three-legged dog. With a flash of vicious teeth, the snarling beast clamped down on one of Teddy's arms and dragged him down screaming.

"I thought I told you to run!" Phipps shouted again at the stunned little faces. "Get out of here! Now!" With those final words, he joined the wild battle between man and animal.

Shaken out of her astonished stupor, Joy yanked the two boys by their collars, pulling them in the direction of the cemetery gates. "Come on!" she ordered.

Hideous cries pierced the night as the three children dashed through the black burial ground in terror.

CHAPTER 25

Arriving on the scene at the cemetery, the police had quickly intercepted three fleeing children—an adolescent girl and two boys.

Thankfully they'd proved to be the same youngsters reported missing from the film set shortly before, and all had been found unharmed. Following the girl's directions, the authorities had soon located another adult victim, however—a city contractor who had heard the ruckus and come to their aid. Luckily, the man had suffered only minor injuries after a stray dog had fought off his attacker.

The police had found little trace of Edward Wannamaker, aka Teddy Danger, anywhere in the cemetery, however. After an exhaustive search, all that had been recovered were a few bits of his torn costume as well as the murder weapon, left just inside the open door of an old tomb. Curiously, they'd also recovered a cell phone in the tomb, identified as belonging to the missing actress Penny Farthing.

Having examined the interior of the tomb carefully, the authorities had found nothing further of interest hidden among the two stone caskets. The injured fugitive had presumably stopped there for a moment to tend to his wounds, or so they had surmised, before making his escape.

Sadly, three others had been confirmed dead at two other locations: two members of the film crew, and a private detective who had perished earlier while conducting a missing-person investigation at the perpetrator's rented residence.

As a result of the ongoing investigation, production of the film *Blackthorne Inn* had been temporarily suspended.

This much, Joy had already read for herself in her father's newspaper.

It was creepy to think that Teddy might still be out there somewhere, but the police were doubtful that someone that recognizable could hide for long.

Stopping by Madame Portia's a few days later, Joy was assured that the man was no longer in Spooking.

"I'm sure of it," the old gypsy told her. "Well, unless my crystal ball is broken, of course, which is highly unlikely. I just had it serviced!"

Joy sat on a squishy old sofa in the gypsy's front room. She kept trying to find a comfortable position, and her constant shuffling was causing clouds of dust to fill the air around her.

"Do you want something to drink, bambina? Or some cookies maybe?"

"I'm not hungry, thanks," Joy lied. Her stomach was grumbling, but she had never forgotten the stale, broken biscuits she'd been offered in the gypsy's submarine house in the swamp.

"Well, don't be shy if you change your mind. Oh, my stars, I'm just so relieved you children weren't hurt!"

Something that sounded like a deafeningly loud Chinese gong rang out, interrupting them.

"The doorbell! Excuse me for a moment," said Madame Portia, getting to her feet.

Joy sat waiting as the old woman toddled off to answer the front door. She looked around the cluttered room, which once again looked like a graveyard for upholstered furniture and crocheted blankets. She hadn't realized just how much of Madame Portia's stuff the crew had removed for the movie, and yet it had still seemed oppressively cramped. Completely restored now to its original state, it felt like they had never even been there.

"Oh, it's you," she heard the old gypsy announce flatly from the entranceway.

"I'm delighted to see you, too, Madame Portia," said a smooth voice that was now only too familiar to Joy. "Do you mind if I come in?"

"Suit yourself."

Joy sat up as Mr. Phipps came into view in the entranceway. There was a bandage on his head from where he'd been hit with the axe handle, and he was holding a large cardboard box. Madame Portia stood behind him with her arms folded, wearing a stormy look on her face.

"Oh, hello," Phipps said, noticing Joy. "Good to see you out and about. How are you feeling?"

"I'm fine, thanks," Joy replied. "How is your head?"

"According to the X-ray, my skull is fractured, which makes it the third time in my life, I might add. Still, I think I got off pretty lucky."

Joy had to agree. She shivered to remember Teddy winding up to bury the axe into the man's body. But instead of running, Phipps had just stood there, unafraid, trying to buy the children time to escape.

"Mr. Phipps saved our lives, you know," Joy told the still surly Madame Portia. "Byron, Morris, and me. We wouldn't be alive without him."

The old gypsy turned to the man, shocked.

"Oh, I wouldn't go that far," Phipps said. "But I will acknowledge that it was fortunate I happened by at the time."

"Yeah, right," Joy replied. "Like you just happened to be walking around the cemetery in the middle of the night? Admit it. You came to rescue us."

But Phipps would admit no such thing. This time, however, it wasn't out of modesty.

In truth, he had been in the cemetery only serving his own purpose—to return Penny Farthing's recharged phone to the tomb where he'd found it. Having stood outside and placed a few silent calls to the actress's friends and family, he had hoped that investigators would trace its signal to the very spot, where they could then focus their search for the missing girl.

Phipps had then placed the phone in the empty sarcophagus. When he'd examined the floor again, he had been shocked to discover that the tunnel had been completely filled in and covered with a heavy paving stone.

It was only then, while fleeing the scene, that he'd stumbled across Teddy in the midst of menacing the children.

Phipps decided that it was better to keep these details to himself. But it did not stop the Spooking girl from sharing her version of events, which continued to paint him as some sort of fearless and selfless hero.

It was a portrait neither he nor the old gypsy recognized.

Nevertheless, Madame Portia's combative demeanor softened immediately. She turned to Phipps, clasping her hands to her chest. "I always knew that deep down you were a good boy, Octavio. . . . How my heart soars to hear this! Come sit, my brave man! I will bring you some cookies forthwith!"

"That's quite all right," Phipps declined. "I can't stay. I've come only to give you a gift before leaving." He then presented the old woman with the cardboard box.

Madame Portia blinked in confusion. "A gift?" she asked. "For me?"

"When we were shooting the movie here, I happened to notice that you still collect those porcelain figurines, just like my mother," he said, pointing at the glass display case in the corner, which was brimming with strange moonfaced little children in various costumes and poses. "And it made me remember what great friends you two were. What's more, it made me think how good you'd always been to her, and how caring, never more so than in her last days, when she was left alone by her miserable excuse for a son.

"So I wanted you to have her figurine collection. I have no use for them, but I thought perhaps they might bring you some pleasure."

Hearing the words, Madame Portia looked stricken. She staggered back to the stairwell and steadied herself with the banister. Then, lips quivering, she inched forward, opening the box Mr. Phipps had placed on the floor. She began carefully unwrapping newspaper from the small object on top.

At the sight of it, her face lit up with joy.

"Look!" the old gypsy cried. "It's the Little Shepherd Girl! This one was always both of our favorites! Did you know there were only one thousand ever made? Oh, thank you! Thank you!"

Delighted by the woman's appreciation, Phipps nonetheless struggled not to make a face as she held up the terrible monstrosity. The figurines were truly among the ugliest things his eyes had ever beheld. "Well, there's more where it came from," he said, relieved to see the same horror reflected in Joy's features.

"But where are you going, Octavio?"

"I'm leaving town. For good."

"No!" the gypsy shouted, dropping the precious figurine back into the box like a rock. "You know you can't do that. You've already spent too many years outside of Spooking as it is!"

"I must go," Phipps said. "I can't stay here, waiting around for the inevitable. I want to meet my fate head-on. Do you understand? I believe my own father would have done the same, had he not needed to keep my mother company."

From the gypsy's face Joy saw it was true.

"You poor dear," Madame Portia said. "I'm so sorry."

"There's no need to be sorry," the mayor's former assistant told her. "I want to go now. I just need to say good-bye to an old friend staying on Cliffside Crescent, and then I'm off. Free at last."

"Wait a second," Joy protested. "Why do you have to worry? The witch is gone, isn't she? Which has to mean her curse is finished! Doesn't it?"

"No, bambina," Madame Portia replied gravely. "The murderous vessel she created in this Teddy Danger fellow has left us. Her evil, however, goes on unsatisfied."

"How can you be so sure?"

"Because this too I saw in my crystal ball," Madame Portia declared, eyes wide.

"Your crystal ball," said Mr. Phipps, rolling his eyes. "Let me guess. The same one you used to cart over to my mother's in a bowling bag. Great."

Joy ignored the remark. "If you don't know for sure that the curse is lifted, you can't leave," she ordered Mr. Phipps. "Not until we figure something out!"

"There's nothing left to be done," Phipps answered. "I've known for most of my life that this day would come, even if I didn't always believe it. And I see now that's why I tried so hard—to make a mark, to do something important. . . . So that when the time came, I wouldn't just disappear.

"But look around. I failed. What does it matter if I stay or go?"

"It does matter!" Joy shouted. "It matters to me!" She felt livid now, glaring at the two adults who just stood there, somberly accepting fate. "There has to be something we can do!"

At that moment there came a voice from the top of the stairs.

"There is something," it said.

All eyes turned upward, to the frail figure of Ethan Alvin Peugeot, clinging to the banister at the top of the staircase. Swimming in his long striped nightshirt, he looked little more than a skeleton, with dark sunken eyes and spindly white limbs.

"There is a way," Mr. Peugeot said, his voice now croaking with the effort, "to lift this curse. . . ."

"Alvin!" Madame Portia cried up at her ward. "What on earth are you doing out of bed? Get away from those stairs! If you fall, *vecchio*, you're a dead man!"

But the bundle of bones did not move back.

"I'm already more than dead enough," Mr. Peugeot replied gruffly. "Which is why we must hurry."

CHAPTER 26

Joy gently held an arm of the brittle old gentleman as her old gypsy friend held the other. At his request Madame Portia had dressed him in his best clothing—a moth-eaten morning coat with moldering old striped trousers and an ascot that sent a puff of dust aloft as she tied it around his shriveled neck.

"Melody always thought I looked handsome in this suit," he said wistfully as he admired himself in the hallway mirror. Hanging off his wasted frame, the clothes made him look like a little boy who'd been playing dress-up in his father's closet. "I used to call her my sweet semiquaver, because even her name made me think of music."

Joy felt herself choke up. "I'm sorry," she said, seeing such sadness in his face.

"Maybe we shouldn't do this," Mr. Phipps told the man whom he now knew—against all sense and reason—was his grandfather, the legendary Ethan Alvin Peugeot. Standing by the top of the stairs, Mr. Phipps watched with a distressed expression as the three slowly made their way down the hall toward him.

"Nonsense," replied the old author. "It is my eternal

shame that I did not do this years ago. Besides, look how nice it is out there. And now that I'm dressed, I feel like a drive."

Mr. Phipps looked out an upstairs window at the golden morning for a moment. He then carefully lifted his grandfather. The man felt light, like a giant hollow-boned bird. Holding the man in his arms like a child, Phipps made his way down the stairs.

Eyes now bright with tears, Joy followed Mr. Phipps, Madame Portia just behind her. At the bottom the old gypsy moved aside the group of curious residents craning to see what was happening. The four then exited through the front door.

The black car awaited, parked half on the grass and half on the path. Without having to be asked, Joy rushed ahead, opening the door of the coupe and putting the seat forward. Maneuvering cautiously, Mr. Phipps managed to prop the man gently up on the backseat and fasten him in.

Madame Portia appeared by the car. "Here, take this," she said, handing Mr. Phipps an antique sequined pillow to tuck behind the old man's head.

"Thank you," Phipps said. He turned to Joy. "And thank you, too."

"What—I'm coming with you," Joy told him.

"I don't know," Phipps replied, his face taut. "It doesn't sound like a good idea."

"Oh, let the girl come," Al called hoarsely from the back of the car. "I would like her company."

Phipps shook his head but nevertheless offered no more

argument. Pushing the seat upright, he turned to Joy and motioned for her to sit. When she was safely buckled in, he got in the driver's side and turned the ignition.

With a growl the black car came to life.

"So this is an automobile," observed Mr. Peugeot anxiously. "I can't believe I'm finally getting the pleasure."

"You've never ridden in a car before?" Joy asked.

"Not once. Of course, I can remember back to the very first models. They were all the same, square and black, nothing more than boxes on wheels, really, that you cranked to start. But I could never work up the courage to climb into one, even later. How it used to annoy Melody to no end! Her roadster was the fastest car in Spooking, yet there it sat lifelessly in the driveway, as I insisted on walking everywhere."

"Wow," Joy replied.

Despite his slightly frightened face, Mr. Peugeot gave a little cheer as the black car backed out toward the street. From the porch Madame Portia and the assembled residents waved to them gravely. Phipps nodded curtly back and then turned the wheel, slowly driving off with Joy and the ailing author.

"She wrote me something before she left," said the old man from the backseat as they passed Ravenwood Avenue. "In her little diary. I was under instructions to read it should she never return."

Joy turned and saw the gaunt-looking author regarding a small tarnished key that hung from a silver chain around his neck.

"But I never ended up opening it," he said, exhaling sharply. "I suppose I was afraid of what I might find inside. She was so angry when she left. I was worried she'd blame me for whatever calamity had come. So when she disappeared, I put the book in a trunk along with her effects, in the cellar."

"I know," Joy answered.

"And you found them," he said, smiling weakly. "Her clothes. They really suit you, you know."

Joy felt herself blush. "Thank you."

"I think she would have loved to have a daughter like you," said the author before falling silent. Joy blinked away tears. She was unable to think of anything to say.

Peugeot gazed out the window. He'd never seen the houses of the Boulevard streak by so. But still, their outlines remained etched in his mind, conjuring up previously forgotten names and faces. Some friends, some foes, their ghosts nonetheless appeared on their porches to wave him off. He smiled back at them all, feeling his face strain with the effort. He was then racked by a terrible rattling cough.

"I still don't see the point of this," Phipps complained, slapping a hand on the steering wheel. "You're too sick to be out. How do you know this will change anything?"

"I don't," the old author admitted. "But I've got a pretty good feeling about it."

Phipps muttered darkly to himself, but continued driving. Soon the houses stopped and the long stone wall of the cemetery appeared out the car's side windows. As a thousand headstones flashed in the sun, the author looked out, remembering how many others were buried in that earth.

He looked for their ghosts, but saw instead only the sunlight playing upon the soil.

The black car wound its way carefully down the crooked road, leveling out and rolling past the bog, as black and buzzing as always, and onward into the orderly streets of Darlington. It was then that Peugeot's eyes went wide. He marveled at the glittering green spaces, the black plains of parking lots, the curious homes that looked like children's drawings, like perfect little dollhouses.

His darting eyes drank in a thousand more delights. Huge billboards of beautiful people, holding up mysterious and unfathomable products. Whizzing traffic full of searing chrome. Streams of pedestrians in strange colorful costumes. These were the dizzying sights of the alien landscape, and for the first time in a long time, the author wished he could capture their likenesses in words on paper.

Finally these visions gave way, replaced by the more familiar pastoral scenes of the countryside, though now stripped of the wild woods that used to stretch as far as one could see. Yet still there was the river, and even a pig farm he once knew, and the same hill where he'd stopped to have lunch when first coming to Spooking as a young man.

And below, a meadow, just as he remembered.

They reached a road, an immense one unlike any other the author had ever seen, extending like a gigantic gray ribbon ahead of them. The black car hurtled forward, terrifyingly fast, until everything became a blur and it felt as if the anchors of time itself had pulled loose and they were now flying forward toward infinity.

But despite their speed, the ghostly roadster roared up alongside, its familiar driver turning to the author with a crooked smile.

She had something important to tell him. He listened carefully as the voice of his sweet love began filling his head, his body tingling with pleasure to finally hear it again.

"Wait!" the author called out to his companions, the words still ringing in his skull. But his feeble voice was drowned out by the noisy car engine.

Barely finding the strength, the author leaned forward.

"The witch's portrait," he croaked into the young lady's ear. "You must burn her likeness to lift the curse. Do you hear me? Burn the portrait!"

He then fell back in his seat, exhausted. But soon he felt his body begin to lighten. The searing pains and grinding aches that had gripped him for weeks stopped, and he felt himself losing substance. Outside, the world turned at once golden, coursing with energy, sprawling out in every direction with both possibilities and impossibilities. Everything became so bright that it became too much to bear. The author closed his eyes, sighing with pleasure at the merciful dark.

Just after the author spoke to her, Joy saw something drawing up beside them—an open-topped old sports car with a long gleaming hood. But turning, she found nothing but an empty lane. Glancing back, she was then shocked to find the backseat empty. Atop a pile of clothing lay the silver chain with the little key attached.

It was afternoon by the time they returned to Spooking. A

heavy silence hung over the car. Phipps took the girl straight to her street, stopping just outside her house.

Joy unbuckled herself. As Mr. Phipps glanced uncomfortably out the driver's side window, she snatched the key from the backseat. She then went to open the door, but stopped.

"How did you know?" Joy asked the old son of Spooking and the mayor's former assistant, who jumped in surprise. "About Alvin and Melody being your grandparents?"

Mr. Phipps fixed Joy with a weary gaze. "Old Lady Zott," he said. "Her family once took in local orphans."

Joy confirmed that she had already heard this part of the story from Peugeot himself.

"Did you ever meet Mrs. Zott?" Phipps asked.

"If I did, I don't remember," Joy admitted. "But for some reason she wanted to leave a copy of *The Compleat and Collected Works* to a Spooking girl with a 'taste for mystery, a thirst for adventure, and an eye for the inscrutable.' It said so in her will."

"The book," Phipps said. "Does it have anything written inside?"

"Yes!" Joy cried out. "'To My Beloved—A.'"

"You have my grandmother's own copy," Phipps confirmed. "The *A* stands for Alvin. Ms. Huxley left it with her son when she gave him up. And my father later read every word, of course, but for some reason left the book with his guardians when he grew up."

"Why?" Joy demanded.

"I don't know. I suppose he was too angry that his parents

had abandoned him, or about the curse, which his kindly caregivers had later revealed to him. Probably both."

The story was incredible, Joy thought. "How do you know all this?"

Phipps laughed. "You definitely never met Old Lady Zott," he told her. "She'd spill the beans on just about every topic to anyone who made it through a full piece of her apple strudel. Which was no easy feat, I can personally attest, because it was like eating a slice of fruit-filled phone book. Anyway, she was a spinster, and the last of her family. I guess she always kept a hold of the book and decided to leave it to a girl a bit like her old friend Melody."

The revelations were too amazing. Joy's book was the personal copy of Melody Huxley, given to her secret son. And now Joy sat staring at the man who shared the aviator's and the author's very blood!

Phipps finally nodded toward her house. "I think you had better get home, young lady," he advised. "Before you are missed."

"Oh," Joy replied as if awaking from a dream. She got out. The black car roared off before she had even reached the path up to Number 9 Ravenwood Avenue.

CHAPTER 27

That evening after dinner Joy retired with her family to the drawing room. Though it was the first time in a while that the Wellses had so gathered, the atmosphere felt notably subdued, as avoiding the topic of the recent horrors left little open for discussion.

"So what's the deal with my trunk?" Joy finally asked, breaking the silence.

"I thought we agreed to let my colleague in the history department take a look at it," Mrs. Wells replied. "To see if it's a genuine find."

"Okay, but what's the holdup?"

Mrs. Wells explained that it had turned out that Professor Keaton had been off on some sort of research sabbatical for the past month, and was returning only next week.

"What's a sabbatical, anyway?" Joy asked.

Mr. Wells answered. "It's basically a paid vacation where you pretend to work," he explained haughtily to his daughter. "Professors—what a spoiled bunch. And people wonder why tuitions are going through the roof!"

Tuning out her mother's angry protest, Joy determined two things—that the trunk was still theoretically within her reach, and that she had only a few days to retrieve the diary from it. Unfortunately, she couldn't simply ask. What would she say? That she felt compelled to safeguard the privacy of the tragic couple, one of whom had vanished that very day?

There was no point. No one would ever believe her. No matter what proof the diary might offer, or what was contained in "The Crimson Pool" or the love letters already in the Peugeot Society's possession, any sort of romance between Alvin and Melody would be considered an irrefutable impossibility. The author was thirty-five years the aviator's senior, after all, and had disappeared when Melody was only a schoolgirl.

But as custodian of this extraordinary secret, it was imperative that Joy find out the truth. Just what was Melody's last message to her lover?

So she had hastily formulated a plan.

"What's wrong, dear?" her mother asked upon noticing her daughter's sudden poutiness.

"Isn't it obvious, Helen?" Mr. Wells replied, his blood pressure still elevated from the thorough chewing-out he had just received. "She's worried about her movie."

It was actually a fair assumption. In truth, as each day went by, Joy was becoming increasingly anxious about the film's prospects.

"I'm sure they'll start up production again," her mother assured her. "Just as soon as they find someone to replace—" Mrs. Wells stopped, swallowing hard. "Once they find someone to play the part of Mr. Blackthorne," she finished.

Joy couldn't help but notice how her mother had been

unable to so much as utter the name of her former singing idol ever since his murderous rampage. Not that anyone could blame her. Although it seemed as if the general public could forgive a sufficiently repentant celebrity just about anything these days, trying to kill a bunch of kids with an axe would likely never figure among them. In fact, immediately following the incident Byron had caught his mother furiously snapping Teddy's entire vinyl discography in half. The shards had ended up bagged and placed on the curb for garbage collection shortly afterward.

"It's not just the movie," Joy replied. "I don't have any shoes that go with my graduation dress," she bemoaned. She caught her head in her hands in a calculated display of despair. "I tried on every pair I have last night, and they all look so stupid."

"Well, that's no surprise," Mrs. Wells replied. It was a well-known fact that she had never admired Joy's taste in footwear, which was made up almost entirely of clunky leather boots from Ms. Huxley's seemingly inexhaustible collection. "Why didn't you say anything before? We could have picked you out a cute pair when we were at the mall."

A cute pair. At the very idea Joy felt like she might barf. But it was important to stick to her plan. "I don't know," she replied with a shrug. "I thought we were looking for shoes for you. Besides, I know we're not made of money."

"That's a good girl," Mr. Wells said. "I'm sure there's something suitable in your closet."

"Oh, be quiet, Edward." Mrs. Wells sighed exasperatedly. "Well, we'll just have to go shopping tomorrow, then."

"Awww," Joy whined. "Does it really have to be tomorrow? I'm *so* tired."

Acting—it really was easy, Joy thought. But maybe she was pushing it. After all, she had been recently traumatized.

Luckily, Mrs. Wells didn't consider this. "I'm sorry, Joy. But tomorrow is the only day my classes finish up early enough. But does this mean you are going to the dance? For sure? Meaning no pretending to be sick at the last minute?"

"Pretending to be sick?" Joy objected, nevertheless a bit unnerved that Mrs. Wells was apparently on to her reliable old gambit. "Not a chance. Like you said, I don't want to regret missing out later."

"All right, then. We'll go and buy you some new shoes. Tomorrow."

As the final component of her plan, Joy then declined her mother's offer to pick her up at home. "Doesn't your lecture end at a quarter to four or something?" she asked, remembering her mother's schedule on the fridge. "Why don't I just walk down the hill and get a bus over to the campus? It will save a lot of time if I meet you at your office."

If Mrs. Wells questioned Joy's sudden enthusiasm for exertion, she didn't mention it. Nevertheless, Joy found herself not completely in the clear. "I thought you hated taking the bus on your own," Mrs. Wells remarked.

"Mom, I'm not a baby," Joy asserted testily. "I'm almost in junior high. I can take a bus, you know."

"Are you sure you want to? What about . . ."

Hearing her mother once again stop herself short, Joy figured it out. "Teddy is long gone, Mom. The police said so. Anyway, like you said, I can't let what happened ruin my life."

"All right," Mrs. Wells said. "You can take my spare office key. If I'm not there when you arrive, don't worry. Sometimes students keep me after class. Make yourself comfortable."

"I will. Thanks."

"Just please be careful."

"Okay, Mom."

Standing outside Teddy's rented residence on Weredale the next day, Joy recalled her mother's simple request: *Please be careful.* Snapping the safety switch off the butane barbecue lighter, Joy knew this probably wasn't what she'd meant.

Unfortunately, sometimes things just needed doing. Lifting up the mat, Joy was relieved to find the front door key still lying in the dust.

"Hello?" she called inside after opening the creaky door. "Anyone home?"

What am I? An idiot? Joy immediately questioned. If anyone—or anything—was lurking inside, wouldn't it be better not to announce her arrival? Well, it was too late now. Steeling herself, she stepped inside.

As she reached the center of the dark foyer, the door suddenly slammed shut behind her.

Leaping in fright, Joy whirled around, certain something hideous was rushing out to get her. However, the cavernous entranceway once again fell into a hush.

Fortunately, the bright afternoon cast enough light

through the transom for her to see. Above Joy's head the crystal chandelier gleamed in a sunbeam. But the cheering sight was dispelled as she looked up the staircase to the darkened second floor.

Joy turned toward the hearth, where the portrait of the woman still hung above in its heavy frame. This time the beautiful sorceress appeared positively evil, her tar black eyes trained hatefully as Joy approached. But the girl with the sunny blond hair did not waver. Instead she drew up beneath the portrait and stared straight at it.

The foyer began resounding with a terrible moan.

"Oh, save your breath," Joy snapped impatiently. Standing on her tiptoes, she yanked the painting off the wall. With a grunt she then wedged it into the hearth. "You've hurt enough people, you stupid old witch. And now," she declared, "it's time to say bye-bye."

With a click Joy fired up the barbecue lighter. The room turned orange as the portrait burst into flame. Choking on black smoke, the girl hurried out into the fresh air.

Heading down the road to Darlington a few minutes later, Joy wondered if she had imagined the otherworldly shrieks that had followed her exit from the mansion. Who knew? Fortunately, they had been immediately silenced when she'd slammed shut the heavy front door behind her. Joy skipped the rest of the way down the crooked road to the bleak-looking bus stop at the foot of Spooking Hill.

Before long the Number 3 appeared.

Her mother was right. She did hate taking the city bus,

she was quickly reminded. As hateful as the Spooky Express was, at least she always got a seat on it. Now, crammed among the noisy high school students, Joy swung helplessly from the handrail with every stop and start.

It was a miracle she didn't throw up.

Gasping for breath, Joy stepped off the stifling transit vehicle just in front of the campus. Worried about the time, she jogged the whole way across the sprawling grounds to the ivy-choked building that housed the philosophy department. With her lungs burning, Joy breezed inside without the slightest challenge from student or faculty member. Then, using the spare key, she quickly slipped into her mother's office.

Inside, Joy found the room to be just as she always had known it—a complete mess piled high with books, and folders sprinkled liberally with loose paper clips and Post-it notes. Nevertheless, in a matter of a minute Joy had uncovered the trunk and retrieved the diary.

After closing the lid, Joy carefully replaced the piles of term papers as precariously as she had found them. Smiling with relief, she then flopped down onto her mother's comfortably padded chair. No one would ever know this little book had even existed, she thought gleefully. Joy looked at the clock and saw she had another twenty minutes before her mother's lecture even finished.

Things had gone perfectly.

Spinning around in the swivel chair, Joy admired the small leather volume. She pulled the little key out from where it hung under her shirt, and she regarded the puny brass lock that had resisted all of her previous attempts to open it.

Take that, she thought, inserting the key.

With a swift turn, the lock clicked open, and all the diary's precious secrets were finally revealed to her.

The following morning Audrey Parker appeared at the front door of Number 9. She was dressed in a sharply tailored jacket and skirt, and she had a large suitcase with her. At the bottom of the path, a cab was pulling away.

Thinking the woman might be moving in, Mr. Wells stood, dumbfounded, in the doorway.

"I'm actually on my way to the airport, but I asked the car service if they could pick me up here, if that's okay. I need to speak to Joy for a moment."

"Of course," said Mr. Wells, relieved. "Come in."

Mr. Wells shouted to Joy, who was out in the backyard trying to get Fizz to run an obstacle course she'd made out of the dried brown clumps of grass clippings. A minute later she joined her parents and Miss Parker, who were waiting in the sitting room.

"Oh, hi," Joy said, surprised to see the woman.

"Hello," Miss Parker said. "Hey, is that your pet toad?" she asked, admiring Fizz's ballooning throat.

"Yes. Except he's a bullfrog, actually," Joy corrected. "I saved him from being roadkill."

"Well, he's cute." Miss Parker turned to Joy's parents, who were hovering expectantly. "Would you mind if I spoke to your daughter alone for a bit?" she asked them.

"Umm, why, certainly," Mrs. Wells replied. Looking

somewhat uncertain, the pair retired to the kitchen none-theless.

Sitting in her father's wing chair, Joy waited patiently for the woman to speak.

"I'm leaving town and heading back home," Audrey said. "But I wanted to drop by first and give you some unfortunate news personally."

"Okay," Joy said, feeling nervous.

"Well, I don't know if there's an easy way to tell you this, but I'm afraid *Blackthorne Inn* is dead in the water," Audrey told her. "The studio has officially canceled production."

"Canceled production?" Joy's eyes went wide with shock. "But why? This was the first Peugeot adaptation that looked like it would be any good!"

"I know it sounds crazy, but it happens a lot, actually. The movie ran into too many difficulties for it to continue. First there was Penny's disappearance, and now this terrible business with Teddy. It was not only running behind sched-ule, it was running out of bankable stars, frankly."

But there had been so much effort invested, Joy bemoaned, in bringing all these people and equipment to Spooking. And now they were going to throw it all away? "What about hiring new actors?" she suggested. "And getting a bunch of even bigger stars?"

Audrey laughed. "It's a bit more complicated than that, I'm afraid. Plus, studio executives are very superstitious people. I'm sure they think the whole movie is cursed at this point."

Well, they were right about that part, Joy knew. The

whole movie had been quite literally cursed from the start. But now that the Witch of Weredale was gone, there was nothing stopping them!

Not wanting to look like a crazy person, Joy kept the matter to herself, however.

"Anyway, they'd rather write the whole thing off and just get on with the next thing," Audrey continued. "And in this business, there's always a next thing."

"Well, that just stinks," Joy replied, looking miserable.

"I know," Miss Parker sympathized. "Listen, Joy, you're a very talented young lady," she told her. "If you really want to be in the movie business, I think you could have a good shot at it. And I can help."

"That's nice of you," Joy replied.

"Actually, I'm not being nice," Audrey confessed. "Spotting the next big star is part of my job, and I really do honestly think you're something special. But this is a tough business, you should know, especially for young people. Which is why I think you should think things over."

"But I don't know what to do now," Joy replied, slumping her shoulders. "I mean, this was such a big chance for me."

"Why don't you just concentrate on your schoolwork and maybe join the drama club? Then, if you discover that you really love acting, give me a call," she said, handing Joy a fancy-looking business card. "If so, you just might have a great career ahead of you. But if you are just hoping to be rich and famous, I'm afraid it's going to come with a lot of heartache.

"Besides, I thought you loved it here in Spooking. Remember

if you did want to become an actress, you'd have to move out to the coast to be close to all the studios for auditions and everything. Is that what you really want to do?"

This much, at least, Joy felt certain about. She didn't want to leave Spooking—not just yet, at any rate. This was the home of E. A. Peugeot, even if no one ever knew it.

"You're a beautiful girl, Joy, with a truly wonderful character. You could go far. But only if that's really what you want."

The sound of honking reached their ears. "That's my car," Audrey declared. "I've got one more stop to make, and I don't want to miss my flight."

Miss Parker headed off, her luggage in tow. Mr. and Mrs. Wells joined them at the door. As usual, Byron sat watching from the stairs.

"Take care, young lady," Miss Parker said to Joy as she descended the porch stairs. "Sorry this one didn't work out. But I'm sure there will be lots of other exciting opportunities in your future."

Her high heels clicking on the path, she then walked down to the awaiting town car. After handing the driver her luggage, she turned and waved to the Wellses as they gathered on the porch.

"What was all that about?" Mrs. Wells asked frantically when they finally were back inside. "What did she mean, 'Sorry this one didn't work out'?"

Joy sighed, bracing herself to relay the news. "The movie's been canceled," she told them. "It's all finished."

"Oh, sweetheart," said Mrs. Wells, holding her daughter

tightly. "I'm so sorry. You must be very disappointed."

Wrapped in her mother's arms, Joy began trembling as something started welling in her chest, and then gushing up like the fountain that had extended for so long the life of the now vanished author.

Burying her sunny blond head, Joy began sobbing.

The movie had been so important to her, Joy realized. Not the part about being an actress or a celebrity, but the possibility of becoming some sort of fixture in her beloved author's world. By playing one of his characters on-screen, Joy believed, she could have then secured her place in his universe forever.

And now it wasn't happening. Now she was simply Joy Wells again, an obscure resident of an obscure town.

But wait a second, Joy thought as she considered this. Hadn't she become something even greater than she could have ever hoped? Wasn't she in fact already a major character in the very last chapter in the life of the legendary E. A. Peugeot?

The only problem was that, because the great author was gone, her exploits would never get written down. But then again, why couldn't they? It was just a story, after all, and stories belonged to everyone. Perhaps Joy could even write it herself someday, chronicling the extraordinary life and times of E. A. Peugeot in a book of her very own! Heck, since most of the research was already done, she had a pretty good head start.

And what did it matter if nobody ended up believing the story? she decided. What difference would it make if everyone assumed her work was just a complete flight of fancy? The astonishing tale of a famous author becoming the improbable lover of a famous aviatrix from another era. There was something endearing about its complete preposterousness.

And if it meant that the world never knew there really were bog fiends and ghost cannons, that there really were healing fountains and jealous witches and vanishing curses, so much the better. Why, even the E. A. P. Society itself didn't actually believe their celebrated author's stories, but did that diminish their love of them?

"It's okay," Joy sniffed. "I'm all right."

"So we're not going to be rich?" Byron asked.

"I'm afraid not this time," Mr. Wells told him. "But we still have everything we need right here at home. Don't we, children?"

Wiping her eyes, Joy nodded.

"Well, maybe," Byron said. "But I still could use a bigger bedroom."

CHAPTER 28

The hot afternoon sun toasted the untended grass of Spooking Cemetery as dandelion pollen gently drifted down onto the headstones.

Across the street, in the disused parking area beside the old music shop, Phipps stood bouncing a tennis ball. Once, twice, three times he bounced it before catching it in his long fingers. He snapped his arm back, threw the ball forward high into the air, and then watched its arcing descent.

The three-legged dog leaped from his side, hopping off in excited pursuit.

Heading along to the cemetery, Joy watched the whole display in disbelief. It had been a long time since she'd enjoyed quiet solitude among the cemetery's headstones, and after everything that had happened lately, she found herself desperately missing it. But she now stood fearfully as the eerie animal ran straight up to her, the slobbery ball glowing neon yellow in its mouth.

"Don't be afraid of Oliver," Phipps called to her. "He wouldn't hurt a fly. But he isn't above eating a person's favorite shoes if given half a chance," he added, drawing up.

"Oliver?" Joy repeated, looking at the creature she had

known as the harbinger, who appeared only when terrible things were about to happen. "He's your dog?"

"Actually, it's a funny story. It turns out he was the Parkers' dog—the parents of my friend Audrey, the casting director who hired you. The Parkers live over on Cliffside Crescent, where I just had dinner for the first time in twenty-seven years. Anyway, they're getting on in years and finding it a bit too much trouble to care for such a big dog these days. Especially one that keeps getting out from under their fence—which is what you like to do, isn't it, you bad dog, you?"

Joy tensed up as Phipps rushed forward and grabbed the dog's huge head in his hands. The dog dropped the ball and bared its teeth at him, snarling frighteningly for a moment before finally licking his face with a long red tongue.

"At any rate, I've agreed to take him off their hands since we get along so well," Phipps told Joy, wiping his face. "Besides, he did save my life. I think I can indulge him in a few games of fetch in return. Here, boy. Here, boy. Who's got the ball?"

Phipps delivered another high toss that sent the animal joyfully scrambling across the cracked remains of the parking area.

"So what happened to him anyway?" Joy asked, admiring the incredible agility of the disabled dog. "Why does he have only three legs?"

"The Parkers used to take him down to that big park in Darlington to chase tennis balls," Phipps began. "Unfortunately, he ran out in the street one day and was hit by a car.

But as you can see, for such a big injury, it didn't slow him down much."

The dog dropped the ball at Joy's feet and began sniffing frantically at her lap, exactly where she'd been stroking Fizz earlier that day.

"Then, why did Madame Portia tell me he was a bad omen?" she asked, leaning over to pat his massive head. Sitting down, the dog closed his eyes and began panting like a steam engine.

"Well, I don't know if you've noticed, but your friend Madame Portia is a fork short of a place setting," Phipps explained. "And that isn't a recent thing either. When I was a kid, she used to have the entire town hiding in their basements whenever someone's budgie got loose. After a while, though, people learned to just ignore her."

"So you've known her all these years?"

"Oh yeah, from way back when she was married to the crazy clockmaker."

"The crazy clock maker?" Joy repeated, her interest piqued.

"She never spoke of him? He kept an entire room full of timepieces that apparently counted down various townspeople's lives. Now, he was a real wet blanket—terribly morose and quite possibly the worst person in the world to get stuck beside at a dinner party."

Joy swooned to imagine what Spooking must have been like when Mr. Phipps was growing up.

"Anyway, Madame Portia and I haven't been on friendly terms for a long time, ever since I left my parents and

Spooking. And since then she's hardly had a reason to warm up to me, especially after I tried to get her evicted from her house in the swamp."

The mention reminded them both about the incident in which Phipps had sawed the submarine-like house from its stilts and sent it rolling into the pond—and so nearly drowning not only the old woman, but Joy and Byron as well.

"I hope you believe me when I say that despite my odious behavior I never meant to harm anyone. I did not even know that you and your brother were inside," he confessed with a shudder. "I can only hope that in time everyone will understand what an overpowering darkness took hold of me, and perhaps forgive me for all the hurts I have inflicted."

Joy looked up at the man who had once been her enemy. She could hardly recognize him anymore as the mayor's assistant, the brute who wanted to destroy her beloved town. His sharp features had somehow softened, and his sinister stoop was gone, and his now floppy hair had become streaked with thick swatches of pure white.

Nevertheless, the disclosure seemed to unsettle him, and he began fidgeting uncomfortably.

"So I guess you heard the movie is canceled," Joy said, changing the subject.

"I did," Phipps confirmed. "And with it my contract with the City of Darlington, with no other positions currently available. Which means you are once again looking at a person without prospects."

"What are you going to do now?"

"I've decided it's time for a road trip," Phipps announced. "As soon as my check from the city clears, I'm going to bundle the Bad Omen here into the car and drive off."

"You're leaving Spooking? But aren't you worried that—" Joy stopped talking abruptly.

"That I might still vanish? No. I can feel it. I feel different, more . . . solid, I suppose."

Joy smiled knowingly in agreement. "Where will you go?"

"Good question. I don't really know yet. Anywhere, I guess. We won't really know until we get there," Phipps said. "I know Oliver here was hoping I'd take him to see a certain person who lives out on the coast. But we'll see. She's a very busy lady, I understand, and might not have the time to hang out with the likes of us."

"Oh, I'm sure she will," Joy replied.

"Well, we'll see. You know, it's curious, though. Now that I finally feel like I'm free to go anywhere I want, for the first time in a long while, I have the strangest desire to stay right here in Spooking. But I think that would be a mistake. At least for the moment anyway. But I think I'll return. Someday."

"Well, I'll be here when you do."

"I believe you will be. By the way, did you know this is it?" Phipps asked, pointing toward Joy's feet. "The very spot where Mr. Peugeot first began trying his hand at the literary trade? It was a bit of a shack, I'm told, and collapsed shortly after my father was given the deed. But I thought maybe you'd enjoy knowing where it all began."

"Wow," Joy answered, feeling her pulse quicken at the very thought. "How amazing."

"Truly." Phipps regarded the girl's excited face and smiled. "Anyway, if you'll excuse me, I need to give Oliver a bath. We have a long ride coming up, and I'm not sure I can bear it unless he gets a proper scrubbing."

"Okay, then."

"Good-bye for now, Joy Wells," Mr. Phipps said.

"Good-bye," said Joy, accepting the offered hand. The man's grip turned out to be gentle, yet pleasingly firm and dry, his fingers still calloused from years of playing musical instruments, she guessed.

Releasing her, Phipps whistled for Oliver, who, with the tennis ball clenched in his teeth, immediately followed his master into the old music shop.

Joy crossed the street and passed through the gates of the cemetery. A breeze had picked up, tossing the feathery pollen around in what seemed like the world's warmest blizzard. Smiling, Joy headed down the west side, away from the terrible scene of that awful night. Here the graves were more recent, the names on the headstones clearly legible. She strolled on for a while until she passed three that were particularly familiar.

Ludwig Zweig. Madame Portia's second husband, the swamp botanist who had liked scuba diving among leeches.

Veronique Phipps. The mother of Octavio, whose husband, Lorenzo, had vanished into thin air.

Gertrude Zott. Once Spooking's oldest resident, she had bequeathed a book to a stranger and so started all of Joy's adventures.

Joy looked up at the endless row of headstones and

monuments to thousands of other beloved souls. And she wondered what their stories might be.

Hearing a noise above, Joy looked up. There were crows, a hundred of them, perhaps, dotting the sky like ink blots. Coming together to form a black cloud, they swirled against the blue sky for a moment before breaking apart and swooping down into the cemetery. Joy watched in awe as they landed on every surface available, perching atop headstones and urns and crosses and angels.

The crows then began cawing, a slaughter of both meter and melody. Was it a point of pride or shame, Joy wondered, to be the least musical of all birds? She listened for a bit, all the while giving them their beady glares right back, and then she ventured onward, deeper into the cemetery.

CHAPTER 29

The pretty lady could stop by only for a few minutes, unfortunately. She was running late and needed to catch a flight, she explained. Outside the Mealey bungalow, a fancy-looking car sat in wait for her, with a uniformed driver at the wheel.

And so, after politely declining tea or coffee or even a glass of lemonade made fresh out of a can that morning, the pretty lady got quickly to her point.

She wasn't making promises, she felt obliged to first explain. And she certainly didn't want to raise their hopes too high.

Still, she'd worked with a lot of child actors in her time and felt the boy had something—a rare gift that had come shining through the dailies of the doomed movie. Specifically, she recalled a scene when the boy had been simply playing with toy soldiers on the floor, and how all eyes in the room had been drawn straight to him as he'd delivered the single most convincing and curiously endearing performance of the entire shoot.

"That kid can act," they'd all remarked, huddled together around a monitor. "That kid looks great on camera."

And so the pretty lady had put a call out to her friend, an agent who specialized in developing young undiscovered talent. He was at this moment eagerly awaiting the tape she had in her purse, excited to see what all the fuss was about.

But the pretty lady had to warn the wide-eyed mother and son. Even if something came of it, exploring such an opportunity would be risky. First they would have to leave behind everything they had known and move out west, where they could be closer to the action. And once there, they would possibly endure a grueling number of auditions and screen tests before even landing the smallest of roles, in a TV commercial, perhaps, or for the pilot of some show that would most likely never see the light of day. It could takes months, she told them, or a year or more even to get a first break.

Nevertheless, on the strength of his performance in *Blackthorne Inn*, the pretty lady thought things might not go that way and could very well happen quite fast, and the boy could find himself landing another movie role before long.

But there was really no way of knowing, of course. It was a gamble.

So it would take a lot of courage, not to mention patience and faith. And without an abundance of all three qualities, she would advise the family to pass on this dream and simply continue with their lives.

The pretty woman then looked at her watch. She was very, very late now and had to go.

Mother and son thanked her for stopping by. They did

very much appreciate her interest and would certainly think about everything she'd said. They would wait for a call from her agent friend. In the meantime they would give it all some very serious thought.

Then with a clicking of heels, she was gone.

Morris sat on the sofa, nervously watching his mother peek through the sheer curtains of the living room window. Even when the car pulled away, she did not move but instead stood there like a wax figure, wearing a similarly unreal smile and unfocused gaze.

"Morris," Mrs. Mealey finally called without moving a muscle.

Morris sat up on the edge of the sofa. "Yes, Mother?" he answered.

"Go to your room," she ordered. "Go to your room and start packing."

The leafy trees of Spooking Park trembled above as Byron and Poppy sat on opposite sides of the merry-go-round, spinning by means of unknown propulsion. The last time he'd visited the playground had been with Gustave, and the little girl had been curiously absent. And the time before that when he'd come with Joy, she hadn't been there. But on his own this time, he'd found her on her usual revolving perch.

They had been sitting in an uncomfortable silence for a few minutes now, ever since Byron had hopped on and asked if she wanted to play with his walkie-talkies.

"I can't use those," she'd informed him after a cursory

visual inspection of the devices. "Sorry," she'd added with a shrug.

Thrown into a huff, Byron had shoved them back into his pockets. He'd then begun glaring off into space as they spun.

"Hey, how is your sister?" Poppy asked him finally.

For a second he considered continuing with the silent treatment, but found he couldn't be bothered anymore. "She's fine," he reported. "But the movie got canceled."

"Canceled? Why?"

"There were a bunch of axe murders on the set, so they had to stop making it."

"Oh, that's a shame," Poppy replied.

Surprised when she didn't ask for any further details, Byron shot an unbelieving look at the girl. Catching his eye, she beamed back at him with that strange toothy smile of hers.

"Actually, it is a shame," Byron continued, immediately looking away. "With all the money she was supposed to make, Joy was going to fix up the bigger room at the back of the house for me. But because she just got to work for a couple of weeks, she only made enough to start a college fund. Or at least that's what my parents say. It's so annoying! I'm sick of my room. It's like living in a closet!"

"I've never seen a movie," Poppy declared. "What are they like?"

Byron looked at the girl to see if she was actually being serious. From her glowing expressionless face, it appeared she was. Man, she was so weird! he thought. Still, there was something about those watery eyes and that pale skin of hers; looking at them together made his heart sort of hurt a bit. Even Lucy Primrose, the beautiful strawberry blond girl he had adored since kindergarten, had never given him quite the same feeling. Anyway, it didn't matter, because Lucy liked Gustave now. In fact, it seemed as though all the girls in their grade liked Gustave for some reason. It was probably his hair.

"What are movies like? I don't know," he said, and sighed, struggling to answer Poppy's question. "A movie is pretty much supposed to be just like real life, I guess, except they take out all the boring bits and leave in just the cool stuff."

"Well, that sounds silly," said Poppy.

"What do you mean?" he asked. "Why?"

"Because the boring bits are the best part of life," she told him.

Byron made a face. *The boring bits are the best part?* Who in the whole wide world believed something like that? Poppy was really too weird, he decided again. How many times had he told Joy just that? And this was the girl she'd once said he should marry?

Annoyed, he turned his attention back to the circling views of Spooking Park, the old library, and the asylum walls across the Boulevard, which hid the ruin beyond. Staring out at the blurred panorama, Byron realized something. He was actually quite bored himself. This was exactly the kind of thing that would never make it into a movie, he thought.

Still, for some reason that he could not explain, he didn't

feel like doing anything else. Turning his head casually, he stole a glance at Poppy. The girl looked up immediately, smiling back at him for a moment before lowering her gaze with a giggle.

Man, she was just so weird, Byron thought. It was like she wasn't real sometimes. And then his stupid heart began hurting again.

CHAPTER 30

Wearing her graduation dance dress and new shoes, Joy began slowly descending the stairs, careful not to trip and fall on the way down. She felt stressed enough as it was, and the last thing she needed was to kick off the evening with a bloodied brow and a limp.

"Oh my! Just look how beautiful you look!" came a cry from below.

Seeing her father standing at the bottom of the stairs, Joy's mouth dropped open. Decked out in a tuxedo, he looked absolutely impeccable, completely unlike the harried lawyer and husband he always appeared to be, and more like a dashing spy on his way to meet a contact at a casino. His wiry hair was neatly but not too neatly parted, and his beard and mustache were trimmed in a way that imparted an almost roguish aspect to him.

"Why are you all dressed up?" asked Joy, suddenly fearing that her father was hoping to accompany her to the dance or something.

"It's the dean's dinner tonight at the university," he explained. "Black tie mandatory."

"You look . . . ," said Joy, pausing as she reached the

bottom of the stairs without incident. "Really good!"

"Thank you, sweetheart. In case you haven't noticed, your mother is one of the most beautiful women in town. I live in fear of having all her colleagues whispering about how she's married to a complete dud."

"Oh, nonsense, Edward," said Mrs. Wells, entering as a vision in a stunning emerald green dress. "Everyone already knows I have a thing for duds." Mrs. Wells laughed at her husband's stricken expression. "But you do look very handsome," she added before planting a long kiss on him.

Joy squirmed, waiting for them to finish.

"Thank you, Helen. You look magnificent as usual."

"I know," she agreed with a devilish grin.

"Where's Byron?" Joy asked.

"He's staying over at Gustave's tonight," her father explained. "We'll drive you down to your school and then pick you up afterward."

"But what if you're late?"

"We won't be, dear," her mother assured her. "We're using you as an excuse to leave before the after-dinner party—when Dean Hargrove starts imploring everyone to 'get their collective academic freaks on.'"

"Yes, that is always painful," Mr. Wells agreed.

Ready to leave, Joy and her parents headed out to the car. Fifteen minutes later they came to a skidding halt outside Winsome. Mrs. Wells looked back at her daughter from the driver's seat and sighed.

"You look gorgeous, dear. Now, just remember to take good care of your grandmother's necklace."

"I will, Mom," Joy replied. She had in fact put a tiny square of tape on the clasp to be certain it couldn't possibly come undone. Looking out the passenger window, she saw a steady stream of nicely dressed children entering the building as other groups stood chatting on the grass. Louden, she noticed, was nowhere in sight.

"Don't you think you should get out?" Mr. Wells asked. "We can't stay here all night. Your mother is blocking the road," he pointed out, nervously looking in the side mirror.

"Oh, people can wait," Mrs. Wells replied. "It's our daughter's graduation dance, after all. Shouldn't we be allowed to savor the moment?"

At that instant someone began honking furiously in answer. Joy released her seat belt and quickly got out. Glancing back, she saw that the beeping vehicle was in fact a white stretch limousine, aggressively inching up on their bumper.

"Thanks for the lift, Mom," she said through the open window.

"We will pick you up just after ten, sweetheart," said Mrs. Wells.

"Okay. Thanks."

There came another three honks.

"Would you go jump off a cliff, moron!" Mrs. Wells shouted back. Joy stepped back onto the curb as her mother pulled away with a deliberate lack of haste.

Oh no, Joy thought. *Ten o'clock.* That meant she would have to suffer through a full three hours no matter what, and possibly all by herself, she began dreading.

The limousine rolled forward, double-parking in the

exact spot Mrs. Wells had just vacated. Joy shot the driver a glare as he got out, but he took no notice as he went to open the rear passenger door.

Tyler exploded out of the dimly lit interior of the limo. "Check me out. I'm rich and famous!" he shouted to onlookers. Wearing a tuxedo T-shirt and a pair of gleaming white sneakers, he stood waiting as the small army of his closest cronies emerged behind him.

The spectacle reminded Joy of the time when she'd gone to the circus and seen a seemingly impossible number of clowns getting out of a tiny jalopy. Shortly afterward, one of them had squirted her square in the face with a soda bottle. But happily these jokers appeared totally oblivious of her. Passing by like she was a ghost, the boys joined the excitable crowd already milling around on the grass.

In fact, as she stood there in her blue velvet dress, no one seemed to notice Joy at all.

What a relief, she thought, exhaling. Maybe she would get through this evening after all. And then, with the movie officially canceled, perhaps she could just get on with her life. Go off to junior high and just be a normal kid, for once.

Hearing a commotion behind her, Joy turned. Seeing Tyler ripping up grass, she flinched. But instead of hurling it at her, he began stuffing it down the collars of his friends' shirts. Before long, a war was on, and the air was full of flying turf.

Joy decided that perhaps she should head inside.

It was funny, Joy thought, but she felt surprisingly giddy

climbing the stone steps of Winsome. Maybe because it was for the last time, or maybe it was because she felt she was in disguise. As she entered the school, everyone just smiled. Did none of her classmates even recognize her?

Reaching the landing, Joy froze. Ahead stood Cassandra and Missy, their eyes fixed directly on her. Behind them a pair of doors opened into the gymnasium. Joy could tell from the thumping music that the dance had already begun.

Keeping her eyes lowered, Joy tried to slip past them.

"Hey, Joy," said Cassandra, catching her arm. "That dress is from It's a Girl Thing, right?"

"Yeah, we saw you trying it on," Missy added before Joy could offer any sort of denial.

"My mother picked it out," Joy answered in way of explanation.

"We thought their dresses were ugly," Cassandra informed Joy. "But that one is gorgeous! We were so jealous when we saw it!"

"Yeah," Missy agreed. "Lucky snag."

"Er, thanks," Joy replied. Smiling back at the pair, she waited awkwardly.

"Oh, and that's beautiful too!" Missy added, peering at the purple sparkling necklace hanging around Joy's neck.

"It was my grandmother's," she explained. "It's an antique."

"Wow. Are those stones real? They look totally real."

"My mother says they're amethysts," Joy told her. "Hey, I really like your hair, by the way," she added. "Both of you guys!" The girls blushed and smoothed down their hairdos, which though usually full and curly had been painstakingly straightened for the occasion. Why anyone would go to all that trouble just to have boring straight hair like hers, Joy had absolutely no idea.

"By the way, sorry to hear your movie got canceled," said Cassandra. "That must really suck."

"Yeah," said Joy with a shrug. "I guess I'm not going to be the next Penny Farthing," she announced, laughing.

"That's good," Missy replied, making a face. "Did you hear where they found her? After disappearing for weeks?"

Joy nodded and laughed, already knowing the story, which Mr. Wells had read out loud from the newspaper just that morning. Apparently the missing starlet had finally been spotted wandering around a garbage dump some twenty miles away from where she'd last been seen in Spooking Cemetery. Looking gray and grimy but otherwise unharmed, Ms. Farthing had claimed to have been abducted by strange humanoids who lived off grubs and worms in a vast underground city. After several weeks, however, the actress's strategy to sufficiently exasperate the creatures with continuous demands had seemed to work, as they'd then dragged her back to the surface and shoved her out into the dump.

The authorities had found little to investigate, however. Unable to locate the entranceway to this supposed hidden world, they'd begun to openly speculate on the possibility that the entire incident had been merely a hoax. Adding to the general skepticism, the sharp-eyed journalist had further pointed out that other than its benign ending, Ms. Farthing's account closely resembled the plot of "What

Lurks Beneath" by E. A. Peugeot. The journalist then revealed that a script treatment of the classic horror story had been recently sent to Marty Newman & Partners for the actress's consideration.

The troubled young woman had since left the country to recuperate at some unspecified island paradise, it was reported.

"Imagine making up a story about being kidnapped by monsters just to get attention?" Cassandra laughed. "What a loser!"

"Yeah," Missy agreed. "Totally."

Cassandra then wrapped Joy in a hug. "Anyway, happy graduation!" she exclaimed. With a squeal Missy rushed forward and crushed the two of them at once.

What was going on? Joy wondered, wincing in pain. Had her mother dropped her off at the wrong school or something? When they finally released her, Joy gently excused herself and headed into the gymnasium.

In all of her years at Winsome, Joy had always thought of the gym as a cinder block torture chamber. Yet somehow the graduation committee had managed to transform it into a pleasant enough space for the occasion. At the ceiling high above, silver balloons danced in the rising heat, and white paper streamers hung in elegant loops. On the wooden floor that had caused Joy no end of scraped knees and bitten tongues, tiny white Disco lights now sparkled. And thanks to the wonders of painted cardboard and construction paper, the basketball hoop had been transformed into a palm tree. Underneath it a small blow-up pool sat filled with small blue plastic balls.

It was supposed to look like an oasis, Joy realized. An Arabian night never to forget. She laughed. To her surprise, she kind of liked the entire goofy effect.

Even the gym teacher, Mr. Hardy, had undergone a transformation, though likely not from the efforts of the graduation committee. Gone were his zipper-fronted Windbreaker and too-tight T-shirt, as well as his short-shorts and knee-high socks. Instead he wore dressy trousers and an actual blazer, Joy noted with awe, along with a pair of shiny brown Oxfords. And where his gleaming whistle—the dreaded Acme Thunderer—had once dangled, a much more muted striped necktie now hung.

Sitting close to Miss Keener, he was even laughing. Joy watched as her now glamorous-looking homeroom teacher cracked jokes to him.

Was there something in the punch? Joy wondered. She recalled a Peugeot story in which the intrepid Dr. Ingram supped from a strange brew offered by a native chief and came similarly unhinged.

"Yo, yo. Whassup, Winsome?" came a booming voice over the loudspeakers. "DJ Star is in the hizz-ouse! And I'm taking your requests all night long. So don't be shy—cuz you know I'm fly!"

The music teacher gave a flourish, and the gymnasium began reverberating with another driving dance beat:

Untss, untss, untss, untss, untss, untss, untss . . .

"Oh, man," said Louden, appearing at Joy's side. "Now, that is just wrong," he declared, motioning to the makeshift DJ booth, where Mr. Star was either popping and locking, or suffering an electric shock from his equipment.

"Is that an alarm clock hanging around his neck?" Joy asked, further noticing it had a picture of that annoying beaver from the movie *Timber!* on it.

"He's either superfresh or was really worried about over-sleeping this morning. . . ."

Joy laughed, stealing a glance at Louden. He was wearing a checked button-down shirt with a vest and cream-colored chinos, not to mention a polka-dotted bow tie, she saw with surprise. The entire look gave him an authentically old-fashioned effect, Joy thought admiringly, like how Dr. Ingram might have dressed himself while resting his shredded nerves at some country estate.

The heck with it, Joy decided, and went on to tell him as much.

"Cool. Thanks. I've never read any books like that, actually, but it sounds kind of interesting. You say the stories are gory?"

"Disgustingly. If you want, I can lend you some," Joy offered. "I have all of Peugeot's stories in one volume. Trust me, you'll love them."

What was she doing? Joy wondered. Did she just offer to let someone borrow her first-edition copy of *The Compleat and Collected Works*, secretly inscribed by the author himself to his lover? She supposed she had done just that.

From the corner of her eye, Joy saw Louden swallow hard. "So anyway," he said, "did you come here with anyone?"

Joy scoffed. "To the dance? No!"

"Me neither."

"I mean, who would want to drag a date along to this dumb thing?" Joy asked, waving dismissively at the décor she had been admiring only a few minutes earlier.

"I don't know," Louden declared, looking around and shaking his head. The two students stood quietly side by side for a minute, watching their classmates starting to gather on the dance floor. Louden then coughed. "Hey, I was wondering: Do you want to go to a movie with me next week?"

Surprised, Joy looked at the boy. There it was, that big grin again, the one she had noticed from the very day he had first come to Winsome. Quickly picturing igloos and icicles and other cooling things, Joy somehow managed not to blush.

"Sure," she answered casually.

"Great. I'll give you a call!" Louden said. His smile stretched so wide it looked at risk of sending the upper part of his head toppling off. "Oh, speaking of movies," he added, "sorry to hear about yours."

"Thanks. But that stuff happens all the time, apparently," Joy told him. "Canceled movies, I mean—not axe murders."

"Yeah, that sounded pretty insane! So the guy really went crazy right during filming?"

"Oh, he went nuts, all right," Joy confirmed. She shivered to remember the mad gleam in Teddy's eye as he swung the weapon directly at her. What if she hadn't ducked in time? She supposed she wouldn't be at this dance, much less having this conversation.

"It's just lucky you and your brother and that kid Morris didn't get hurt."

Joy agreed. Except it wasn't all luck. There was, of course,

Mr. Phipps, who had almost given his life coming to their rescue. She pictured the shadowy son of Spooking who had once struck such fear into her heart, and wondered if he was at that very minute roaring across the country with Oliver lolling his tongue out the window of the mighty black car. She hoped so.

Seeing Louden's expectant face, Joy went to tell him the terrifying details—the collapsing porch, the swarm of bats, and the final drama in the cemetery. But she stopped herself. Because the crimes were not only under investigation but had been perpetrated by a famous person, the Wells had been strongly advised against speaking to anyone about the events that had transpired. Unless, that is, they liked the idea of an army of reporters and TV cameras camping out on their front lawn.

Joy's family had all agreed it was something they could do without. Still, it was Louden she was talking to, an old schoolmate and a new friend. What harm could it do? But no, she'd promised her parents, she remembered. It was better to play it safe for now.

Besides, she could always tell him later. And she would have plenty of time when they were at junior high together.

"Anyway, do you think you're still going to be an actress after this?" Louden asked, thankfully dropping the subject.

"I don't know." Joy shrugged. She did sort of like the idea of acting, the part about helping to tell stories for a living. And who would mind a chance at becoming rich and famous while they were at it?

But having slept in until eleven that morning, now Joy

wasn't so sure. Could she really endure going back to those awful crack-of-dawn calls? Maybe she just wasn't a morning person.

And with the possible exception of having your own trailer, most of it was a bit of a drag, Joy thought. The few days she'd worked, she'd waited around for hours and hours in full costume and makeup just to deliver a couple of lines. And then they would make her say the same things over and over and over again until her tongue finally felt like it was about to crack.

But that wasn't the worst part. In order to pursue a career in acting, Joy would have to move, Miss Parker had told her, to a completely different coast! And after everything that had happened, she now knew for certain that Spooking was even more amazing and mysterious than she had ever guessed. Having finally made its way into the hands of experts, Melody Huxley's trunk alone was already causing considerable excitement.

Who knew what adventures Joy would miss if she picked up and left?

"No, I think I'll stick around here," she told Louden. "At least until I finish high school. Then we'll see what happens. But I do want to see the world, someday."

"That's pretty much my plan," said Louden. "Hey, do you want to get some punch or something? I don't know if you want to dance a bit, but I'm pretty bad, I think. I mean I've never tried, in public at least."

With a laugh Joy admitted to the same secret shame. Relieved, they got some punch and stood safely behind the palm tree. From there they watched as overexcited graduates began busting out their best moves. Soon the dance floor became packed with girls grooving and boys trying to outdo one another with ridiculous acrobatic stunts.

It didn't take long before the gym became one big sweat-box. Gasping for air, Joy and Louden headed outside. Joy caught a few eyes following her as she exited the gym with Louden, and even caught a knowing smile from Missy.

At first she felt embarrassed. But then, as she stepped outside with the first boy she knew to ever properly rock out a bow tie, she realized it was just a smile, and that smiles were usually good things.

The pair walked on, talking about their hopes for the next year, and all the things they wouldn't soon miss about Winsome. The list carried them a few blocks.

"I hope the place has a cafeteria," Louden remarked, turning the conversation to junior high school and what it might be like.

"Aren't school cafeterias supposed to be gross?" Joy asked.

"It can't be much worse than that ham sandwich gas you have to breathe every day down in the Winsome lunchroom."

"I hate the tuna fish smog, personally."

"Hey!" Louden protested jokingly. "I always have tuna fish!"

Before long they arrived at the nearby park, passing the spot where Joy's mother had rear-ended Mr. Phipps's car. The whole thing felt like it had happened ages ago.

"We should head back," said Louden, noticing how far they'd come.

"Can we sit on that bench for a bit first?" Joy asked. Her new shoes were now killing her feet, and she needed a break.

The two of them sat down and gazed out on the quickly darkening playing field. In the distance a lone player chased a glowing white soccer ball. Joy looked beyond to the far-away line of houses, with their porch lights now on and their living room windows alive with flickering TV light.

Maybe Darlington wasn't such a terrible place, Joy decided. Could a place where people lived in peace and loved their children truly be that bad? Probably not. Besides, not everyone down here was a jerk, it had turned out.

Joy looked up at Spooking Hill, now black against the evening sky. Lights were twinkling up there, too, she saw. She could remember once seeing them from this distance and believing a few to be will-o'-the-wisps, the ghostly lights she'd read about in one of Peugeot's stories. But now they didn't look mysterious. They just looked like home.

The sight instantly made Joy think of Melody Huxley's diary. Having decided to keep it a secret for now, Joy had hidden the book under some old E. A. P. Society newsletters in her desk drawer. But each night, once her home fell silent, she retrieved the little volume and pored over its contents by lamplight.

Upon first unlocking its hasp, Joy had been disappointed to discover that the diary had been used more as a sketchbook than as the receptacle of secrets she had been expecting. But soon she'd become transfixed by what she'd found.

Joy lost herself in the detailed drawings of the old airplanes Ms. Huxley had presumably flown, and the strange and exotic plants she'd encountered, and of course all the unfortunate animals she'd stalked through tangled jungles and dark forests across the globe. Beside each such image, corresponding notes were scribbled in the margin.

The remainder of the book was devoted to a series of tiny landscapes—heartbreakingly beautiful places where Ms. Huxley had lingered long enough to paint. Endless burning deserts, hulking snowcapped mountains, and lush tropical islands ringed with bands of pink sand.

Though wonderfully rendered in miniature, all were unfamiliar to Joy except for the last effort. There, the aviatrix had deftly captured the unmistakable silhouette of Spooking Hill, inking it against an indigo sky that was just beginning to sparkle with stars—exactly the view tonight, Joy realized in wonderment.

The page after this little painting contained the final sheet of the illustrated diary, Joy knew only too well. The diary bore no further images but rather a sample of the adventure-woman's handwriting. But unlike the volume's many other annotations, this time the words were neither inked in a hurried scrawl nor smudged from the book's hasty closing. This time they were spelled out with great care and left to properly dry, with each letter placed as delicately and deliberately as a flower in a garden.

> *Dear Alvin,*
> *You are the most beautiful sight I've ever seen, and all the adventure I could ever want. I will love and miss you forevermore.*
> *—Melody*